"I could read to ~~took Bryce by su~~

"You don't have to d~~

"Really, the help wanted section of the *Maple Grove Gazette* is not as large as I had hoped. You finish what you're working on." She bent down so she was eye level with Camden. "Would that be okay, little man?"

Camden eyed her suspiciously. "Do you know how to read with voices?" he asked with his head tipped to the side.

"I am excellent at reading with different voices. Should we try?"

Camden nodded and handed her the books.

"I got this," she said to Bryce before she followed Camden to his reading corner.

Was this really happening? Bryce tried to go back to his nanny search, but the alternating sound of Willow doing funny voices and Camden belly-laughing was too distracting. It had been too long since he'd heard those sounds coming out of his boy.

It made his heart ache.

Dear Reader,

This is it! The last book in the Stop the Wedding! series is here. I've enjoyed creating a little chaos around what's usually the happiest time in someone's life. In *His Texas Runaway Bride*, Willow Sanderson is about to marry into one of the most powerful families in Dallas. The problem? Willow realizes moments before she's supposed to walk down the aisle that she doesn't want to get married. Afraid to stand up for herself, she decides to run.

The small town of Maple Grove, Texas, seems like a good place to hide out until she can muster up the courage to face the consequences of running away. Enter single dad sheriff Bryce Koller and his son, Camden.

The best part about writing romance is finding a way to give the characters I love the happily-ever-after they deserve. I promise that Willow and Bryce will get theirs...eventually! The other fun part of writing romance is throwing a few obstacles in the way. I hope you'll laugh, maybe shed a tear, but in the end, get that warm, fuzzy feeling that everything is going to be all right!

I love to connect with my readers. You can find me on Facebook at Facebook.com/amyvastineauthor or Twitter @vastine7. Please stop by my website amyvastine.com and sign up for my newsletter as well!

Xoxo,

Amy Vastine

HEARTWARMING

His Texas Runaway Bride

—

Amy Vastine

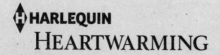

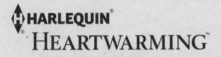

HARLEQUIN®
HEARTWARMING™

Recycling programs for this product may not exist in your area.

ISBN-13: 978-1-335-49090-2

His Texas Runaway Bride

Harlequin Enterprises ULC
22 Adelaide St. West, 41st Floor
Toronto, Ontario M5H 4E3, Canada
www.Harlequin.com

Printed in U.S.A.

Amy Vastine has been plotting stories in her head for as long as she can remember. An eternal optimist, she studied social work, hoping to teach others how to find their silver lining. Now she enjoys creating happily-ever-afters for all to read. Amy lives outside Chicago with her high school–sweetheart husband, three teenagers who keep her on her toes and their two sweet but mischievous pups. Visit her at amyvastine.com.

Books by Amy Vastine

Harlequin Heartwarming

Stop the Wedding!

A Bridesmaid to Remember
His Brother's Bride
A Marriage of Inconvenience
The Sheriff's Valentine

Return of the Blackwell Brothers

The Rancher's Fake Fiancée

The Blackwell Sisters

Montana Wishes

Visit the Author Profile page at Harlequin.com for more titles.

To all those people pleasers out there—
never settle for someone else's happiness.

CHAPTER ONE

"YOU ARE THE loveliest bride I have ever seen," Hilary Sanderson said as she stared at her daughter's reflection in the mirror with damp eyes.

"Mom, stop. You can't start crying before the ceremony even begins."

Of course, Hilary wasn't the only one about to break into tears. Willow squeezed her hands into fists to stop them from shaking. Was she really going to go through with this? The dark cloud of doubt that had been hovering over her for weeks seemed ready to unleash a violent storm of regret if she did. Yet, here she was, standing in the bridal suite in her wedding gown, about to walk down the aisle.

"Your dad and I are so proud of you. I hope you know that."

Willow's eyes widened for a second before she forced a neutral expression. She turned to face her mother. "Proud of me for what? Marrying Hudson Carpenter?" she asked with a tilt of her head.

The last thing Willow felt was proud of herself. She had spent years in school to become a pediatric nurse only to throw it all away as soon as Hudson asked her to. Hudson wanted her to stay home and start having his babies. He had a plan for the two of them and he didn't really bother to ask her if she shared that same vision. He just assumed she did. Hudson assumed a lot of things because no one ever questioned a Carpenter. That included Willow.

Willow had grown up doing what was expected of her. First, it was what her parents expected, and now it was what her soon-to-be husband expected. That was what a dutiful woman did. Her parents had always provided for her. She had grown up wanting for nothing. She was marrying a man from one of the wealthiest families in Dallas; surely she would want for nothing the rest of her life. Why would she complain? Why would she question their decisions? So what if they impacted her life so significantly?

"Proud of you for being you, darling," her mom replied, placing a hand on her shoulder.

"You have always been such a good girl. You deserve the wonderful life Hudson is going to give you."

How does someone refuse something that they are so very lucky to have received? Why did Willow want to refuse it so very badly?

She stared at herself in the mirror, at the dress her mother had chosen for her. The white lace was more sophisticated than the simple satin dress Willow had liked best. Hudson Carpenter needed a bride who stood out and rose above the rest. It didn't matter which dress made her feel confident. Her parents were paying for it. How could Willow even consider wanting anything else?

She twisted her finger around the tendril of hair that had been perfectly pulled from her updo to frame her face. Hudson's mother had suggested she wear it up because that was how he liked it. It was better to please him than disappoint. It didn't matter that Willow thought it would be prettier down like she had imagined when she pictured herself on her wedding day.

It didn't matter how Willow felt. About anything.

"I feel like I need a minute alone. Would

that be okay?" she asked, in desperate need of some privacy.

Her mother paused for a moment and seemed to be trying hard to read her daughter's expression. Satisfied that there was nothing to worry about, she smiled brightly. "Of course, sweetheart. I'll go make sure your father is ready to walk you down the aisle."

"Thanks."

Willow had no bridesmaids to chase out of the room. Hudson had decided that his brother and sister would be the only ones to stand up for them. He wanted things simple. Too many of the Dallas elite had a dozen bridesmaids and groomsmen to make them look popular. Hudson didn't want to look popular. He felt all that did was take the attention away from the bride and groom. They were the only two that mattered anyway.

It didn't matter that Willow wanted her best friend Portia at her side or that she and her college roommate had promised to be in each other's weddings when they happened.

She plopped down on the ivory chenille couch that looked like it had never been sat on and held her head in her hands. Why did this all feel like she was about to make the biggest mistake of her life?

It was times like these that she missed her Grandma Rose the most. Grandma Rose was Willow's favorite person on the planet. That woman had such a colorful personality. She told the best stories and always gave the best advice. Grandma Rose would have known what to do in this situation.

Grandma Rose had been the one to encourage Willow to pursue an education and had reminded her that she could be anything she wanted to be. She had enjoyed the finer things in life but appreciated that some of the best things didn't cost a thing. She had loved her life in Dallas but sometimes longed for the simpler life she'd left behind.

Grandma Rose had grown up in a small town southwest of Fort Worth called Maple Grove. She'd often share stories about her childhood, which had been very different from Willow's. Growing up, Grandma Rose had gotten dirty trying to catch frogs by a pond. Her family hadn't had a lot of money, but no one seemed to mind. Their house wasn't large, but it was full of the people Rose had loved. She'd shared a room with her older sister, and they used to stay up late at night talking about their favorite books and silly things like which boys they thought were cute. They had eaten dinner together as a family every night and gone to church on Sundays.

Willow had grown up in a big, fancy house that had every material thing she could want inside it. Only, it never felt like the home that Grandma Rose had described, filled with laughter and love instead of expensive furniture and crystal chandeliers. Her mother loved her, but it often seemed Hilary's mission in life was to make sure *everyone* loved Willow. From an early age, Willow was in pageants and the goal was always to be the prettiest, the wittiest, the most articulate. The ultimate goal had been to shine bright enough to gain the attention of the right people—like her mother had won the attention of her father. They were the beautiful wife and daughter of Gregory Sanderson. That was supposed to be enough.

Willow's stomach roiled. She was about to walk down the aisle and marry someone who was going to put her in a house with expensive furniture and crystal chandeliers. If she married Hudson, she was going to spend her life making sure she was a pretty accessory for him to show off to his friends and business associates. Her breathing became irregular. She didn't want that. She didn't want to marry Hudson.

She scanned the room. Three windows looked out to a garden. Her mother's purse sat on the side table by the enormous vase of silk flowers. Willow only had one chance to get away and if Grandma Rose were still alive, she would have wanted her to take it. Her mother always kept cash in her wallet for emergencies. This was definitely that.

With shaking hands, she requested a ride to the bus station on her phone and dug through her mother's wallet. She opened the window and heaved the suitcase she'd packed for her honeymoon out into the garden. Her heart pounded in her chest as she gathered all the tulle from the skirt of her dress. She jumped out and started to run.

"CAN I HAVE the rainbow sprinkles cake pop today?"

"You can definitely have one, bud." Sheriff Bryce Koller held open the door to the

Coffee Depot for his four-year-old son. They were greeted by the delicious aroma of fresh ground coffee and the sound of the owner's classic rock playlist.

Camden hopped over the threshold. He loved going to the Coffee Depot. The cozy shop was their favorite spot to hang out on Sunday mornings after breakfast and church. The Depot had a little bookcase in the corner full of books for all ages to read.

Today, Bryce was going to use the time to find himself a nanny on some website that Gretchen, the desk sergeant at the station, had told him to check out. Supposedly, this site screened all the applicants for people so they didn't have to worry about all that.

"Well, look who finally made it. I was starting to think you two weren't coming today." Louie Brenner was the affable owner of the Coffee Depot. He and his daughter had run the place going on six years.

"We're running a little behind today, but we made it," Bryce said. Truth was it had been a rough morning. Camden had struggled to fall asleep last night and then, after finally conking out, woken up a few hours later because he wet the bed. This morning, he was a total bear: didn't want to wear the clothes Bryce picked out for him, drank three glasses of OJ because he was so thirsty and the eggs weren't cooking fast enough, complained about his shoes hurting his feet, wouldn't sit still long enough to get his hair combed. They ended up missing their usual church service and had to go to the later one.

This was why finding a nanny was imperative. Keeping up with the household chores and working full-time, while being mom and dad to Camden, was too much for him to handle.

Camden tugged on his arm. "Daddy, I need to go." He bounced on his toes and tugged on his shorts. That meant he needed to go *now*.

"We'll be right back, Louie," Bryce said, snatching Camden up into his arms and moving quickly for the restroom. The consequence of drinking too many glasses of juice was needing to go to the bathroom a hundred times.

They washed their hands and headed back to the counter. An unfamiliar woman finished paying for her order when they got back in line. She tucked a couple of folded dollar bills into the tip jar and stepped aside to wait for her drink.

"Okay, what can I get for my favorite customers today?" Louie always wore a big smile and a blue apron with the Coffee Depot logo on it. There was no need to check the chalkboard menu that hung behind him. Bryce always got the same thing.

"I would like the largest cup of your dark roast with my usual amount of cream and sugar, and this little guy would like a glass of chocolate milk and a cake pop, please."

"With sprinkles!" Camden reminded him.

"Ah, yes, with sprinkles, *please*."

"Please!" Camden repeated.

Louie's face fell. "Oh, buddy. I am so sorry, but that nice lady in front of you got the last cake pop with sprinkles."

Camden did not understand. "But I want a cake pop with sprinkles."

"How about we get a cookie this time?"

"I want a cake pop with sprinkles!"

Bryce crouched down so he could be eye to eye with his son "Buddy, there are no more cake pops with sprinkles. We can get something else."

"Hey, I'm sorry. He can have this cake pop," the woman said.

Bryce stood back up, mortified. "He can pick something else. Please don't worry about it."

"It's fine," she assured him. "I won't be able to enjoy it, knowing he wanted it. Here you go, bud." The little paper bag that they had put the cake pop in crinkled as she handed it to Camden.

Bryce didn't recognize the kind woman. She wasn't from around here because Maple Grove was small enough that everyone knew everyone. She had dark brown hair pulled up into a ponytail and was dressed in a little white dress covered in a lemon print. He would have guessed she was younger than him but not by much.

"Thank you very much. What do you say, Cam?"

"Thank you!"

She had a pretty smile. "You're very welcome. It was no biggie."

"Let me buy you something else from the pastry case," he offered. She shook her head, but he insisted. "Please. You can't let him take your treat and not let me get you something in return."

Her eyes darted from the case back to Bryce. "Oh, what the heck. I'll take one of those chocolate croissants. No dress to worry about fitting into anymore."

Bryce squinted. She was wearing a dress that seemed to fit just fine. Not that he was looking at how this woman was fitting into her clothes. She was attractive, but he did not have time for romance in his life. He smiled politely before turning his attention to anything other than the woman whom he was not attracted to and her perfectly fitted dress.

"One chocolate croissant, coming up," Louie said, his smile always reaching his eyes.

"Thank you," the woman said, pulling Bryce's gaze back to her. "You really didn't have to do that."

Bryce got out some cash to pay for his now complete order. "Are you passing through or visiting someone here in Maple Grove?"

She played with the string that was tied around the waist of her dress. "Um, no. I, um, don't have anyone to visit here, but I am not just passing through, either."

He furrowed his brow at her answer that didn't provide any clarity whatsoever. "You just woke up one morning and decided to move here?"

She seemed to think about it for a second before that smile was back. She scrunched up her nose. "You would be surprised at how close that is to what actually happened."

"Would I?"

"I think you would. My grandmother grew up in Maple Grove. It's why I wanted to come here."

"Who's your grandmother?"

"Her maiden name was Rose Everly. It's been a long time since she lived here, though. I'm not sure you'd know who she is."

"I don't know a Rose Everly, but I know a Charlie Everly and his family. Maybe they're related."

She brightened. "Really? I don't know much about my grandmother's family, but she used to talk about this town and her love of it. It made it seem magical to me when I was a little girl. I couldn't think of a better place to make a fresh start."

Bryce wasn't sure what it was about this woman, but the energy she exuded was like standing in the sun after a long, dark winter. He'd lived in Maple Grove his entire life and never thought of it as magical.

"Well, I hope it turns out to be everything you want it to be," he said, taking his change from Louie.

"Me, too," she replied with a wistful sigh.

Louie handed her the croissant, and Caroline, his daughter, called out the woman's name. "Willow."

"Willow," Bryce repeated to commit it to memory. Willow turned her head at her name being spoken a second time. "It was nice to meet you, Willow."

"Bryce, your coffee and water are up," Caroline said, placing the two cups on the counter by Willow.

"Bryce," Willow repeated with an amused grin.

"We weren't very good at introducing ourselves, were we?"

She softly snickered as she dropped her gaze to the floor. "I guess not."

"Bryce Koller. Nice to meet you," he said, sticking out his hand to shake. Poor Willow, however, had her hands full with a drink and her pastry. He retracted his hand. "Sorry. I wasn't thinking there."

Willow gave her head a little shake. "No worries. I'm Willow."

"No last name? Are you like those famous people with only one name?"

Camden came running over and slammed into his leg. "Dad! I can't find my favorite book. It's gone!"

Bryce smiled at Willow, who took that opportunity to find herself a table. *Well, that was awkward.* "Let's look again together. I bet we can find it." He grabbed their drinks. "Here, take your water."

Camden took the water in one hand and his father's hand in the other, tugging Bryce over to their corner. "It's not here, Dad. I can't find it. Maybe someone stoled it. Can you catch them? You're the sheriff."

Bryce was the sheriff but busting book thieves was not really his top priority. "Let's give it one more look, bud."

Getting down on his knees, Bryce searched the bookcase with Camden. Sure enough, his favorite book was there. Bryce slid it out of its spot. "Here it is, Cam. Mystery solved."

Camden snatched the book out of his dad's

hand and hugged it against his chest. He skipped over to the comfy chair in the corner that was his spot on Sundays.

"Excellent work, Sheriff," Willow said with a wink from her table nearby. She had the local paper laid out before her.

Bryce rose to his feet. "I'm trained to handle difficult situations like these."

She nodded. "I'm sure. I can only imagine how many books have been recovered thanks to your diligence."

"More than I can count."

Willow's giggle was a sweet sound that Bryce found himself wishing he could hear again. She bit down on her lip and stared back down at the newspaper. He wanted to wipe the crease that formed between her brows. He pushed that feeling away, unsure where it came from.

Camden was busy "reading" his favorite book and Willow was clearly done conversing, so Bryce settled in at the table nearest his son and took out his laptop. It was time to do some nanny shopping.

The website Gretchen referred him to was a bit overwhelming. There were several questions to answer and his first search rendered no matches. He was prompted to change some of his filters. Three candidates were found.

Candace Harper, age sixty-eight. She had raised five of her own children and had fifteen grandchildren, who all lived in north Texas. Promising start. She had experience with children. That was a plus. She needed all major holidays off and might have to take a few days off a week to help with her grandchildren. Sometimes the child or children in her care might come with her and sometimes not.

That was a no for Grandma Candace. She had her hands full.

Bridgette Garrison, age twenty-two. She had spent two years in college studying early education. That was a plus. If she was a live-in nanny, she would require a private living space and be allowed to have overnight guests.

Sorry, Bridgette. Bryce wasn't going to have random friends of hers spending the night at his house.

"Dad, will you read me these books?" Camden asked, holding his favorite book and a new one.

"Can you give me a couple minutes, bud?

As soon as I finish doing this, I'll read as many books as you want."

"I want you to read to me now."

Bryce had to remind himself that four-year-olds didn't always understand the concept of being patient. "I know you do, but I am asking you to look at the books on your own for a little bit longer. Dad really needs to finish this."

"I could read to him." Willow's voice took Bryce by surprise.

"You don't have to do that."

"Really, the Help Wanted section of the *Maple Grove Gazette* is not as large as I had hoped. I can do it so you can finish what you're working on." She bent down so she was eye level with Camden. "Would that be okay, little man?"

Camden eyed her suspiciously. "Do you know how to read?"

"I do. I finished all the grades in school and even went to more school. Reading was my best subject."

"Do you know how to read with voices?" he asked with his head tipped to the side. Camden loved it when Bryce did the voices of characters. It made him giggle like nothing else.

"I am excellent at reading with different voices. Should we try?"

Camden nodded and handed her the books.

"I got this. You finish what you're doing," she said to Bryce before she followed Camden to his reading corner. She sat down next to him on the comfy chair and opened the first book.

Was this really happening? Bryce tried to go back to his nanny search, but the alternating sound of Willow doing funny voices and Camden giggling was too distracting. It had been too long since he'd heard those sounds coming out of his boy. It made his heart ache with joy and sorrow.

Bryce closed his laptop. Maybe fate had stepped in and put exactly who he was looking for right in his path this morning. Willow glanced up at him and noticed he was no longer glued to his screen.

"All done?"

"You mentioned you were looking in the Help Wanted section of the paper. Are you looking for a job here in Maple Grove?"

"I am. I only have so much money and the B and B in town isn't cheap."

"You're staying at Glenda and Ken's B and B on Apple Tree Lane?" There was only one bed-and-breakfast in town and not even Bryce could afford to stay there long-term.

"Yes, sir. It was the only place that had a room for me when I got here. Most people make sure they have a job and a place to live before they move somewhere. I'm doing things a little backwards."

This might have been the wildest idea he ever had, but something told him to give her a chance. "I think I might not only have a job for you but a place to stay as well. I have two questions, though."

Her face lit up. "Are you serious? Ask away."

"Since this was a little bit of an impulsive move on your part, can I trust you're going to stick around for more than a couple weeks?"

"I plan on staying as long as I can afford to stay here. I don't have any desire to go back to where I came from."

Bryce knew he should ask why she didn't want to go back, but they'd get to that question later.

"Okay, second question is have you ever

been arrested? And don't try to lie because I am the sheriff in this town and I will be looking you up later."

Willow held her hand up as if she was swearing on a Bible in court. "I have never been arrested. I have gotten a couple speeding tickets in my lifetime, but that's not, like, permanently on my record, is it?"

And just like that, Two-Ticket Willow was hired.

CHAPTER TWO

MAPLE GROVE WAS MAGIC. Just like Grandma Rose had made it seem. Willow had somehow gotten herself a job and a place to live all on her first full day in town. It was as if her grandmother's spirit had guided her right where she needed to be.

"Is this all you have?" Bryce asked as he placed her suitcase into the back of his truck.

Could it be more obvious that she had run away? Willow held tight to the black garbage bag that held her wedding dress. Her mother would freak out if she knew that the four-thousand-dollar dress was balled up in a garbage bag instead of on a hanger in a garment bag, but Willow had to work with what she had. "That's it."

"Do you want me to put that back here, too?" He reached for the garbage bag.

"I'll hold on to this if that's okay."

He held up both hands and backed away. "Yeah, no problem."

Willow climbed into the huge pickup truck. The cab had two rows of seats. Little Camden was strapped into his booster seat in the back. "Hi, Camden."

He turned his head away, hiding a huge smile on his face. "Hi, Willow."

He was adorable. How lucky was she that the job was going to be hanging out with this cutie all day?

"All set?" Bryce asked as he got settled in the driver's seat.

Willow nodded.

Speaking of cute...

Bryce was attractive, but not in the same way she found Hudson attractive. Hudson had been polished. Designer pretty. He had a skincare routine and spent hundreds of dollars on haircuts. His nails were perfectly manicured and he smelled divine. Hudson ran to stay in shape and had a runner's body—long and lean. Bryce was the complete opposite. Rugged. Natural. He probably used the same soap on his face that he used on the rest of his body. He had a five o'clock shadow and a light pink scar on his right temple. Bryce worked out to stay strong. He was all muscle.

His navy blue T-shirt was stretched tightly across his chest; his biceps were a work of art.

Not that she was paying attention to those kinds of things, because she wasn't. He was her new boss. She needed to stay focused on doing a good job and finding a way to support herself until she figured out what in the world she was going to do with her life now that she had blown up the old one.

"I have a car you'll be able to use. You'll have weekends off, unless I'm needed at the station for an emergency. But my neighbor can also help out in those situations. I don't want to make you feel like you won't get time for yourself."

"No worries. I am happy to help out whenever you need me." For the first time in her life, Willow had no social life to keep her busy, no demands from her parents, no image to uphold. It was kind of liberating.

Maple Grove was definitely a small town. The drive from the bed-and-breakfast downtown to Bryce and Camden's house took minutes. They pulled into the driveway and Willow admired the two-story white colonial house and the mature trees that shaded it. It had steps dead center leading to a wide front porch. Two rocking chairs sat in one corner and colorful flowerpots sat empty on the other side. Six tall windows were flanked with black shutters.

Bryce unbuckled Camden before going to the back to grab Willow's suitcase. Camden led the way to the front door.

"Your room is on the first floor with Cam's. I'm upstairs," Bryce explained as he unlocked the door.

Willow stepped inside their world and was immediately greeted by a very friendly golden retriever.

"What's this guy's name?" she asked, attempting to pet him while hanging on to her garbage bag and trying to keep him from jumping up on her.

"Banjo, down. Come on, now. That's no way to make a first impression."

Banjo was a good listener because he dropped to the ground on command.

"Hi, Banjo."

"Did I mention we have a dog?" Bryce looked absolutely remorseful. "You aren't allergic, I hope. I am so sorry I did not check with you before I basically let him pummel you."

"Not allergic. I love dogs. I've never had one, but I always wanted one."

"I promise he will behave himself. Right, Banjo? Let's show you around."

The stairs leading to the second floor were right there in the entryway. To the right was a formal dining room. There was a stillness in that room that gave the impression that no one ever ate in there. The hall led to the living room that was clearly the heart of the home. This was where they lived. Camden's toys were scattered in one corner. The couch looked worn in; she'd surely sink into it, all comfy-cozy. A wood-burning fireplace was on the back wall. To the right of that was a huge kitchen with a window seat in the breakfast area that had views of their backyard where there was a play set and tire swing.

"The bedrooms are back this way," Bryce said, heading to the left. He switched on the hall light. "This is your room," he said. nodding to the right before pointing to the room at the other end of the hall. "That's Camden's room. I keep a monitor in my room upstairs, so I have eyes on him all night. He's been having some trouble sleeping. Sometimes I end up crashing on the couch, so don't be alarmed if you find me there in the morning."

Willow poked her head in her room and flicked on some lights. This was clearly the master bedroom. There was a large king-size bed and an en suite bathroom that had to have been newly remodeled. It had a gorgeous claw-foot tub and a walk-in shower. The dark wood double vanity had a white marble top and elegant satin brass hardware and faucets.

"There are towels and such in the linen closet in the bathroom. Feel free to use whatever you need."

There were two doors in the space between the bathroom and the bedroom. One was open to an empty walk-in closet and the other was closed. Willow put her hand on the knob.

"Don't!" Bryce shouted, causing her to nearly jump out of her skin. He immediately seemed filled with regret. His voice softened. "That's off-limits. Don't go in there. The other closet is all yours."

Willow's heart was beating a million beats a minute. "Sorry. Of course. This is a beautiful space for a nanny. I feel like it's almost too much. I hope your room upstairs is as nice as this."

"Let me show you around the kitchen," he said, ignoring her comment altogether. She shouldn't question his kindness. Grandma Rose's magic was still working in her favor. This was more than she could ask for.

She tossed the garbage bag full of her past mistakes into the empty closet and followed him to the kitchen. The kitchen took up the whole length of one side of the house. It had a massive island and an adequate amount of cabinets. Willow was used to the all-white kitchen back at her parents' house. It had always felt very sterile. This one had warm brown cabinets with chunky brass hardware. She loved the contrast of the white counters and walls.

"Part of the job will be taking on the meal planning and cooking. I will add you to my account at the grocery store and they'll let you charge everything to me."

Cooking? That was not Willow's strongest skill. In fact, she was best at ordering take out. How hard could it be, though? There had to be plenty of videos online that could show her how to make the basics.

"Fantastic," she replied, plastering on a fake smile. "Can you make me a list of things y'all like to eat, so I have an idea of your tastes?"

"Good idea." Bryce opened the door to the laundry room. "Here's where you can do your laundry. You'll only be doing yours. I'll take care of me and Cam."

"Dad, I'm thirsty. Can I have some apple juice?" Camden asked, pulling open the refrigerator.

"How about some water?" Bryce walked over and closed the door. "You've had enough sugar today." He retrieved a cup from the cabinet next to the sink and filled it with tap water. Willow would have to learn where things went in here.

"I typically work from eight to five Monday through Friday. However, because I'm sheriff, I'm on call twenty-four seven, three hundred and sixty-five days of the year. Luckily, Maple Grove doesn't see too much action, but there are times I may be called away outside of my regular work week. Like I said, my neighbor, Mrs. Holland, is willing to help out if ever there's a need. You just let me know. I want to respect your boundaries."

"I appreciate that." Willow found him to be extremely respectful. Other than scaring the daylights out of her when she almost entered the forbidden closet, she found him to be quite the gentle giant.

"More water, please," Camden said, holding the empty glass out for his dad.

"I swear this kid must be growing. He eats and drinks more than I do." Bryce refilled Camden's cup.

"Good to know," Willow said, taking a seat at the island. "Does Camden have any allergies or medical issues I should know about?"

"None that I'm aware of. He's healthy as a horse."

"You said he's been having some trouble sleeping. Is there an issue there?" Her nursing instincts told her to ask.

Bryce cleared his throat. "Hey, buddy, can you go pick up your toys in the living room so Willow doesn't trip on any of them?" After a tiny protest, Camden did as his father asked. Once he was out of the kitchen, Bryce placed both hands on the island and stared down at the counter instead of making eye contact with Willow. He swallowed hard. "Cam lost his mom about a year ago. It's been tough and the town doctor had warned me that I might see him regress a little bit. He's restless at night. More recently, he's been wetting the bed in the middle of the night. I'm hoping having another adult in the house full-time will help get him back on track."

That answered the questions she had about Camden's mom. "I am so sorry for your loss," she said, reaching across the island and putting her hand on his.

His eyes shot up and met hers like a scared animal. He pulled his hand away. "Thanks. It's been really hard on him, but I think he'll be okay in the end."

Looked like it wasn't only Camden that the loss had been hard on. Clearly, he wasn't ready to go there with a stranger. They both had some secrets that needed to stay secrets. She could respect that.

BRYCE WAS EMBARRASSED that he had jerked away from her touch like that. He hoped she hadn't noticed that he was reacting so poorly to talking about April. He knew it was going to come up eventually.

"It makes sense that he'd be responding to the loss by having some developmental setbacks. We'll monitor his fluid intake later in the day and we can get the bedwetting under control real quick, I bet," Willow said confidently.

"You have experience with this kind of thing?" Bryce realized he hadn't even asked her what she did before she came to Maple Grove.

"Uh, I do. I've worked with kids before in my old job."

"What kind of work did you do?"

She seemed apprehensive to share. "I was actually a nurse at a children's hospital."

Bryce couldn't hide his surprise. "A nurse?" He should have been happy about this, but given the way Camden felt about doctors, nurses, and hospitals, it gave him pause.

She misconstrued his concerned expression. "I can provide you with some references. I left on good terms, I swear."

"All cleaned up, Dad," Camden announced. "Can I show Willow my play set out back?"

"I would love to see your play set. Lead the way, little man." Willow reached for his hand and followed him to the French doors that led out back, with Banjo not far behind.

Seeing Camden holding a woman's hand put a giant lump in Bryce's throat. He tipped his head back and glared at the ceiling. "I hope this is the right thing to do, April. I figure you wouldn't let this happen if it wasn't," he whispered.

He watched out the window as Camden climbed up the ladder and slid down the bright yellow slide. Willow high-fived him and Bryce could tell Camden asked her to take a turn. She didn't hesitate even though she was still in that lemon print dress. She climbed right up there and slid down, much to Camden's delight.

This was the right thing to do.

His phone rang. It was June.

"I am sitting on my back porch and listening to that boy of yours laugh while playing out there with a young lady I have never seen before. Are you trying to tell me I'm fired?"

Bryce loved June. She'd been like a second mother to Camden, especially when April got sick. Her support had meant the world to him because his parents were in Amarillo, near his sister, and April's mom was unreliable at best. He could not have asked for a better neighbor. "I am finally done taking advantage of your kindness. I hired a nanny."

"Well, that was fast! I thought I would have a couple more weeks with my buddy Cam."

"She might need your help these first couple weeks. I told her you are a godsend and that I couldn't have survived the last year without you."

"Oh, Bryce. You know I think of you and Camden as family. I loved April like she was my own. There was nothing I wouldn't have done for you this past year."

The lump in his throat was back in full force. "Thank you, June," Bryce pushed out around it.

"I look forward to meeting this new nanny. I hope she's exactly what you need."

So did he. "You are always welcome to stop by. Let's give her today to find her bearings. Maybe you could drop by tomorrow to help her while I'm at work?"

"I will do that. Enjoy the rest of your Sunday, Bryce."

"You, too."

Camden and Willow were now swinging on the swings. She was showing him how she pumped her legs to get her to go higher without being pushed. Camden always wanted to be pushed, but there he was trying his best to do what she was doing. The smile on his face was priceless.

Bryce went back to the island and rummaged in the junk drawer for a pen and notepad. He started his list of favorite meals. Once he finished that, he made a general schedule for the week. One of the neighbors had convinced Bryce to sign Cam up for a T-ball league that started this week, and June had him in a weekly gymnastics class. He wrote down the names of a couple of friends in the neighborhood who had kids Camden liked to play with sometimes.

Before he knew it, an hour had passed. Willow and Camden came back inside laughing and out of breath.

"I'm thirsty. Can I have some apple juice now?" Camden asked.

"I can get it for him," Willow offered just as Bryce set down his pen.

"Thanks. The cups are—"

She didn't need his help, though. She went right for the cabinet with the cups. She was a fast learner.

"What's for dinner?" Camden asked after he downed his entire cup of juice.

"I was thinking we would order pizza tonight since it's Willow's first night and she shouldn't be tortured by my bad cooking."

"That sounds like a great plan," Willow said with a clear sense of relief.

"You're that afraid of my cooking?" Bryce asked, knowing she should be.

Embarrassment colored her cheeks. "Oh my gosh, no. That's not what I meant. I love pizza. I would eat anything. I'm sure you're not that bad a cook. It's not that hard to cook, right?"

She seemed like she was actually asking. "I'm kidding. Although you should be more afraid of my cooking than you are. It's not good. I think you have to be born with a cooking gene and I was not. I have watched videos on YouTube and tried following recipes that say they're easy. No luck."

"No luck, huh? Even when you watched the videos and did exactly what they said?"

"Even then. Bad cooks are bad cooks."

Willow fidgeted with that string tied around her waist again. "Gotcha. Pizza it is."

She was difficult to read. It was going to take some getting used to having another adult in the house again, especially one who was basically being hired to mother his child. He needed this to work out.

"Can I have a snack and more juice?" Camden asked. "I'm so hungry."

"Do you want to show Willow where the snacks are?" Bryce asked Camden. He was going to have to be a big helper these first few days. They were kind of throwing Willow right into the fray without much preparation. Bryce refilled Camden's cup with some water.

"Over here, Willow." Camden ran for the pantry and came out with a bag of cheese crackers.

"Did you want something to snack on?" Willow asked Bryce, holding a bag of crackers. She was thoughtful. He liked that.

"I'm going to wait for the pizza, but thank you. I made you some lists while you two were out there playing."

She came over and sat next to him at the island. She had a light sheen of sweat covering her skin. Camden and Banjo had given her quite the workout. She opened her bag of crackers and put one in her mouth. "Mmm, these are pretty good."

"You've never had cheese crackers before?"

Her laugh was light. "I haven't. Is that weird?"

"I guess not."

"You only guess?" Her eyes danced with

amusement. "That means there's a possibility that it's weird."

She made him chuckle. "Fine. I can with absolute certainty reassure you that it is not weird. At least not *super* weird."

Her face fell along with her shoulders. "Wow, thanks for that. Your nanny is only a little weird, Cam. Not super weird."

"I like weird things," Camden said, looking up at her with those big brown eyes that were just like his mom's.

"Well, that's perfect, then," Willow said, ruffling his hair. "All right, let's see these lists."

How was it that she fit in so perfectly from the start? This had April's touch written all over it.

"Knock, knock!" a voice came from the front of the house. Bryce's shoulders tensed immediately. There was only one person who felt it was completely acceptable to walk into his house without actually knocking.

Banjo barked like it was a burglar.

"Grandma!" Camden shouted as April's mom rounded the corner. Her eyes fell right on Willow.

"Who the heck is that?" she snarled.

CHAPTER THREE

WILLOW COULD FEEL the pure disdain coming from the woman Camden called Grandma. She glared at Willow as if she was some kind of miscreant.

Bryce got on his feet and put himself in between the woman and Willow. Grandma's hair was a wild mess of dark brown curls streaked with gray and she was wearing a loud, multicolored, striped dress that looked more like a costume than her Sunday best.

"Delia, this is Willow. I hired her to be Camden's nanny."

Camden wrapped his arms around his grandma. She squatted to give him a hug back. "You hired a nanny to take care of my grandson?"

"We talked about this. I told you I was going to do that."

"Instead of letting me, his flesh and blood, watch over him?" Delia's instant dislike for Willow made sense now.

Willow wondered why Bryce had not mentioned that Camden's grandmother lived nearby. He seemed to rely on the neighbor more than his mother...mother-in-law, maybe.

"We've talked about this, Delia. You know why that is not an option and we're not going to go over it in front of Cam."

"You think because you're the sheriff you can boss me around?"

Bryce shook his head. "Why don't you come in and let me get you some water? Camden can show you some of his new art projects."

"Have you been coloring again, Cammy?" Delia asked.

Camden took her hand and walked her into the living room where he had some coloring sheets taped to the far wall.

"I feel like I should give y'all a minute," Willow said. She was used to this kind of family tension. It was part of the reason she'd run away from her own wedding.

"Yeah, why don't you go to your room and I'll let you know when dinner is here," Bryce said, his expression hard and controlled.

Willow made a quick escape back to her new bedroom. Surely, he would have to explain everything later. Something told her this wasn't the last time she was going to come face-to-face with an aggressive Grandma Delia.

She took a seat on the bed and wished she could go on her phone and see what was going on in the world. She knew that if she turned it on, Hudson would be there faster than lightning. He had to be trying to track her down. She could only imagine how angry he was. No one told Hudson no, and she had done that without words but with her actions. Her parents were also probably searching for her. She hadn't meant to humiliate them in front of their friends and all of the Carpenters, but what other choice had they given her? There had been no way out but to flee.

Now she was here in Maple Grove and suddenly in the middle of someone else's family drama. Bryce's wife was dead. Her mother was unhappy with his parenting plan. What other bombs were waiting to go off around here?

She decided not to dwell on it and unpacked the few possessions she had instead. It was almost comical how few things she had to hang in the closet. Her toiletries took up little space on the vanity in the bathroom. This was such a beautiful space. Everything seemed brand-new. Willow wondered why Bryce would choose not to use these rooms for himself.

Willow could hear some more arguing and then a slam of the front door. She waited a few moments and then poked her head out to make sure the coast was clear. Bryce and Camden were sitting on the couch while Banjo lay at Bryce's feet. The television was on and a cartoon was playing. Bryce had his head tilted back and his hand on his forehead as though he was nursing a headache.

"Is it okay if I grab some water?" she asked, stepping into the room.

Bryce's head snapped forward and his gaze latched on to her. "Yeah, she's gone. You're free to move around the house again."

"Can I have some more water?" Camden asked. "I'm so thirsty."

Bryce began to get up, but Willow waved him off. "I've got it. Relax, I feel like you need to after that visit."

"You have no idea," Bryce said, following her into the kitchen anyway. "I should explain. I planned to explain after Camden went to bed tonight. There are things you should know about his grandma."

He stood close, so close it was hard not to touch. The look of exhaustion on his face made her want to take him in her arms and tell him everything was going to be all right. He was a big, strong guy, but she could see there was still a person who needed some care and comfort under all that.

"I can wait until he goes to bed." She filled up Camden's cup and handed it to Bryce.

"Thanks for understanding. I feel like I really made the right choice in hiring you. I'm glad you showed up at the Coffee Depot this morning."

"And bought the last cake pop with sprinkles?"

He smiled and she felt triumphant for the moment. "Right, that's what started it all."

Willow felt this pull in her chest. She liked the way he looked at her and had to tear her gaze away from those blue eyes. She filled up her own glass with some water and drank it down as if she needed to put out a fire.

"I'm going to call for pizza. Any topping requests?" he asked.

"I like everything except pineapple and onion on my pizza. So go nuts."

"Camden will only eat cheese. It's nice

to have someone to share something a little more adventurous." He backed away and delivered Camden his drink.

Do not fall for your hot boss, she had to remind herself. One day ago, she was about to walk down the aisle and marry another man. Obviously, that had been a huge mistake. She wasn't sure she had ever truly been in love with Hudson. It didn't matter, though. Bryce was her boss. She couldn't mess up the good thing she had here by letting her silly feelings get in the way.

BRYCE WATCHED WILLOW eat pizza as if she had been denied food for months. She was on slice number three and showed no signs of slowing down.

"It's good, right?"

She picked up her napkin and wiped her mouth. "It's delicious. I can't remember the last time I had pizza. I think I've been living on kale and tilapia for way too long."

"Kale and tilapia?" Bryce was going to make sure those two things never ended up on the dinner menu.

"Yeah, I was watching my weight. Or I should say my mother was watching my weight, but that is now over and I am going to enjoy food again because life is too short to eat kale."

Willow did not appear to be someone who had to watch what she ate. She was dainty. Petite and slim. Her mom sounded…interesting.

"Do your parents live in Texas?" he asked, curious to see what she'd share. He truly did not know much about her or where she came from.

She quickly took another bite of pizza and nodded her head.

"Can I have some more milk?" Camden asked, having finished two slices of his personal cheese pizza.

Willow glanced at her watch. "What time is bedtime?" she asked.

"Bedtime routine begins around seven."

Willow gently patted Camden's hand. "I think we need to cut you off, little man. No more drinks tonight."

"But I'm thirsty!"

"I know. It's going to be the hardest tonight, but once we get this routine set, you'll be able to stop drinking at this time every night like it's the easiest thing ever."

Camden put both hands on his neck. His eyes started to fill with tears. "I'm so thirsty. I just need a little water. Please, Daddy."

"I think Willow is right, bud. We don't want an accident like we had last night."

"I won't. I promise. Please, Daddy," Camden pleaded.

Bryce hated when he begged. It was so hard to deny this little boy anything, given everything that he'd been through in the last year. "What if he just had a little bit?"

Willow winced. "It's up to you, but setting a cutoff time is really important. It will help us determine if it's intake or something else."

"Something else?"

She lifted a shoulder. "I mean maybe there's a bladder issue. I don't know. We would need to rule out the intake before we jumped to that. That's what a doctor would tell you."

"Please, Daddy." Camden began to cry. One little sip of water wasn't going to tip the scales in the wrong direction.

"Just a little bit, but then no more tonight."

Bryce got up from the table and consciously didn't make eye contact with Willow. He didn't want to see the judgment that had to be there. He filled Camden's cup with a little bit of milk. He was growing. That had to be why he was eating and drinking so much. He didn't have a bladder issue. He was dealing with some emotional baggage left behind by his mother's untimely passing.

He placed the cup in front of Camden, who snatched it up and finished it off in less than a second. "That wasn't enough, Daddy."

"Well, it's going to have to be. No more drinks tonight. Why don't you go back into the living room and finish coloring?"

Reluctantly, he did as he was told. When Bryce mustered up the courage to look Willow's way, she was hyper-focused on the pizza on her plate.

"I know what you're thinking," Bryce said. She was too polite to say anything first.

"You are his dad. You always get the final say on everything. What I think does not matter," she was quick to reply, still staring down at her plate.

"He's had a rough year. It's hard to be super firm with him. I know I need to be firm at times, but I'm still working on it."

Finally, she lifted her gaze. He didn't see judgment. It was worse. He saw pity. It was a common occurrence. Everyone in town knew what had happened to April. Even a year later, people still looked sorry for him. It sure didn't take long for the nanny to be like everyone else.

"You'll get it. I'm here to help now," she said, causing his heart to skip a beat. That was unexpected. Her words felt like a warm hug. It had been so long since someone other than Camden had hugged him.

"Thank you," he said, meaning it more than he could explain.

After dinner, they went over the weekly schedule. He explained that June would be coming over in the morning to help her get a handle on things when Bryce wasn't around to answer questions. At seven, Bryce got Camden ready for bed.

"What a busy day we had, huh?" he said to Camden as he switched on his nightlight.

"Is Willow going to be here in the morning?"

"She is. She's going to be here every day. She's going to help me take good care of you like Mrs. Holland used to, but she's going to stay here instead of going back to her house like Mrs. Holland did."

"She's nice. I'm going to show her my animals tomorrow." Camden had quite the collection of miniature animal figurines. He liked to line them up and pretend they were in an animal parade.

"I think she'll like that a lot."

"And I'm going to show her where we keep the ice cream."

Bryce raised his eyebrows. "Oh, are you? Not because you want ice cream but because you want to be nice and let her know where it is, right?"

"I can have a little bit. Not a lot."

He made Bryce smile. "A little bit and only *after* you have lunch."

"You can have some, too."

"Daddy is going to be at work tomorrow, remember? Mrs. Holland is going to check on you and Willow to make sure y'all are doing okay. If you need anything, you can tell Mrs. Holland and she will make sure I know, okay?"

"Okay, Daddy."

Bryce brushed the hair from the little boy's eyes. His hair had been so blond when he was a baby. April had thought he was going to look exactly like Bryce, but the older he got, the darker his hair got. Soon enough it would be the same chestnut brown his mother's had been. Bryce saw April in Camden all the time. He had her mischievous grin, her inability to wait for anything. Her eyes, her hair. Her heart.

"Get some sleep, bud." Bryce kissed him on the forehead and went to the door. He switched off the lights and closed the door, leaving it open three inches, the mandatory gap necessary for Camden to stay in bed.

Willow sat on the couch, her legs curled underneath her. Banjo was lying next to her on the couch, even though he knew he wasn't allowed on the furniture. The dog seemed to like her. Willow paged through one of Camden's coloring books.

"Feeling the urge to color a picture tonight?"

She was startled and laughed. Setting down the book, she smiled. "No, but I was trying to find the one I was going to color tomorrow with Camden."

"I like that you're trying to be prepared," he said, taking a seat on the other end of the couch. "Banjo, get down, boy. You know better than that." The dog hopped off the couch and lay down by Bryce's feet. Banjo followed directions when the boss was around, at least.

"I'm sorry. I didn't know he wasn't allowed on the couch. He jumped up here like he owned the place."

"Don't worry about it."

"I'm trying to make a good first impression. Eventually, once you're used to having me around, I'll be sitting here with a glass of wine, watching the latest reality TV dating show, forcing you to tell me who you'd eliminate if you were the bachelor."

He tried and failed to hold back a smile. "So much to look forward to."

They sat in silence for a moment. Bryce wasn't sure where to start even though he knew where he should begin. "I should explain about Delia," he said.

"Grandma Delia."

"She's my mother-in-law. Her relationship with me is complicated. Her relationship with her daughter was complicated April's whole life. Besides that, we noticed Delia becoming more forgetful around the same time April got sick. She still refuses to go to a doctor. April tried, but she got so sick so fast she couldn't manage her illness and her mom's at the same time."

"How difficult for her and you," Willow empathized.

He hadn't thought about this in so long. It had been so hard on April. For Bryce, Delia's issues were just another thing he was helpless to make better. Another reminder that he was useless.

"Delia has a boyfriend named Lee, who does his best to look after her, but her memory issues make her an unsafe person for Camden to be alone with. That being said, I would never deny her the opportunity to spend time with her grandson, especially since we lost his mom."

Willow nodded. "That makes sense."

"If she ever shows up here when I'm not home and offers to take Camden somewhere, it's imperative that you call me. She is welcome to come in and under your supervision see Cam, but she is not to be left alone with him or be allowed to take him anywhere without me."

"Got it."

"I can give you my cell number and the number at the station where you can talk to someone who can get me a message right away if I don't answer my cell. I should get your cell number as well." Bryce pulled out his phone ready to enter her number into his contacts.

"Um." Willow pressed a hand to her cheek. "I, uh, lost my phone, actually. I was going to get a new one today and all this happened and I totally forgot."

"Oh." That was strange. In today's world, people were attached to their phones day and night. It had, however, been a whirlwind of a day, so maybe it wasn't as strange as he thought. "We only have one cell phone provider with a store in town. You're going to have to go to Stephenville to get one with the major brands. I could take you there after work tomorrow. I don't know how you would feel about going on your own with Camden. Maybe June could stay with Camden while you went?"

"The place in town is fine. I was ready to change providers anyway. I'll get one tomorrow first thing."

Bryce couldn't quiet the voice in his head that told him something was up. "Don't you have that thing that lets you search for your lost phone remotely? You can use my laptop if you want to."

"No, I didn't have it set to do that. I'm almost positive that I lost it on the bus that brought me here. I need to get a new one."

"I'm happy to let you use my phone to call the bus company and see if someone turned it in. I'm in law enforcement, I know all about stolen phones, but it's possible that some kind bus rider turned your phone in."

She pulled her legs out from under her and set her feet on the ground. She looked ready to bolt from the room. "Uh, I called them from the B&B. No luck. It's not a big deal. I'll go first thing in the morning and get a new one. You'll have a way to get a hold of me as soon as possible."

That was all that mattered. He needed to know that he could get in touch with her at any time. He was leaving her in charge of the most important person in his life. Was he losing his mind by moving a woman he knew nothing about into his home, allowing her to watch his child?

"Do you need anything from me to do that background check you were planning on doing?" she asked as if she read his mind.

"Your last name would be good. Maybe I could see your driver's license, so I know those tickets didn't end with you losing your license."

She seemed unfazed by his request. "I have never lost my license. I am a very good driver, by the way. Those speeding tickets were from many years ago when I was a new driver. Grown-up me is much more cautious and law-abiding," she said before disappearing into her bedroom.

Maybe he had no reason to be so suspicious. She was a good person. He would run her license and surely find nothing of concern.

"Here you go," she said, handing him her Texas driver's license. She was from Dallas.

"You're a city girl, huh?"

"Yeah, born and raised."

Willow Sanderson from Dallas, Texas. Granddaughter of Rose Everly. Here to start a new life. What was wrong with her life in Dallas? Why did she leave her job at the children's hospital? Was she hiding something or not? He would find out before he left Camden alone with her.

CHAPTER FOUR

WAS IT AGAINST the law to lie to a sheriff if when telling that lie, the person was not under arrest? Willow sure hoped not. It wasn't like he could run her driver's license and find out she hadn't lost her phone. It was currently hiding in the black garbage bag with her wedding dress. Why did she say she lost it? Why didn't she just say it was broken? She knew she couldn't tell him she was a runaway bride. He'd question her motives for being there. He might think she lacked good judgment.

Maybe he'd be right.

Willow knew he had made a call to someone, but he hadn't heard anything back by the time she decided to retire to her bedroom. Someone was running her driver's license and would find out she was a normal, rule-following citizen capable of caring for a child for a few hours a day.

She thought of other ways he might try to

snoop into her background. He could look her up on social media, but all of her accounts were private. He wouldn't be able to glean much from that. It was bad enough that she didn't have a good reason to explain why she left her job, one she had worked hard to get. She didn't want him to figure out that she had run away from her wedding. It would make her look flaky.

The knock on her bedroom door made her jump anyway. "Come on in," she said, sitting up straight.

"Sorry. I wanted to give you your license back. I had one of my deputies run it at the station and nothing of interest came back. You were not lying when you said you have no criminal record. I probably should have told you earlier that tickets are removed from the record after three years here in Texas. You, miss, have probably had a clean driving record for a while." Bryce handed her the license.

Willow was relieved that there was nothing to worry about. Her parents hadn't reported her as a missing person or had the police put out an APB or whatever it was called. She was safe and sound.

"Let me know if you want anything else from me. I am an open book," she said, hoping it sounded convincing, so convincing that he wouldn't take her up on the offer.

Bryce nodded. "I'll let you know. For now, I'll let you get some sleep. Camden is going to be ready to go bright and early. I hope you're prepared."

"Piece of cake."

Famous last words.

At three in the morning, she woke to the sounds of Bryce and Camden talking. Bryce reassured Camden that he wasn't mad; it was an accident. Camden must have wet the bed again. She would have to be firmer about the drink cutoff time moving forward if they were going to work this out.

At seven in the morning, Camden knocked on her door.

"Come on in, buddy. Is everything okay?"

"My dad is in the shower and I'm really thirsty. Can you get me some orange juice and make me breakfast?"

Bryce hadn't been lying. Camden was ready to put her to work first thing. "Let me brush my teeth and get human. I'll meet you in the kitchen in a few minutes, okay?"

"Okay, but I'm really thirsty."

"I promise, I'll only be a couple minutes," she said, dragging herself out of bed. It was one kid. She was used to managing several. Nursing wasn't exactly the same as being a nanny, but it couldn't be that much harder. At least this kid was healthy. He didn't have to take any medicine. She didn't need to take his vitals on the regular.

One bad thing about only having her honeymoon suitcase was that her vacation wear was not kid-friendly. Nothing Hudson wanted to do was ever casual. She had dresses and jumpers, a few bathing suits, an embarrassing amount of lingerie.

Willow certainly couldn't make breakfast in her silk nightgown. She put on a floral maxi dress. It was supposed to be her walk-around-a-Greek-island dress but was about to become her hang-out-with-a-four-year-old dress. She swept up her hair in a ponytail and brushed her teeth.

She stepped out of her room at the same time Bryce exited the hall bathroom in nothing but a towel. Apparently there was no bathroom upstairs. His chest was even more impressive when it was not tightly covered in fabric. His blond hair almost looked the same color as Camden's when it was wet.

"Sorry, Camden is waiting for me in the kitchen. He's ready for breakfast or so he tells me." Willow could smell the soap Bryce must have used in the shower. It had a fresh scent that stuck to his skin.

"Yeah, he's a big fan of breakfast. And lunch, snack, dinner, after-dinner snack…"

Willow laughed. Why did he have to be good-looking and funny?

"I'm going to go get that started while you, uh, put some clothes on."

"Good idea." He smirked and somehow the temperature in the house went up a hundred degrees.

Willow had to avert her eyes and remind herself that she was here to take care of Camden, not ogle his father.

"Okay, buddy," she said, slapping her hands together when she got into the kitchen. "Breakfast time. How about some cereal?" Willow could make cereal. That was easy. Bowl, cereal, milk. Easy-peasy.

"I don't like cereal," Camden replied. "Can I have some orange juice and some scrambled eggs?"

"Scrambled eggs?" That was not as easy as cereal. Was there anything she had to do to the eggs besides scramble them? What should she use to scramble them? Was there a special tool? Maybe a whisk. Did she have to add anything else? She really needed to get that new phone pronto so she could google these things. "Let's start with the orange juice."

Drinks were easy. She poured him a small glass and he finished about one second after she set it in front of him.

"Can I have more?" he asked.

"Okay, but let's try to drink this next one a little slower." She added some more to his cup. "What if instead of scrambled eggs we had toast with jelly. That used to be my favorite when I was little."

Camden scrunched his nose. "Toast? That's boring."

"Plain toast might be boring, but toast with jelly is delicious. I could also cut up some banana. What about that?"

"I like eggs best. Or, I know! Let's have pancakes!"

Pancakes? That sounded even more complicated than eggs. "What if once your dad comes downstairs, we ask him where the best doughnut place is and we get doughnuts for my first day? That could be fun, right?"

Camden's face lit up like it was Christmas. "Doughnuts? I love doughnuts!"

She still had plenty of the money she had stolen from her mother's purse, thanks to Bryce's offer of free room and board. It had to be enough to buy doughnuts and a new phone.

Bryce entered the kitchen in his sheriff uniform and Willow almost dropped her glass of orange juice. Bryce in a uniform was almost more butterfly-inducing than shirtless Bryce, and shirtless Bryce fluttered a lot of butterfly wings.

"Dad, we're going to get doughnuts."

Bryce's brow furrowed. "We're doing what now? We don't have to get doughnuts, Cam. Willow is here to make you breakfast."

"She said we can get doughnuts when you come downstairs."

"I suggested that since I need to run to town to get a new phone that maybe afterward, we could stop and get some doughnuts instead of wasting time making breakfast and cleaning up and all that jazz. Just this morning because, you know, I need a new phone, like, right away since you have to go to work." She took a sip of orange juice to stop her mouth from spitting words out.

Bryce scratched the back of his neck. "I don't know the exact time the cell store opens, but I can almost guarantee you it is not seven thirty in the morning."

"Right. It's that early. I didn't realize. Well, we could get the doughnuts first and then get the phone." She twirled her hands in one direction and then twirled them in the other. "Reverse the order of things. The doughnut stores are open this early, aren't they?"

Bryce pulled his phone out and did a quick search. "Cell phone store opens at nine. I think I know what's going on here."

Willow was about to die of embarrassment. She had to admit that she had no idea how to cook anything. Scrambled eggs might as well be crème brûlée.

"Camden, I know you love doughnuts, but we have to remember that Willow is not here to feed you all the goodies in the world."

"But Dad—"

"No but, buddy." Bryce turned his gaze on Willow. "He was already plotting last night how to get you to eat ice cream with him later today. This little guy has a massive sweet tooth. Please don't feel like you have to indulge him. It's okay if we just have something at home."

"I had suggested something a little healthier like cereal," Willow said, praying Bryce could convince Camden that cereal was the breakfast of champions.

"What about that brown sugar oatmeal that you like, Cam?" Bryce suggested.

"Can I have blueberries on top?"

Bryce looked to Willow. "I think we can manage that," she replied. Blueberries on top were the easiest part of this plan.

"I'll grab the oatmeal packets if you want to heat the water in the kettle," Bryce said, heading for the pantry.

Heating water in a kettle, also easy. She could also do that. Couldn't get simpler than boiling water. No one messed that up.

Bryce handed her two packets of oatmeal, both of which stated clearly how much water to add to the oatmeal inside. She sighed a sigh of relief.

"I am going to have to grab and go. Mondays are always a little busier for me first thing in the morning. You have all my numbers, and June said she'd stop by sometime this morning. I wrote out directions for you so you can get to town later and replace your phone. Y'all good?"

"We're good," Willow replied.

"Bye, Daddy," Camden said, holding his arms open for a hug. Bryce didn't hesitate to pick him up and hug him tightly. Camden squeezed his dad around the neck. The two of them were adorable together.

"You be good for Willow. We want her to stay, right?"

Camden let go of his dad but stayed in his arms. "Right," he said, flashing a big ol' smile.

Bryce kissed the side of Camden's head and set him back on the stool at the island.

"Call me once you get your phone and if you need me before that—"

"Ask June. I've got this, Sheriff." Willow gave him a thumbs-up.

Bryce nodded once. "Of course, you do. All right. I will see y'all tonight." He grabbed his keys off the counter and headed out.

Willow was officially in charge.

BRYCE HAD NEVER been so distracted at work before. Rationally, he knew that things were fine. He was the sheriff; if something terrible happened, like the house set on fire, he would literally be one of the first people to know about it. If something less life-threatening but still disturbing happened, June would surely call and let him know.

He checked his watch. It was ten thirty. Wasn't Willow's plan to go get the phone right away? The cell phone store had been open for an hour and thirty minutes. How long did it take to buy a new phone?

"Excuse me, Sheriff." Deputy Sam Regan knocked on his door but walked in since it was open. "Do you have the job assignments for the spring festival?"

Bryce shuffled through the neat stack of papers on his desk. That list was there somewhere. He located it and handed it to his deputy.

"Are you okay, boss? You look a little frazzled, which is not like you."

Frazzled was a good way to describe how he felt. "I'm fine. Just have a new nanny looking after Camden and hoping everything's going okay."

"You got yourself a nanny? I thought your neighbor was helping you out."

"June was my saving grace after April passed, but I couldn't take advantage of her kindness any longer. She's almost eighty. The woman deserves some peace."

"Where did you find a nanny?"

"I gave him a caregiver website," Gretchen said, coming in behind Sam. "So it worked out, huh? You hired someone super quick."

She seemed so proud of herself for solving one of his problems that he couldn't bear to tell her the truth. Bryce was also embarrassed to say that he'd plucked a stranger right out of the Coffee Depot and put her in charge of his kid instead of choosing a fully vetted candidate with references and such.

"Yeah, I lucked out and found someone who was available to start right away."

"I think that's really great. One less thing for you to worry about," Sam said.

Right, childcare was supposed to be one less thing to worry about, not the thing he obsessed over all day. Bryce's phone rang with an unknown number. It had to be Willow. He held up his phone. "It's the new nanny. I need to answer this."

"I'll come back," Gretchen said.

Sam shook the paper in his hand. "Got

what I needed." He closed the door behind them as he exited.

Bryce answered the call, "Hello?"

"Hey, it's Willow. I got my new phone and wanted you to have the number."

Bryce was relieved to know he would be able to communicate with her when he wanted or needed to. "Everything going okay?"

"Yeah. The people around here are so sweet. I have yet to meet someone who isn't the epitome of kindness. It's got to be this town, because my grandma was the same."

"I'm glad you're finding everyone to be cordial. Maple Grove has always been my home, so I assume I'm a bit prejudiced, but it's a great town to be in."

"So far, it's a ten out of ten. I'm going to stop at the grocery store and do some shopping. June is watching Camden. She thought it was best that she stay home with him while I ran errands."

A ten out of ten. That was good. She already had June helping her out. He had told her to ask for help if she needed it.

"I hope that's all right with you," Willow said, sounding concerned at his silence.

"Yeah, that's fine. I'm glad she was able

to help you out." He knew that June wouldn't have offered if she hadn't wanted to spend some time with Cam.

"Is there anything else you need me to do while I'm out?"

This was a strange new dynamic. June had been helping him for the last eleven months, but her sole responsibility was watching Camden. Having someone help him manage the household was kind of nice.

"We made a pretty good list last night. I can't think of anything else off the top of my head, but if I do think of something I'll text you on your new phone."

"It's so good to have a phone again. You don't realize how much you rely on your phone until you can't use yours."

"It's not so bad to be unplugged sometimes. Wish I could do that."

"True. Well, you enjoy the rest of your day. We'll see you tonight at the house."

"Bye, Willow." Bryce ended the call and sat back in his chair. He could breathe a sigh of relief. Maybe childcare was truly one less thing for him to worry about.

There was another knock on his door and Gretchen poked her head in. "Sheriff, Carter

Robinson called. He says cattle from the Mills ranch are on his property again and that he'd like you to come out and talk to Eugene."

"He won't do the neighborly thing and call Eugene to let him know some of his cattle busted through the fence?"

"Says Eugene knowingly permitted them to come on his land and block the road. Says last time this happened, Eugene argued with him about Texas being an open-range state and said Carter needed to get over it. He wants you to respond."

Bryce grabbed his hat and headed out to encourage Eugene to come get his cattle. Texas was a free-range state, but counties were allowed to pass a stock law, effectively making them a closed-range county. Carter was correct: Maple Grove was in a closed-range county.

He found the two men engaged in a shouting match when he arrived on scene. Bryce steeled himself for this altercation and stepped out of his vehicle.

"Gentlemen, please calm down and step away from one another."

"Sheriff, I'm tired of this!" Carter shouted, throwing his arms in the air. "This guy thinks he can run his cattle across my land and not have to pay for damages."

Eugene folded his arms across his broad chest. His dark brown cowboy hat shaded his face. "It's called free-range. Look it up. I don't have to fix anything on your land. Plus, they didn't do no damage to your property, you big baby!"

Good thing Willow wasn't there to witness these two. They weren't being very kind at the moment.

Carter was having none of Eugene's nonsense. "Actually, we're a closed-range county, you nincompoop!"

Eugene raised the fist. "What did you call me? I will make sure that you never rest a day in your life!"

Bryce stepped in between the two men and placed a hand in front of Eugene but did not touch him. "Mr. Mills, you need to calm down. Let's talk about this like reasonable adults." He turned to Carter. "I need you to take a step back as well. Why don't you each find your own safe space and I'll talk to each of you separately?"

Bryce had a pretty good handle on what was going on. Eugene was mistaken about the law and Carter believed he was being will-ingly ignorant about it. Bryce started with Eugene.

"Mr. Mills, unfortunately, you are incor-rect about us being open-range. This is a closed-range county. Also, to be clear, even if we were an open-range county, you cannot knowingly let your cattle roam wherever they please, and if they break someone else's fence and destroy property, you are liable, sir."

"I didn't knowingly do nothing! I'm here, aren't I? I came when I found out they broke out of our fence. All this guy had to do was call me and I would have come and got them. He didn't need to call the police. I don't un-derstand why he's such a stubborn jerk!" he shouted over Bryce's shoulder at Carter.

"There is only one stubborn person here and it's you, you curmudgeon!"

"What did he call me?" Eugene tried to push past Bryce and go after Carter again.

"Mr. Mills, please stop. I'm standing right here and I am trying to explain the law to you so you don't have to deal with me again, nor will you have to pay hundreds and hundreds of dollars in damages. If you assault Mr. Robinson, I will have to take you in and that will make today even worse for you and me."

Eugene, thankfully, did not want to go to jail today. He agreed to round up his cattle and fix his fencing. He acknowledged that the law in Maple Grove did not allow for his cattle to roam free and eat Carter's green Bermuda grass or block the road. Bryce didn't leave until the road was clear and all of Eugene's cattle were off Carter's land.

Bryce suggested Carter take pictures of the damage and contact a lawyer if he was serious about seeking damages. He also encouraged him to bulk up his own fencing to prevent this in the future.

He got in his truck and headed back to the station. Surprisingly, an hour had gone by and he hadn't worried about how Camden was doing once. He thought about stopping by the house to check on them but talked himself out of it. Willow was a capable adult. She didn't need him hovering. Plus, June was probably still hanging around.

Just as he parked in front of the station, his phone rang. Willow was calling. "Hey, there. How are things going?" he asked.

"Fine," she said, her voice one octave too

high. Bryce could hear Banjo barking like a mad dog in the background and something else, like an alarm. "I just had a quick question. A hypothetical question. Hypothetically, if the smoke detector were to go off in the kitchen, that wouldn't, like, notify the fire department, would it? It's not like that triggers them to send anyone over here, right?"

Bryce could feel her anxiety through the phone. "Willow, did you set the smoke detector off?"

"Banjo, come here, boy," she said. The dog hated when the smoke detector was set off. The beeping drove him up the wall and led to him barking his head off until it was turned off.

"Willow, what's going on?" Bryce asked, restarting his truck and pulling out onto the road.

"I may have had a slight issue while I was grilling up some grilled cheese for Camden's lunch. By the way, was he tricking me when he said you put mayonnaise on the outside of the bread?"

"Tricking you? He was not tricking you. We do use a little bit of mayonnaise on the outside of the bread instead of butter to help make the outside of the sandwich brown and crispy."

"Oh. Brown and crispy sounds delicious. Banjo! Where are you going? Come back! Sorry, Bryce, I'll call you back. Don't worry. Everything is fine!"

Apparently, Bryce was going to be taking his lunch break at home.

CHAPTER FIVE

"ARE YOU SERIOUS, BANJO?" Willow had lost the last bit of patience she could muster. The dog had been freaking out since the first beep of the smoke detector. She'd assumed that he would relax if she let him outside, but no such luck. Instead, he had run around like he was being chased by a ghost—and now he wasn't even in their yard anymore.

It shouldn't have been this difficult to make lunch. It was grilled cheese for goodness' sake. Of course, Camden had insisted that his dad used mayo not butter on the outside of the bread. Maybe that was what caused it to burn so fast. Or maybe she had stepped away longer than she thought she had.

Camden had needed help with the button on his shorts after he used the bathroom, and before she could get back to flip the sandwich, the smoke detector had gone off. She'd turned off the stove and opened all the windows, but the darn detector would not stop beeping and the dog would not stop barking. Camden was yelling, "Make it stop!" with his hands over his ears. There was so much smoke and no fire. Willow had panicked and called Bryce, afraid that he was going to hear the fire department was headed to his house.

"How are we going to get Banjo back?" Camden asked, his hands on his head.

"Your dad is going to fire me." She shouldn't have called him. There was no way he believed that was a hypothetical question. He also would be a fool if he thought everything was fine and under control.

Banjo came flying back into the yard and sat in front of Willow with his mouth open and his giant pink tongue hanging out as he panted. "Good boy," she said, cautiously stepping closer. She petted his head and quickly grabbed his collar.

"You've never had fire trucks show up when the smoke detector has gone off before, have you?" she asked Camden.

He shook his head. She should have started with him instead of his dad.

She needed to figure out how to turn that smoke detector off. It probably wasn't a good idea to beat it to death with a broomstick. Suddenly, it went quiet inside the house.

Willow took a deep breath. *Thank goodness.* The kitchen must have aired out.

"What is going on?"

Willow spun around, letting go of Banjo, who made a beeline for his master. Bryce stood on the back porch with his hands on his hips.

"Dad, the grilled cheese turned into smoke. You should have seen it! It was everywhere!"

That wasn't exactly what happened, but it probably seemed that way. How did one little sandwich make enough smoke to fill a whole room?

"Sorry, you didn't need to come home. I had it all under control." The words sounded as false as they were. Bryce's hardened expression didn't change, meaning he didn't believe her, either.

Willow trudged up to the house as Bryce gave Camden a hug and inspected him for damage. It wasn't like she'd burnt him to a crisp.

The kitchen was still a bit hazy when they went back inside. Camden sat at the kitchen table. "Are you going to have lunch with us?" he asked his dad.

"I thought I'd better join y'all for lunch today," Bryce replied, inspecting the kitchen as if it was a crime scene.

Willow picked up the wet, and now cool-to-the-touch, burnt grilled cheese and tossed it in the garbage. Her first instinct had been to spray it with cold water. Little did she know that pouring cold water on a hot pan was bad for the pan and didn't do much to stop the smoke.

"I did not mean for you to feel like you need to come home and check on us," she said. "I promise you I was not even close to setting your house on fire. Everything is fine, as you can see."

Bryce stood beside her and picked up the warped frying pan. He said nothing but lifted his eyebrows and stared at her.

"I'm going to buy you a new frying pan."

He set the pan down and walked around the island. "I like to come home for lunch sometimes. Even on days when hypothetically nothing is going on and everything is fine."

Willow could feel that her cheeks were

pink with embarrassment. "Can I make you a sandwich?" she asked, grabbing the bread off the counter.

"I would love a sandwich, but I can make it myself."

"Can someone make me a sandwich, too? One that's not burned up and turned into smoke?" Camden asked.

"I got you, bud. How about a turkey and cheese sandwich, not grilled. I think we are going to skip grilling things for a bit. Willow, can I make you one?"

Willow wanted the earth to open up and swallow her whole. She shook her head. She was too humiliated to eat with them. "I'm going to clean up while y'all have lunch together."

Bryce made himself and Camden a sandwich and joined his son at the kitchen table. "How have things been going, bud? Are you having a good day with Willow?"

"Yeah it's been fun," Camden said. "We're gonna build a whole town with my blocks after lunch and Mrs. Holland said she's going to bring over an apple pie for dinner."

"Oh, that's awful nice of her," Bryce said. "How long was Mrs. Holland here today?"

Not long enough. Willow should never have assured their neighbor, who just happened to be amazingly competent in the kitchen, that she would manage fine on her own.

"She left when I got home from the store," Willow replied as she stood at the sink, wetting a sponge. She turned around and wiped down the island. "She is very sweet. I can see why you adore her."

"No problems at the grocery store?" Bryce asked. "You were able to charge everything to my account?"

A true small-town mom-and-pop shop, Cattleman's Grocer was like walking into a different time period. Long-time residents had accounts that they settled up monthly. Grocery stores in Dallas did not do that. "They were so great, and I had no trouble charging it to your account.

"Good. Guess what, Cam? I got to see the plans for the Spring Festival today. It looks like it's going to be super fun this year."

Willow glanced in their direction. The Spring Festival was coming up? She'd heard all about the Maple Grove Spring Festival from Grandma Rose. She used to say it was one of her favorite events of the year.

"What's a spring festival?" Camden asked.

"You probably don't remember last year's. The whole town celebrates the start of spring. They're going to have tons of rides and games and a Ferris wheel."

Camden cocked his head to the side and scrunched up his little forehead. "What's a Ferris wheel?"

"It's this giant wheel that has a bunch of seats for people to sit in so they can go up and around like this." Bryce used his hands to demonstrate.

"My grandma used to talk about the festival. How cool that they still do it after all these years?"

"It's one of the biggest events here in Maple Grove. There's a farmers' market, a carnival, live music each night… I'm really excited to take Camden this year because he's old enough to ride some of the rides and play some of the games."

"My grandma used to tell me she would get pink cotton candy on a paper cone when she was little. Do they still do that?"

"What's cotton candy?" Camden asked with big eyes.

"They take sugar and spin it really fast until

it turns into thin strands of yumminess," Willow explained. "Then they take those stands and wrap them around into a big, fluffy mound. It looks like a cloud on a stick. Sometimes it's pink, but I've seen blue and purple before. It depends on what flavor it is."

"I want that!" Camden's sweet tooth was going to be in seventh heaven.

"Cotton candy has been at the festival as long as I have," Bryce said. "And I have been to many Spring Festivals."

"I'll share with you, Willow. Can we go on the Ferris wheel together, too?"

He warmed her heart. She'd burned his lunch, but he still liked her. "I would love that."

Camden's grin was electric.

"What about me?" Bryce asked. "Who's gonna go on the Ferris wheel with me?"

"Oh, Daddy!" Camden giggled. "I'll go on the Ferris wheel with you and with Willow. We can go on the Ferris wheel a million times."

"A *million* times?" Bryce feigned being shocked by this request. "Trust me, you aren't going to want to spend all your time on the Ferris wheel. There's so much to do."

Camden rubbed his eyes. Willow had noticed he looked tired today. Maybe it was because he'd kept waking up in the middle of the night after wetting the bed. Bryce had said the same thing had happened the night before.

"Maybe you'd like to take a nap this afternoon," Willow suggested, as she took the empty plate away from Camden. "You look a little tired, bud."

"Willow's right, little man. Maybe you should take a little nap after lunch and then y'all can build with your blocks."

"I was actually going to check his temperature after he finished eating. I was wondering if he was coming down with something. A fever could also be a sign that he has a bladder infection."

Bryce reached over and placed the back of his hand against his son's forehead. "He does feel a little warm to the touch. Does he need to see a doctor if it's a bladder infection or is that something we can get medicine for over the counter?"

"I'm not sick!" Camden climbed off the chair and stomped through the living room toward the bedrooms. "I'm just tired!"

"Sometimes when someone is sick it makes them feel tired," Willow said, following after him. "It's not a big deal if you're sick. We just need to make sure so we can help you feel better."

"I don't want to go to the doctor. I'm not going." He stormed right into his bedroom and closed the door.

BRYCE KNEW EXACTLY why his son hated going to see the doctor. His mom had gone to the doctor when she was sick and then she'd died. He didn't blame the child for thinking the two things were connected.

"I didn't mean to make him upset," Willow said, coming back into the kitchen.

"It's not you. It's doctors. He has developed a fear of them since his mom…" Bryce couldn't finish that sentence.

Understanding registered on Willow's face. "Oh, got it. I'm so sorry."

Bryce shook his head. He didn't want her sympathy. He was so over sympathy. "I shouldn't have brought it up in front of him. I should have waited to talk to you until after he went to take a nap. It was my fault."

"Let's just keep an eye on it. Maybe it's

nothing, and if it is something, maybe it's just a bug that his little immune system will take care of all on its own."

That was a solid plan. To be honest, Bryce didn't like going to the doctor anymore, either. The last thing he wanted to do was take Camden in and get news like he did when April got sick.

"Can I show you something?" he asked, standing up. He motioned for Willow to follow him over to the smoke detector. "If, hypothetically, the smoke detector was to go off because of a mishap and not because there was a fire, all you have to do is press this button right here and that will reset it. It gives you a few minutes to clear the smoke out and calm Banjo down."

Her smile was full of gratitude. "Thank you. Hypothetically, if that were to happen, I will do that instead of calling you and making you worry."

"Did you really think it called the fire department?" he asked, unable to hide his smile.

She covered her face with a hand. "I know, I'm a fool. I started to think that maybe it was like the fire alarm at school. I don't know. This has never happened to me before."

"Well, that's good to hear. I was hoping burning food was not your usual cooking style."

She dropped her hand, yet still looked mortified. "Right. Definitely *not* my cooking style."

He believed her until later that day when she pulled a smoking pan of lasagna from the oven. Bryce jumped up and pressed the reset button on the smoke detector just as it went off and Banjo started barking.

"I don't know what happened," Willow said, setting the well-done pasta dish on the stovetop. She waved the potholder over it. "The directions said to broil it."

"How long did you leave it under the broiler?"

"Too long, I guess." Her bottom lip trembled and her eyes welled with tears.

Bryce didn't want her to cry. "It's fine. Let's just peel the burnt cheese off. I'm sure the rest of it is good."

"You think that will work?" she asked.

"I don't see why not."

Without hesitation, she reached into the pan and grabbed a corner of the burnt cheese, pulling until the nerves in her fingers finally registered that she was burning them. She dropped the hot cheese and screamed, "Ouch! Shoot!"

Bryce went to the freezer to grab some ice. Willow ran to the sink and turned on the water, sticking her fingers under the stream.

He wrapped a couple of ice cubes in a paper towel and held it out for her. "Here, put this on it."

"No, no. You should never put ice on a burn," Willow said. "Use cool water, not cold. Otherwise, you can damage the skin even more."

That was news to him. "Are you sure? This is what my mom always did when we burned ourselves."

"I'm sure. I will take that paper towel, though."

Bryce handed it to her and she wet it before wrapping it around her fingers. Willow closed her eyes and took some deep breaths.

"Are you okay?" Camden asked.

Her eyes opened and she turned in his direction. "I'm fine, buddy. I'm embarrassed, but I'm fine."

"We all have touched something hot without thinking," Bryce said in an attempt to make her feel better. "How about I take care of the lasagna?"

She managed a small smile. "Thanks."

Bryce grabbed some tongs and peeled off the burnt cheese. "There we go. Unburnt lasagna."

"Did you make garlic bread, too?" Camden asked.

"Ah, the garlic bread. Maybe that was what was supposed to go under the broiler. Not the lasagna." Willow tapped on her phone and scrolled through something on her screen. "Oh my gosh. Yeah, the broiling was for the bread."

"I think we should eat the bread at room temperature. I think the oven needs a rest," Bryce said, positioning himself in front of the oven. He could not handle any more smoke alarms going off today.

They sat down at the table and Bryce served everyone a slice of cheese-less lasagna and French bread. Willow had to hold her fork with the three fingers on her right hand that weren't wrapped in wet paper towel. It couldn't have been easy and Bryce was tempted to cut up her food for her. But he figured that would only make her more embarrassed, so he let her do it her way.

"Banjo is not going to like me if I keep setting off the smoke detector. Maybe tomorrow, we can have a salad for dinner."

Camden's little face scrunched up as if she had suggested they eat mud. "Salad? For dinner? Just vegetables?"

"Salads can be delicious! We can go to the market and get different kinds of lettuce and peppers and cucumbers."

"Cucumbers? What's that?" Camden asked.

"You've never had cucumbers? Oh, we definitely need to have a salad tomorrow with cucumbers. You're going to love them!"

Bryce decided not to burst her bubble, but there was no way Camden was going to love cucumbers. He hated pickles. Didn't like the texture. Cucumbers were basically flavorless pickles. He'd wait to tell her after Camden went to bed.

They finished their dinner and Willow wouldn't let him help her clean up. "Go spend some time with Camden. I'll just put everything in the dishwasher. I've got this."

This was why he'd hired himself a live-in nanny. Bryce had wanted someone to help him out around the house so his time at home could be spent with his boy.

"Want to show me the town you built with Willow today?"

Camden's eyes lit up. "We made it so good, Dad. Wait till you see it. I made the biggest city in the world. It even has a zoo."

"That sounds pretty awesome. What else is in your town?"

Camden took him by the hand and showed him the city of blocks and toys. He was very proud of his zoo, which consisted of all the animals he had talked about wanting to show Willow last night. He also had a grocery store, the sheriff's station and a school in his town.

"Willow made this. It's a hospital. She said that it's not scary. That there are lots of nice doctors and nurses who help us when we get hurt or sick. The doctors and the nurses take care of people until they get better. Sometimes they can't get better, so they have to go to heaven like Mommy."

Bryce's chest tightened. Who gave her permission to talk to him about hospitals and his mother?

"But the doctors and nurses don't make people go to heaven. Just sometimes they can't stop it," Camden continued. He picked up one of his action figures. The toy's leg had a Band-Aid wrapped around it. "Like when this guy gets hurt in a fight, he goes to the hospital and they give him some medicine and they clean up his boo-boo and they wrap it up so it doesn't get yucky. Tomorrow, he will be all better!"

"Willow told you all that?"

"Yep."

"What if you had to go see a doctor? How would you feel about that?" Bryce asked, curious as to how Camden would answer.

Camden shrugged but kept playing with his bandaged action figure.

"What else is in your town?" Changing the subject seemed like the best plan at this point. If Camden was done talking about doctors, so was Bryce.

Just as they finished checking out the town, Willow came out of the kitchen. "He did a great job on the zoo, didn't he?"

"It's all very impressive. We'll have to chat about the hospital when Cam goes to bed."

Her brows pinched together. "Okay. Camden, did you show your dad how the nice doctor fixed your superhero's leg?"

"Yep," Camden said, jumping on the couch. "I think that he needs to have a bandage on his arm, too. I think it's broken."

"We can take care of that tomorrow when he comes in for his checkup."

"Can I have some water? I'm thirsty." Camden batted his eyes at her as though he knew it would work.

Willow's gaze shifted to Bryce.

"Remember we said no more drinks after dinner? We're doing a test tonight to see if we can stay super dry all night," Bryce said.

Camden flopped on his back and kicked up his legs. "But I'm so thirsty!"

"I know, buddy, but I really need you to try."

"I don't want to try tonight. I want to try tomorrow." He sat up and looked over at Willow. "What are those bubbles doing?"

Bryce and Willow both glanced in the same direction as Camden. A mound of bubbles was slowly creeping out of the kitchen and into the living room.

"What in the world?" Bryce ran into the kitchen to find suds pouring out of the dishwasher. "What did you do?"

"I put the dishwashing soap in the little

dispenser and hit Wash. Why is it leaking all over?'

Bryce stepped gingerly into the foam so he didn't slip and pressed Cancel on the dishwasher. "Dish*washing* soap or dish*washer* soap?"

Willow's nose was scrunched up. "What's the difference?"

Who had he hired to be his nanny? Someone who didn't know how to cook or clean and overstepped her boundaries with his kid? Bryce was starting to think this may have been the biggest mistake of his life.

CHAPTER SIX

DISHWASHING SOAP—liquid soap that went into a sink full of water to wash dishes.

Dish*washer* soap—a tablet that went in the dishwasher to wash dishes.

Willow was an intelligent person. She had a degree in nursing and had managed to keep herself alive her entire adulthood. Her lifestyle, however, had not been very domestic. Hudson would have been quite surprised to find out that she wasn't going to be the picture-perfect housewife.

Growing up, they'd had a cleaning lady and a cook. When Willow went to school and started working, she ate on the run half the time and ordered in the other. There were never dishes to do, so no need to know about things like dishwasher versus dishwashing soap.

There was a knock at the back door. June waved and Willow could hear her say, "Good morning!"

Willow unlocked and opened the door, letting Bryce's sweet little old neighbor into the house. Banjo came over, tail wagging. They exchanged a head pet for a quick sniff and he went back to his spot on the floor near Camden.

"Good morning, neighbor. How are you this morning?" Willow asked.

"I cannot complain. How are you doing, little man?" June asked, giving Camden's hair a ruffle. He had finished breakfast and wanted to do some coloring at the kitchen table.

"Good. Do you want some doughnuts? Willow bought us doughnuts for breakfast."

"Oh boy, I wish I'd known! I would have skipped my cereal this morning."

Willow had wanted to avoid any and everything that had to do with cooking this morning, so she had gotten up early and bought doughnuts. Bryce hadn't been as excited as Camden.

"We have plenty of leftovers. You can take one home for later if you like," Willow offered.

June took a seat at the table. "I may take you up on that."

"Did Bryce ask you to come over?" Willow

had a sinking feeling that there was a reason their elderly neighbor had stopped by other than being friendly.

"No, no. I don't want you to feel like I'm checking up on you. You have to understand that Bryce retired me without much notice. I need to ease myself out of this relationship."

As if she didn't feel bad enough, Willow realized that not only was she woefully underqualified to be a live-in nanny, she had stolen part of the job from one of the nicest people in the world. "Well, I'm warning you now not to get attached to your new-found freedom because I am pretty sure that Bryce is going to let me go, if not tonight then by the end of the week."

"What? He would never."

Willow let out a long, low sigh. "Do not be so sure. I am a bit of a menace in the kitchen."

"What's a menace?" Camden asked, looking up from his coloring book.

"Someone who is nothing but trouble," Willow answered. She had no doubt that was how Bryce thought of her. He had been so angry last night that he couldn't even speak. They had cleaned up the kitchen in silence. When they finished, he'd put Camden to bed and gone straight upstairs to his room without even saying good-night. "And in the kitchen, I am nothing but trouble."

"You're good at coloring in the kitchen," Camden said with a smile. His kindness was almost too much.

"I appreciate that, bud."

"Well, I happen to be fantastic in the kitchen. I am happy to help you figure things out. Sometimes getting used to someone else's kitchen takes some time."

"Honestly, I don't think I'd do much better in my own kitchen. I don't have a ton of experience with cooking." Or using major appliances like dishwashers, apparently.

June's forehead wrinkled, and her tone was incredulous as she said, "You can't be that bad."

"I set the smoke detector off twice in one day. Lunch and dinner."

The older woman's eyes went wide and her head jerked back. "Oh, dear."

Camden set down his crayon. "My hands feel weird," he said, capturing Willow's attention.

"What do you mean they feel weird?"

"Like they have bubbles in them."

"Bubbles? Like last night?"

"Bubbles?" June had a perplexed look on her face. Willow would have to explain that one later.

"Like bubbles are popping inside my hands," Camden said.

His hands were tingling, perhaps? She placed her hand on his cheek to check for a fever. His skin was warm, but he was not burning up.

"Maybe we should take a little rest on the couch. If you aren't feeling better soon, I think we might need a nice doctor to help us out."

Camden got up. "Can I have some more juice during my rest? I'm thirsty."

Willow smiled and grabbed his cup. "Sure, bud."

"You are always so thirsty," June said. "I've never seen a little boy drink so much liquid in a day."

Willow paused. She had only spent a couple of days with him, but Camden did drink a lot and often. He also went to the bathroom multiple times a day. He'd been wetting the bed. He was exceptionally skinny, even though he ate like he was a grown man.

"How about some water for now, okay?"

Camden didn't argue. He took his water to the couch. Willow covered him in a light blanket and gave him some books to page through.

"He's been drinking a lot for some time now?" Willow asked, returning to the kitchen table. June nodded. "Has he always been so skinny?"

"Oh, goodness, no. He used to be the cutest little pudge. April used to call him her chunky monkey."

Willow's nursing instincts kicked in. She drummed her fingers on the table. "Bryce hasn't taken him to the doctor in over a year, has he?"

"Camden's been afraid of doctors since April got sick. He thought the doctors made her worse. He's had a couple of meltdowns about it. It's been hard on Bryce. He figured since Cam was healthy, there was no reason to go until they absolutely had to."

Avoiding the thing that made a person anxious was actually the worst thing to do to help ease fears. "I think they absolutely have to."

"You think something's wrong?"

"I won't know for sure until they run some tests."

June grimaced. "Tests? I don't know how Camden will react to that. Or Bryce. The last time someone they loved went in for tests, they got very bad news."

Willow understood their fear, but it didn't change her concerns. If she was right, this wasn't something that would get better on its own. Camden was going to need medical intervention.

"Maybe you can help me figure out how to make a dinner that I can't burn. That will help me win back a little of Bryce's trust, so he'll listen to what I have to say."

"I can do that," June said with a wink. "If there's one thing I know how to do, it's how to fill a hungry belly."

June walked her through the prep for a chicken casserole that she could keep in the refrigerator until dinnertime. She gave Willow clear directions about time and temperature. No broiling needed.

"Besides casseroles, another thing that can be your friend—a Crock-Pot. You stick the ingredients in after breakfast and leave it alone until dinner. Like magic, everything will be perfectly cooked."

"Just throw stuff in a pot and I'm done? I love that idea," Willow said with a laugh.

"I'll teach you all the tricks," June promised. If Willow still had a job tomorrow, she would be sure to take her up on it.

She glanced over at Camden on the couch, where he had fallen asleep. Banjo was on the couch, cuddled alongside him. She knew she should tell the dog to get down, but they were too cute. Some rules could be bent.

RULES WEREN'T MADE to be broken. That was the point of them. They were there so people knew what to do and what not to do. Bryce thought the black-and-whiteness of it was kind of perfect. Most people followed the rules. Others had a tendency to break them over and over.

Like Daisy Sikes.

"I don't understand what's wrong with hanging some flyers around town letting people know that I walk dogs. How is that a crime? Since when is trying to get some work against the law? How are teenagers supposed to make money if they can't promote themselves around town?" She had a stack of flyers in her hand. She flailed them around as she spoke.

Daisy was fifteen and ambitious. She had hoped she could convince all of Maple Grove to save the sea turtles last year. It was a tough sell, seeing as how there weren't a whole lot of sea turtles in Maple Grove. She had tried this flyer business a few months ago when she wanted to advertise her friendship bracelet business. She also broke curfew regularly. She often "forgot" where skateboarding was and was not permitted. She and a friend had been caught breaking into an abandoned farmhouse, thinking it wasn't against the law if no one else lived there.

"We've had this conversation before, Daisy. You can't post your flyers on public property. You also can't post them on private property without the permission of the owner of said property."

"I can't post them on public property?" She raised her arms in the air. Her dark hair was blowing around her face. "It's public. Doesn't that mean that it belongs to all of us?"

"There is a public ordinance in Maple Grove that prohibits advertising on public property. Why don't you ask Holly over at the dog groomer's or Doc Griffin if you can post over at his vet office? People with dogs definitely go there and would be the customers you're looking for."

"But if he says no, I can't stick one on the light post right in front of the clinic?"

"You cannot."

She folded her arms across her chest, defiant and frustrated. "Can I pass them out to people on the street?"

"Well, we've been through this one as well. You are allowed to pass them out to people on the sidewalk, but you can't block people from passing by or force people to take them because that leads to littering, which is also—"

"Against the law. *Everything* is against the law in this town!"

"Listen, I'll take a flyer," Bryce said, holding out his hand. "I'll post it in the sheriff's office. Maybe some of the people who work there need a dog walker."

Daisy rolled her eyes and frowned. "Yeah, right."

"Hey, I have a dog. Maybe you can walk my dog."

"Really?" Her expression softened just a bit.

"Why not? Banjo loves walks and I don't get him out as often as I should."

Daisy beamed. "Great, how many times a day should I come over?"

Bryce hadn't been thinking this would be a multiple-times-a-day kind of job. "Why don't we start with a couple times a week? Maybe Wednesdays and Fridays?"

She pulled out her phone. "Okay, wow, I guess you don't love your dog as much as you think you do, but we can work with that. I start tomorrow, so I'm going to need your address."

As Bryce gave his address to one of the biggest delinquents in town, he started to wonder when he had become the guy who welcomed random people into his home to take care of the people and animals dependent on him. He needed to stop doing that. He also needed to fire Willow. June would probably be happy to take over babysitting duties until he could hire someone from the actual caregiver site Gretchen had given him.

"Thanks, Sheriff," Daisy said sincerely. "It's cool of you to help me out even if it is your stupid laws that make it impossible for me to get any other business."

Bryce couldn't help but chuckle. "Have a good rest of your day, Daisy. Stay out of trouble so *I* don't have to bug *you* again."

"See ya tomorrow," she said, taking off on her skateboard that she was not supposed to ride on the downtown sidewalk.

Bryce didn't have the energy to chase after her. He watched until she turned off the main street and on to a side street where it was perfectly acceptable for her to be on that thing. Banjo didn't know what he was in for tomorrow.

Thankfully, it was time to go home. As much as Bryce was relieved to be off duty, he dreaded going home. He hoped Willow hadn't set anything on fire or decided it was time to talk to Camden about the birds and the bees or something equally not her place to talk to him about. He also wasn't looking forward to having a conversation with her after Camden went to bed about how she needed to find herself another job and a place to live. He would let her finish out the week and pay her for her time. That should at least help her pay for a room at Glenda and Ken's B and B for a couple of days while she figured things out.

The house was still standing when he pulled into the driveway. Things were quiet. Banjo wasn't barking, the smoke alarm wasn't going off. He walked in and was immediately assaulted with the delicious aroma of something cooking in the kitchen. Camden and Willow were putting together puzzles in the living room. Banjo noticed Bryce was home first and sauntered over with his tail wagging.

"Daddy," Camden said, glancing up to see where Banjo went.

"Hey, buddy. What are y'all doing?"

"We're doing puzzles."

Bryce stepped farther into the room. Willow jumped to her feet and gave him a nervous smile.

"How was your day?" she asked. "Dinner is going to be ready in a couple minutes. Can I get you something to drink or do you want a few minutes to unwind or whatever?"

She was anxious with good reason. At least she seemed aware that yesterday had not left a good taste in his mouth, figuratively and literally.

"My day was good. I'm going to run upstairs and change out of my uniform and wash up for dinner." He started to turn but stopped. "You aren't broiling anything tonight, right?"

She let out a breathy laugh. "No broiling tonight."

"She's not a menace today, Dad," Camden said.

Bryce's brows pinched together. "A menace?"

"He meant to say everything is good. We're all good down here. You go get changed. I'm just going to check on dinner. We can meet back here in a few minutes." Willow clapped her hands together as if they were breaking from a football huddle.

As Bryce walked up the stairs, he started to have second thoughts. Maybe yesterday was a fluke bad day. Camden seemed happy and he appreciated that she seemed to engage with him instead of plunking him in front of the television. Of course, she could have known he was coming home soon and turned off the TV just so he would think that.

He massaged the back of his neck. Confrontation was part of his job. It was something he did every day. It didn't mean he liked it. He really didn't like it when it was highly likely that the person he was going to confront would cry. He hated making people cry.

Once he had changed out of his uniform, Bryce splashed some water on his face and stared at himself long and hard in the mirror. He needed to do what was best for him and his son. He needed to have someone reliable, someone who understood Camden was *his* son and that he had final say on how to handle Cam and his issues.

Willow had to go.

"Do you want to do the forks next?" he could hear Willow say as he approached the kitchen.

Camden was helping to set the table. "Do we need spoons?"

"I don't think so. I can't think of anything we would eat with a spoon," Willow replied. "Unless you want some Jell-O with your chicken."

Camden wrinkled his nose and stuck out his tongue. "Jell-O on my chicken? Gross!"

Willow and Camden's laughter filled the kitchen like music. "Not on your chicken, you silly. With your chicken. On the side."

"Yes, please."

"We're having chicken, huh?"

"Chicken casserole. It's one of June's recipes. She swears you'll love it."

"June stopped by again, did she?"

"I think she feels like I stole her job. She's very nice about it, but she misses spending time with Camden. She's so nice I let her come over whenever she wants."

Bryce hadn't thought about June being upset about losing her babysitting job. He figured she'd be relieved.

They sat down and Willow set the casserole dish on the table without burning herself or anyone else. It smelled amazing. Bryce hoped that it tasted the same. He'd just begun serving Camden when the little boy popped up.

"I gotta go to the bathroom!"

Bryce didn't hesitate, jumping up to follow him to make sure he made it. Unfortunately, he did not. Camden began to cry out of frustration.

"It's okay, little man." Bryce tried his best to stay calm. Being mad didn't make anything better. "We'll get you all cleaned up and then we can eat."

"I should have thought to have you go before we sat down. I'm sorry, Cam," Willow said from the hallway.

Bryce glanced over his shoulder at her. "Can you grab some clean underwear and his pajamas for me? They should be on his bed."

She nodded and dashed into his room. Bryce cleaned Camden up and Willow returned with the dry clothes. Ten minutes later, they were back at the kitchen table, eating dinner.

"We need to talk when Camden goes to bed," Willow said.

He was surprised she brought it up. He assumed he was the one who would have to initiate it. She was most definitely going to cry about being fired. He wasn't going to be able to go through with it. Maybe they could talk about boundaries and he could give her one more chance. "We do."

Dinner was a million times better than the night before. Willow chose to hand-wash the dishes tonight, avoiding the dishwasher altogether. Camden was exhausted after showing Bryce all the pictures he had drawn earlier in the day and sharing a story about Banjo stealing part of Willow's lunch off the table.

"Sounds like you had a good day," Bryce said as Cam got ready for bed.

"It was good. I got bubbles in my hands,

so Willow and I played doctor. She said I should know what's going to happen when I have to go."

Bubble hands? Doctor? "When you have to go where?"

"To the doctor."

Bryce's body shook and flushed with heat. The vein in his neck pulsed. He took a deep, shaky breath. "She told you that you were going to go to the doctor?"

"Yeah, she said it won't be scary. She knows lots of nice doctors."

It was almost impossible to hear anything else Camden said. All Bryce wanted to do was go out into the living room.

Willow was so fired.

the son or 172, you play that trophies thing
with him make would know what to speak.

The attorney was kicked in and raised her
armrest that city, "Yes, that's what I want
to tell a little you something your now.

(Bryce say sudden with her Girl came
as me relate set and not and arms and chest

CHAPTER SEVEN

THE MORE WILLOW thought about it, the more
she was sure she was correct. She needed
someone to run some tests, but the signs were
much too clear for her to be wrong.

"Willow." Bryce's voice was a soft growl.

"That was quick. He was tired, huh? I
think I know why." She spun around and the
hairs on the back of her neck lifted. An over-
whelming desire to flee consumed her when
she saw his face.

Bryce moved toward her slowly, deliber-
ately. His jaw was clenched so tight she wondered if he was hurting himself. "I am going to
let you sleep here tonight, but you will pack up
your stuff and you will leave here tomorrow."

Willow flinched as her chest tightened. Her
thoughts were muddled, her mind racing, trying to make sense of his anger. "I know yesterday was kind of a disaster—"

"Did you tell my son that he was going to

the doctor? Did you play that hospital game with him so he would know what to expect?"

The adrenaline kicked in and helped her focus her thoughts. "Yes, that's what I wanted to talk to you about. I think Camden—"

Bryce's eyes glinted with fury. "Camden is four years old and suffered an unimaginable trauma when he lost his mother. I don't know who you think you are, but the fact that you're okay with telling a little boy, who you've known for all of two days, that he needs to go to the doctor makes me want to kick you out of my house right this second."

"Bryce—"

He cut her off as he unleashed his frustration. "I knew I should have said something last night when I heard you talked to him about hospitals and doctors and heaven. I get you were a nurse before you came here, but you had no right."

"Bryce—"

"Did you ever think about the stress you're putting on him for no reason?"

"I think he has diabetes," she blurted out before he could interrupt her again. Bryce froze and went silent. "He has all the major symptoms. Frequent urination, especially at night. The bedwetting. The excessive thirst. He's tired all the time. He's so skinny. June said he's definitely lost weight. Today, he told me his hands had bubbles in them. I think he meant that his hands were tingling. He admitted to me that sometimes his feet feel that way, too. He's hungry all the time. His breath smells fruity. I can go on and on. He needs to see a doctor. You need to have him tested."

Bryce stood there like a statue. The only thing moving was his chest, rising and falling with heavy breaths. "Diabetes? He's four years old."

"Type 1 can show up at any age, but the big spikes in onset are between ages four and seven and then again between ages ten and fourteen."

Bryce shook his head. "Just because he likes sugary things doesn't mean he has diabetes."

"Type 1 diabetes is not caused by eating too much sugar. No one is going to judge his eating habits. They had no impact on him getting it if that's what it is," she tried to explain.

"He's having a hard time because the anniversary of his mom's passing is coming up. Once we get through that, he'll be fine."

The denial was strong. Willow understood his need to rationalize what was going on and his desire for this not to be a lifelong disease. "There are really simple tests to rule it in or out. A simple blood test is all they'll probably do at first."

Bryce raked a hand through his hair. "I don't think being a nurse qualifies you to diagnose my child with a serious medical condition. Maybe you're better off working with kids who are actually sick. Maybe you don't understand normal kid stuff."

He went from being eerily still to fast-moving. He stormed past her and into the kitchen. Yanking open the refrigerator, he grabbed a Coke and popped it open. He chugged it down, standing in front of the open fridge.

Willow understood his fear. She had dealt with many parents who weren't ready to face what their children were up against. "I know this sounds kind of scary, but it's super important for you to find out as soon as possible. If it is diabetes, the longer it goes untreated, the sicker he's going to get."

Bryce wiped his mouth with the back of his hand and closed the refrigerator. Tossing the empty soda can into the garbage, he again rushed past her. He paced around the room. "He won't go to the doctor."

"That's why I practiced with him today. I showed him how someone would listen to his heart and check his pulse. We talked about needles and getting a fancy bandage when he was done having blood drawn. He's going to be scared, but he'll go if you tell him it's important and that he's going to be totally safe."

Bryce shook his head as he gripped the back of his neck. "He won't. He's terrified."

"We practiced. We've been talking about how nice doctors and nurses are. I've been prepping him. If you show him that there's nothing to be afraid of, he'll go."

"You'll leave in the morning. I will call June and she can watch him until I find someone new."

As much as it stung to be fired, Willow couldn't let him neglect Camden's health. "I'll leave if that's what you want, but you have to call the doctor in the morning, Bryce. I can't stand by and let your fear keep Camden from getting the medical care he needs."

He pressed a hand to his chest. His nostrils flared. "My fear?"

"Yes, *your* fear." Willow's own fear caused

her heart to race. Her chin trembled and shoulders tightened. She was a people pleaser. Her entire life had been spent doing what she was told so those around her saw value in her. Being confrontational was not a skill she possessed, but Camden's health was too important for her to roll over and keep her mouth shut.

"I can give you a ride back to the B and B on my way to work," he replied, walking right out of the room. She could hear his heavy steps as he raced up the stairs.

The urge to flee was back. Avoiding another conversation with Bryce was preferable. She had been as firm as she could about what Camden needed. She would follow up with June to make sure Bryce did what he needed to do. Willow's heart sank. She couldn't leave without saying goodbye to Camden. Staying until morning was the right thing to do for a boy who had lost too much already.

She went into her room to start packing. It was a good thing she hadn't gotten herself too settled. It didn't take her long to have everything neatly folded in her suitcase. Maybe Maple Grove wasn't as magical as she thought it was. Maybe she'd been wrong to come here.

ALL THE WEBSITES said the same thing. Camden had all the symptoms of diabetes just like Willow had explained. They also said that if he didn't get treatment, he could develop another disease—diabetic ketoacidosis, which could kill him.

Bryce felt like he couldn't breathe. The thought of something being wrong with Camden made him nauseous. The possibility that he was sick scared Bryce so much he could cry. He couldn't handle this. Not without April. She was the one who took care of Cam when he was sick. She was the one who knew how to make him feel better when something was wrong.

Something was most definitely wrong.

Bryce went downstairs. His hand shook as he raised it to knock on Willow's bedroom door. He rapped lightly.

Willow opened the door, her eyes wide with worry. "If you want me to leave tonight, can we at least wake Cam up so I can say goodbye?"

"I need you to tell me what else you know about diabetes."

Willow pressed her lips together. She put a hand on his chest and pushed him back a little. "Let's talk." She turned off her room lights and stepped around him.

Bryce followed her into the living room, where she sat on the couch. She pulled her knees up to her chest.

"You're a nurse. You've seen kids with diabetes. You think Camden has diabetes?"

"I have and I do."

The lump in Bryce's throat was too big to talk around. He could feel the burn of tears in his eyes.

She unfurled herself and moved closer to him. Placing a hand on his knee, she kept her voice low. "It's a manageable disease. There have been so many advances in how they regulate insulin. He'll be able to live a normal life."

Bryce blew out a puff of air. "Normal. Nothing will be normal if he's sick."

"I know it's scary after everything you went through with your wife, but this isn't going to be like that. If he has diabetes, he isn't going to die. He'll have to give up his sweet tooth, but he's going to be able to live a full and happy life."

Emotion overwhelmed him. Bryce rubbed his jaw as he fought the tears. "Will you come with us to the doctor? Can you help me figure all this out?"

"Absolutely. Whatever you need. I'll be there." Her hand moved from his knee to his back.

His guilt made it difficult to accept her comfort. "I'm sorry for being so angry. I shouldn't have taken my fear out on you." He needed her to know that he felt regret along with all the other emotions swirling inside him at the moment. Instead of chastising her, he should have been thanking her for preparing Camden to go to the doctor. He didn't deserve the comfort she was offering him.

"I'm sorry you're going through this hard time. We'll figure it out, though. Between my grandma and Camden's mom, we have some pretty amazing guardian angels looking out for us."

Goodness, that was exactly the kind of thing April would have said. She had believed in all that stuff. Bryce had lost a lot of faith after she died. He wasn't sure Camden being sick was going to convince him he was wrong in being sure no one was watching over them.

Bryce called Doc Wight first thing in the morning. He was the only doctor in their small town, which meant it wasn't always easy to get in to see him. As soon as he heard the reason for Bryce's call, he made room for Camden later that morning.

"You're not going to work today?" Camden asked as they ate breakfast.

"I'm taking the morning off because we're going to go visit Doc Wight. He's going to make sure that we're doing all the right things to help you feel your best."

"I don't feel sick today," Camden said, pushing his eggs around his plate. "Maybe we should go another day when I need help."

He may have practiced going to the doctor with Willow yesterday, but that didn't mean he was fully on board with doing this for real. "I know it's kind of scary to go to the doctor, but like Willow told you, it's super easy and he can make things better."

"I have tumbling today. I can't go today." This was what Bryce had feared. He didn't want to go and was going to work himself up if they kept pushing.

"I know they are going to miss you at tumbling today, but I bet we can ask the doctor if we can use his stethoscope so you can listen to my heart or maybe you'll want to listen to your dad's. I bet his is really loud," Willow said, bringing Camden more water.

"That sounds like an excellent idea," Bryce said. "You could try being the doctor when we're there."

With his elbow on the table, Camden propped his head up on his hand. "I want to listen to my heart."

Willow glanced at Bryce with a satisfied smile. "That would be fun, too. You're going to do awesome at the doctor today."

Bryce wished he could say the same about himself. His nerves made it impossible to eat. His head was spinning with a million questions. What if he blanked out when he got there and forgot to ask the important stuff? That wasn't going to happen because he had Willow coming with him and she was a nurse. She would know what questions to ask if he forgot. Thank goodness he hadn't truly fired her last night in his rage.

"Can I have some juice?" Camden asked. "I don't want water for breakfast."

Juice was going to be off-limits if he had diabetes. A lot of foods he loved were going to be big no-no's if Willow was right. That was going to be extremely hard for a four-year-old to understand. The kid lived for sugar, and that was his worst enemy at the moment.

"We don't have any juice," Willow replied. I told you that already. You could have some milk if you don't want water."

"Can I have chocolate milk?"

Willow shook her head. "Sorry, bud. You can have white milk because it will help you grow big and strong."

"I'll just have water," Camden said in defeat.

"It's going to be okay," Willow whispered to Bryce when breakfast was finished and she was washing dishes.

Bryce wanted to believe that was true, but it was a hard sell this morning. He set the rest of the breakfast dishes by the sink. "We'll see. I don't know what I'm going to do if he melts down about going to the doctor. The last time I tried to take him for his yearly physical, his panic attack caused me to have a panic attack. We couldn't even get in the truck."

"We're not going to let that happen this time. This time, we're going to make it fun. It's going to be so fun there is nowhere else he's going to want to go."

She wasn't lying. Willow made going to the doctor seem like they were headed to an amusement park. Bryce feared she was building it up too much and there was no way it was going to live up to Camden's expectations. That would only lead to him refusing to go later, when Bryce was going to need his cooperation the most.

"Can I bring two stuffies with me? I think Elephant also might need a checkup," Camden asked as Bryce strapped him in his booster seat. He already clung to his stuffed tiger, who apparently had a broken tail that needed to be bandaged by the doctor.

"Ah…" Bryce looked to Willow.

"How about we bring your elephant next time?" she suggested. "We don't want to have all the fun the first time. We need to spread it out, right?"

That was good thinking. It gave him something to look forward to when they had to go back. If they had to go back. Bryce said a silent prayer that they wouldn't have to.

Camden agreed to bring his elephant the next time. The drive to Doc Wight's office was short. It didn't give Bryce much time to reel in all his dread and panic. He took a deep breath and reminded himself what Willow had said last night. Camden would be looking to him for clues about how to act. If Bryce was a nervous wreck, Camden would be one, too.

"I hope we get to squeeze the ball on the blood pressure cuff. I bet you can squeeze it harder than your dad," Willow said to Camden, her tone light and cheery. Her enthusiasm was contagious.

Camden smiled. "I can."

"Oh, we'll see about that," Bryce said, trying to sound as excited as Willow.

Doc Wight's wife sat behind the reception desk. "Sheriff Koller, right on time."

"Thanks for squeezing us in," he replied.

"Doc will be ready for you in just a minute. Can I have you make sure all the insurance information is correct?" she asked, handing him a clipboard full of papers. "And if you could fill out the patient registration form and sign the consent form, the office protocol and the authorization releases, that would be great."

Bryce hated paperwork. This was the stuff April always handled. She had all of their social security numbers memorized and had known things like the date of Camden's last checkup.

"You got this," Willow whispered, giving him a thumbs-up before turning her attention to Camden. "Let's read a book to your tiger while we wait."

Camden glanced at Bryce, checking to see if he should be anxious or not. Bryce forced a smile, and Camden went with Willow to pick out a book. He couldn't have done this without her. She was so calm, and he could tell that Camden felt her positive energy.

Doc Wight escorted his previous patient to the reception desk. "I want to see you back here in six months. We'll make sure that nothing has changed."

Eli Fisher shook Doc's hand. "Will do. Thanks, Doc." Eli turned to leave and noticed Bryce. "Howdy, Sheriff."

"Eli," Bryce replied with a nod.

Eli crossed and uncrossed his arms in front of him. "Marianne and I have been meaning to check in on you. See how you're doing. You know how things get, though."

Bryce learned that no two friends handled death the same. There were the ones who managed their own grief through action. They cooked for him. They came over and cleaned for him. They offered to run errands. The second group were the friends who texted. It was as if seeing Bryce might cause them some discomfort, so they only communicated with him through text. Next up, there were the criers. Those were the ones he'd bump into around town who would immediately get teary-eyed. They would hug him and share something they missed about April. Then, there were the ones who avoided him altogether. Eli and his wife fell in that category.

Marianne and April had been friends. Sometimes the four of them would get together for dinner and such, but the women were closer to one another than the men were. The last time Bryce had seen or heard from them was at April's funeral.

"I know how it can be," Bryce said, letting him off the hook.

"We should have you over for dinner. Catch up."

Bryce knew that was never going to happen. "Sure. That would be great."

Eli promised to connect and took off. Bryce hated the criers, but accidental run-ins with avoiders was almost worse.

"Camden, you're up, big man," Doc Wight said with a clap of his hands.

Camden and Willow stood up, but Bryce was glued to his seat. Getting up meant putting everything into motion, and he wasn't sure he was ready to do that. Right now, he could still deny that there was something wrong.

Willow walked right over and held out her hand. She offered a small smile with no judgment. "Let's do this."

Bryce swallowed hard and accepted her hand up.

CHAPTER EIGHT

"Is it okay if Camden's nanny comes back with us?" Bryce asked. "She was a nurse back in Dallas."

Willow could hear the anxiety oozing out of him. So could Doc Wight.

"Absolutely. You can bring anyone you want, Sheriff. How nice that Camden's got himself a nurse for a nanny. I've been looking to hire a nurse for six months. I haven't found one yet."

Willow was well aware of the nursing shortage in Texas and around the US. It was another reason she had felt so terrible about leaving the Children's Hospital back in Dallas. She knew how hard nurses were to come by and that finding someone to replace her wouldn't be easy.

"You run this practice all by yourself?" she asked as he led them back to his exam room.

"I do. If you have any nursing friends looking for a job, please send them my way. I'd love a physician's assistant, too, if you know one of those." Doc Wight had a friendly smile and a shiny bald head encircled by a ring of what was left of his white hair. His thick, black-rimmed glasses magnified his eyes when Willow looked at him straight on.

"I'll put a word out."

"Thank you, Miss—"

"Willow. My name is Willow."

"She's related to someone named Rose Everly," Bryce said, clearly good with talking about anything other than what was going on with Camden. "Grew up here years ago."

"Rose Everly…" Doc pondered the name. "Any relation to Charlie Everly?"

"We're not sure yet. Plan to ask him next time I see him," Bryce replied.

"Rose was my grandmother. She passed years ago but always spoke so fondly of Maple Grove."

"Well, welcome to our small town, Willow. Now, I want to check out this cool guy here. How's it going, Camden? Long time no see."

Camden squeezed his tiger a little tighter and pressed his lips together.

"Cam is hoping that after you get done checking him out, you'll be able to help his tiger. Poor guy got his tail stepped on. We think he needs a bandage," Willow explained.

"Oh my! Maybe we should check out Mr. Tiger first. Want me to take a look?" Doc held out both hands and Camden cautiously placed the stuffed animal in them. "Ah, I see. I think I know exactly what Mr. Tiger needs. Would you mind helping me, Cam?"

Camden couldn't hold back his smile. "Can I listen to his heart?"

"You can do more than that." Doc patted the paper-covered exam table. "Sheriff, can you put Camden up here so he can assist me with this?"

Bryce lifted Camden up and sat him down on the table, causing the paper to crinkle. Doc handed the tiger back to Camden. He grabbed his otoscope from the wall and placed a new ear tip on it.

"Let's make sure he doesn't have anything other than stuffing in his ears."

Doc and Camden took turns—Doc looked in Camden's ears before letting Camden look in the tiger's. They checked blood pressure and temperature. Doc listened to Camden's heart and lungs and then let Camden try on the tiger. He tapped on the stethoscope so

Camden heard something. Doc checked Camden's abdomen and asked Camden to do the same to the tiger. Together, they wrapped Tiger's tail in some gauze.

Willow was impressed with how good he was with the little boy. Not all general practitioners were good pediatricians. Doc Wight was one of the good ones. He managed to get his basic wellness exam done without Camden really noticing.

"Okay, so we've solved Mr. Tiger's problem. Let's talk about Camden," Doc said, looking at Bryce, who sat next to Willow. His leg bounced nervously as he worried his bottom lip with his teeth.

Willow nudged Bryce to answer. He snapped out of his catatonic nervousness the best he could. "Like I said on the phone, he's been showing lots of symptoms of, you know…"

Willow could sense he didn't want to say the word diabetes. She decided to step in and talk medical professional to medical professional. "At first, I thought maybe he was coming down with something. He presents as tired, he's had a slight fever. But I've noticed other things that caused me to think it might be something else. Frequent urination, excessive thirst. Enuresis. His dad confirmed there's been some weight loss even though he's hungry all the time. Fruity-smelling breath. Cam told me yesterday that his hands and feet tingle."

Doc listened intently and nodded. "That's a lot. I think we should do a simple blood glucose test today. I assume he had breakfast?"

"Eggs and toast. No juice this morning. Water only," Bryce said.

"Good. I would stay away from the sugary stuff while we're investigating. If the first test comes back high, we'll do a fasting glucose test."

"This could all be related to that stuff we talked about last time, too, couldn't it?" Bryce asked. "The emotional stuff."

"I know we talked about some behavioral changes you might see, but what Nanny Willow is describing is not behavioral. These are physical symptoms that are probably not related to his emotional well-being, but we're going to do the blood test and that will tell us if we're wrong." Doc came over and put a hand on Bryce's shoulder. "I know the possibility of a diagnosis like this probably has your stomach in a knot, but I am going to help you through it, whatever *it* is." He stepped away and started to prep for the blood draw. "And you've got yourself a nurse as a nanny. That could not have worked out better."

Willow wasn't sure if Bryce had come to a final decision about her employment. He had been grateful for her knowledge at the end of the evening, but there was a long list of reasons he might not want her to continue as Camden's nanny.

Bryce rubbed the back of his neck. The guy was wound so tight it was no wonder he had exploded last night. "It's almost like someone knew we were going to need one of those," he said, giving her a little glimmer of hope.

"Nanny Willow, do you think you could help Cam and me with this next very important part of our appointment today?" Doc asked.

Willow popped up to her feet. "I would love to."

"Cam, I'm going to be honest with you, this is not going to be the fun part, but it's the most important. We need to check your blood. That means we're going to have to give you a little squeeze and a little poke. Nanny Willow, can I borrow your arm for a second?" Doc asked.

Willow held out her arm as Doc showed Camden what he was going to do.

"No, thank you," Camden said after he got to the part about putting the needle into his arm. "I'm ready to go home now."

"We talked about this yesterday, remember?" Willow said. "This is the part where you have to be really brave like your action figure."

"I'll be brave next time."

Willow did what she could to wordlessly encourage Bryce to step in. The look he gave her back said he didn't know what to do. She tried to communicate not to let Camden chicken out.

He took a deep breath and stood up. "You know who's always brave?" Camden shook his head. Bryce's shoulders slumped. "Me, you silly! How about I share some of my brave with you, bud?"

Camden thought about it and nodded. Bryce picked him up and took his spot on the exam table. Setting Camden in his lap, he gave him a kiss on his head.

Willow moved to the other side of the table. Her goal was to help Camden feel like he was in control. "Do you want to do a countdown or should we play with your tiger so we don't notice what the doctor is doing?"

"Countdown," he said after reflecting for a second.

"Wow, you are brave," she said with a wink.

Doc Wight tied the tourniquet. "This is the tight squeeze." He cleaned the spot on the underside of Cam's elbow. "A little bit cold and wet."

"Okay, are you ready to count down?" Willow asked. Camden nodded. Bryce, Willow and Camden all began to count down from five. "Five, four, three, two, one."

"And a pinch," Doc said before sticking him with the needle. It took a few seconds to draw enough blood to be tested. "Okay, all done."

"That wasn't bad," Camden said when it was over.

Doc covered the spot with a bandage. "You were awesome." He gave Bryce a tight smile. "I'll call you when I get the results back."

"Thank you, Doc."

"It was my pleasure. I have to warn you, Sheriff." Doc wagged a finger at Bryce. "If you don't treat Nanny Willow right, I am going to steal her away and make her Nurse Willow."

Bryce glanced over at Willow. His eyes were clouded with the same remorse from last night.

"I'll remember that," Willow said.

BRYCE WASN'T SURE how he was supposed to concentrate at work after spending the morning at the doctor. At the same time, he was glad for the excuse to be out of the house. Every time he looked at Camden, he imagined the hardships he was going to face if he was diabetic. Would the kid ever get to enjoy trick-or-treating at Halloween? Could he have a birthday cake on his birthday? Would they not be able to celebrate a home run when he was in Little League by getting ice cream like Bryce used to do with his parents? They lived in a sugar-obsessed world. How could a kid who wasn't allowed to have sugar survive?

"How are things going with the new nanny?" Gretchen asked when he came out of his office to refill his coffee cup.

"They're going." He couldn't say more than that without having to explain about a million different things.

"Is she cute?" Sam asked.

Willow was beautiful. She had been dressed in a fancy hot pink romper and some strappy sandals today. Bryce was beginning to wonder if the woman even owned a T-shirt. Willow was more than cute, but he was not going there with Sam.

"I'm not answering that, Deputy."

"You didn't really answer my question," Gretchen complained. "Does Camden like her?"

"Camden loves her. She's really good with him."

Gretchen raised a brow. "Why do I feel like there's a *but* at the end of that sentence?"

"But she's not cute?" Sam thought he was being funny. Bryce disagreed and shot him a look that made his feelings known. Sam held up his hands. "Got it. You aren't answering that one."

"Why is it always about looks with you, Sam?" Gretchen tapped a pen on her desk. "Can't you see the value in a woman beyond her appearance?"

"I see the value in you and I never mention your appearance," Sam snapped back.

Gretchen's eyes went wide. "So you're saying I'm not attractive? I can't believe you!"

"I didn't say you were unattractive. I said I *value* you."

"But you don't value my looks?"

"I thought you didn't want me to value looks!"

Bryce did not have the patience to listen to their bickering. The two of them had been friends since elementary school. Sometimes they acted like husband and wife and other times, like right now, as if they were brother and sister. They could fight about everything and anything.

He retreated to his office and shut the door, muting their voices a bit. His phone rang and Willow's name appeared on his screen. He answered it, hoping nothing was wrong.

"Hey," he said. "Everything okay?"

"Uh, there's a teenage girl here claiming to be Banjo's dog walker. She said you hired her to come on Wednesdays and Fridays. You didn't mention a dog walker to me."

Bryce had totally forgotten about Daisy. He had planned to give Willow a heads-up last night, but last night had taken a turn for the worse and Banjo's walk had slipped his mind completely.

"Sorry, I did hire someone to walk Banjo a couple times a week."

Willow lowered her voice. "She's got a skateboard. Is that okay?"

Bryce pinched the bridge of his nose. "Can you put her on the phone really quick?"

Willow passed her phone to Daisy. "What's up, Sheriff? Don't tell me you're backing out of our deal."

"I am not backing out of anything. You can take Banjo for a *walk*, which means *you* and the dog should be walking. Okay?"

"Fine." Bryce could almost hear the eye roll that accompanied her reply.

"Can you give the phone back to the nanny?"

"He wants to talk to you," he heard Daisy say before Willow was back on.

"All good?"

"All good. She promises to walk with the dog. Sorry again for not mentioning it."

"No worries," Willow said, her voice light and forgiving. "I just didn't want to mess up and give your dog away to a stranger."

He appreciated that. He hung up with her and sat back in his chair. He also appreciated that Willow never complained, she made adjustments with ease, and she never wanted him to feel bad about anything he did or didn't do. She was smart and funny. She couldn't cook and had no idea how to use major appliances. But she *was cute*.

He pinched the bridge of his nose again. He'd known this woman for a handful of days. He was not going to think about whether or not she was cute. She was Camden's nanny. Period. He would not become some cliché who fell for the nanny. His heart wasn't ready for that kind of thing anyway.

Gretchen knocked on his door. "Can I come in for a second?"

He waved her in.

"Are you okay? I know you aren't a talker, but I feel like something is going on. You never call off work unless it's something major. If it isn't the nanny, then it has to be Camden."

Bryce let out a long, deep breath. "I had to take Camden to Doc Wight's for a blood test."

Gretchen's face fell. As much as she loved being right about things, he could tell she hated being right about this. "A blood test for what? It's not like—" She stopped before saying April's name.

Bryce shook his head. "It's not like April. It's not cancer. We're testing him for diabetes."

"Diabetes?" Her eyes bulged. "How in the world did you come up with that?"

Bryce sat forward and put his elbows on his desk. "I didn't. The nanny noticed the signs. She used to be a nurse in Dallas."

"Well, that was lucky. I am so glad I told you to go on that site to find someone."

"Honestly, Gretchen, I sort of struck out on the nanny site. I met Willow at the Coffee Depot on Sunday and hired her on the spot."

Gretchen seemed more shocked by this news than the possibility that Camden had diabetes. "You hired a woman you met at the Coffee Depot? That is not like you, Sheriff. You don't do things on a whim like that." She narrowed her eyes at him. "She's cute, isn't she?"

Shaking his head, he held up his hands. "This is not about her being cute. I hired her because of the way she interacted with Camden. And she's a nurse, so it all worked out the way it should."

"Fine, I believe you, but when I finally

meet this woman and she's super cute, I am going to question everything I ever believed about you, Sheriff."

"She's very pretty, okay? But that is not why I hired her. I don't care if she's pretty or not. I care about Camden and…" Bryce sucked in a breath and tried blinking back the tears "… I'm scared to death what this diagnosis means for him. I don't want my boy to have a hard life, you know?"

Gretchen went from annoyed with him to sympathetic in an instant. "Oh, man. I'm sorry, Sheriff. You know I think the world of you and your boy. Camden is going to have you, me and everyone in this town who loves you and him looking out for him. He's going to be fine and he's going to have a great life."

Bryce rubbed his jaw and nodded, unable to speak. There were a lot of people in Maple Grove who cared about them. Camden was going to have tons of support getting through all this. That was what Bryce needed to remember.

He was just about to leave for the day when his phone rang. It was Willow.

"First, I need you to know that Camden

and I have walked around the neighborhood three times. She's gone."

"Who's gone?"

"The dog walker. She never came back from the walk."

Bryce put his hat on and grabbed his keys. He'd hired a delinquent to walk his dog and she'd probably sold him off for the cash. After some quick goodbyes, he got in his truck and made his way to all of Daisy's known hangouts. It didn't take long to find her behind the high school where the kids had turned some land into a makeshift skateboard park.

Banjo was lying down with his tongue lolling out of his mouth as he panted. Some of the kids started to scatter as soon as Bryce pulled up in his truck, but Daisy paid him no mind until she heard the slam of his door.

"Is there a reason you chose not to walk my dog back home?" he asked. "Come on, Banjo."

The dog got to his feet and slowly made his way over to Bryce. Daisy skated over to where he was standing as well.

"I was going to walk him home. I get paid by the hour and you only hired me for two days a week. A girl has to make a living, you know."

She was a piece of work. "You don't get to dognap my dog for the day and charge me for it. I am paying you to walk him around the block. I pay per walk, not per hour."

"Wow, Sheriff. I didn't take you for the kind of guy who would take advantage of a poor girl trying to make ends meet."

Bryce dropped his chin and glared at this budding con artist. "Don't start with me, Daisy. You better not be pulling this with other people in town. Your dog walking business is going to be over before it even begins."

"Why do you have to constantly ruin my life?" Daisy dramatically threw her head back and raised her arms up to the sky.

Bryce had talked to Daisy's mother enough to know that the kid didn't have an easy life, but she was doing a great job of making it harder on herself than anyone else. "Do you need a ride home?"

She stepped on the back of her skateboard, flipping it up into her hand. "I've got a ride, thanks."

"Banjo will see you on Friday. For a walk around the block. Maybe twice around if you're feeling generous." Bryce opened the door to his truck. "Come on, Banjo. Up. Let's go home."

CHAPTER NINE

BRYCE CAME INTO the kitchen Thursday morning with a smile on his face. Willow wasn't sure why, but she was glad for it. After the day he'd had yesterday, she knew he needed something to smile about.

"No surprise guests I should be aware of today?" Willow asked as she cut up an apple to add to Camden's breakfast.

"The dog walker does not come back until Friday. If Daisy shows up, tell her you're not authorized to allow any extra dog walks."

"She's a character. I think in the short period of time she was here, I may have agreed to buy some friendship bracelets. In fact, I might be in a pyramid scheme because I think she told me I'm supposed to sell the bracelets to my friends. She sort of caught me off guard and talks a mile a minute."

Bryce shook his head as he opened the

refrigerator to grab the milk for his cereal. "Daisy has a way of doing that."

He sat down at the island. Willow found herself admiring how good he looked in his uniform. He was absolutely the guy she'd want to come rescue her if she were in danger. There had to be other ladies in Maple Grove who felt the same.

"Okay, I'm trusting you that no one is going to show up to wash your car or mow your lawn," she said, giving him a hard time.

He rested his tanned forearms on the island. "The only thing I can't guarantee is that June won't stop by because she can't seem to give up her Cam time."

"I have no issues with June. She is welcome any day, any time." Willow hoped she would come by so she could talk to her about some recipes that would work well with Camden's new dietary needs. "I was thinking… Camden has his first T-ball game at four. What if I packed a picnic dinner and you met us at the baseball park after work?"

Bryce's blue eyes stared back at her for an extra beat. It made her skin feel warm and her stomach funny. "I think that sounds like a plan. I had planned to swing by to see him play."

"Awesome. Picnic in the park it is. What do you think, Cam? Are you excited for a picnic?"

Camden nodded as he shoveled some more oatmeal in his mouth. She placed the bowl of sliced apples on the table.

Willow didn't want to ruin Bryce's mood, but it was very likely he was going to get a call from Doctor Wight today regarding Camden's blood test results. If she was right about it being diabetes, she wanted to get a jump-start on supporting Camden the best she could. She didn't want to step over any lines Bryce might have, however.

"One other thing I wanted to run by you before you go to work," she said, lowering her voice a tad. Bryce gave her his full attention. "I know a doctor back in Dallas, a pediatric endocrinologist. That's the kind of doctor who would specialize in treating diabetes. Would you be okay with me touching base with him and asking him a few questions?"

The easy smile he had worn when he came downstairs was gone. "What kind of questions?"

"I thought it might be good to pick his brain about what to expect moving forward. He might be able to give me some insight into what's new out there in terms of treatment. He can also tell me what questions you might want to ask your doctor so you feel good about where things are headed. I don't want to overstep, but I also want to help you in any way I can."

Bryce rubbed his forehead. "I don't know, Willow. I appreciate you wanting to help, but maybe we should wait to hear back from Doc Wight first before we go bothering people."

"I totally get that. I know that you are hoping for the best, but sometimes it's good to prepare for the worst. Why don't you let me do that part, while you stay positive?"

"You trust this doctor?"

Willow nodded. "I do. He's a well-respected doctor at the hospital I used to work at. I think he could be an excellent resource."

He took a deep breath and let it out in a sigh. "Go ahead, but I don't want to know what he said until I hear back from Doc Wight."

"Got it." Willow had no problem meeting that condition. She understood how scared he was about this. Their life was going to change if she was right about this.

Bryce and Camden finished their breakfasts and Bryce headed to work. It didn't take long for June to knock on the back door.

"How did things go yesterday?" she asked Willow after greeting Camden with a hug.

"Camden was a rock star at the doctor yesterday. He helped Doc make sure Mr. Tiger was in tip-top shape."

"I got to listen to his heartbeat. It was loud!" Camden shared. He also showed off the bandage on his arm that he had refused to take off last night. "And I was super brave when he had to poke me. It didn't hurt at all."

"Wow, very impressive," June said with a tilt of her head. "Of course, I knew you would be amazing."

"Now we wait to see if he needs another blood test to confirm it is what I think it is," Willow said, pouring June a cup of coffee. She had learned over the last couple of days that Bryce bought "the good stuff," according to his neighbor.

"And how is Bryce doing with all of this?"

"He's anxious, of course. But he did a really great job of not showing it yesterday. It helped things go smoothly."

June added a little sugar to her cup. "It's a good thing he found you. I would never have thought to send them to the doctor. You are an angel sent from Dallas."

Willow chuckled. Maybe running away from Dallas had been the right thing to do after all. She may have hurt Hudson, but maybe helping Camden would even out her karma. "I'm super happy Camden is going to get what he needs to be healthy and maybe a little bit glad I made myself useful so I don't get fired in the first week."

"Me, too." June held up her cup and Willow clinked hers against it. June reminded her so much of her Grandma Rose. It was too bad June hadn't moved to Maple Grove until after her grandmother had left town. They seemed like they would have been friends.

Willow took advantage of having June there to make her call to Dr. Theo Nandi. What she hadn't told Bryce was that she and Theo had dated briefly when she first started at the hospital. They had ended things on good terms, so Willow felt like she could call in this favor.

Back in her room, she turned on her old phone and quickly searched her contacts for Theo's number before shutting it down again. She didn't know why she was being so paranoid. It was very possible that Hudson wanted nothing to do with her and had no intentions of looking for her.

She texted Theo first so he would know who was trying to reach him.

Hey, Theo, it's Willow Sanderson. When you have a minute, could you give me a call at this number?

Surprisingly, her phone rang almost immediately after the text was delivered.

"Willow Sanderson? Is this for real?"

"It's for real. Why wouldn't it be?"

"Are you kidding me? People have been talking about your disappearing act all week. Some of us were worried you were dead when we heard no one could get ahold of you. Where are you?"

Oh boy, the rumor mill at the hospital had made it to the doctors already? She had invited some of her former coworkers to the wedding, so she knew word was bound to get out. She didn't expect it to make it to special-ists like Theo already.

"I'm fine. I'm somewhere safe and sound. I need some time to clear my head and figure out what I want to do with my life, because getting married wasn't it."

"No one is going to believe that I am talk-ing to you."

She knew this was the risk in calling him. "I know I created a lot of drama, but I am try-ing my best not to make any more. I need to pick your doctor brain for a minute or two, though. Do you think I could do that?" she asked, trying to steer the conversation where it needed to go.

"What do you need a pediatric endocrinol-ogist for exactly?"

"I have a four-year-old little boy present-ing with all the symptoms of type 1 diabetes. I could really use your help in guiding this little guy's dad through what to expect, what questions to ask his doctor, what's available in terms of insulin management."

"So you quit your job at the hospital to marry Mr. Fancy Pants and now you're in hiding and playing nurse to a diabetic four-year-old? Willow, how am I supposed to keep this to myself?"

"Actually, maybe you can help me with one other thing," she said, knowing that by the end of the day someone at the Children's Hospital was going to know that she had talked to him. As long as he didn't know where she was, not too much damage could be done. "Could you get a message to Portia and tell her to let my parents know that I am alive and well. That I am sorry for leaving the way I did, but I will explain everything when I'm ready."

"You haven't talked to your parents since you ran off?"

He didn't need to make her feel any more guilty that she already did. "Can you help me out or should I find someone else?"

"I will let Portia know. Now, what can I do to help this little buddy of yours?"

Theo answered all of her questions and was a fount of knowledge, just like she knew he would be. Bryce would be able to talk to Doctor Wight armed with some information of his own when the time came.

When she got off the phone, she found

Camden giving June a pretend physical exam like the one he had helped Doc give Mr. Tiger.

"How's she doing, Dr. Cam?" Willow asked.

"She's gonna need two shots," Camden announced. "Sorry, Mrs. Holland. It won't hurt bad. Just a pinch."

"Oh, goodness. I hope I can be as brave as you were," June said, playing along.

"Knock, knock," a voice came from the front of the house. "Where's my favorite grandson?" Willow and June exchanged apprehensive looks as Grandma Delia waltzed in. "Who are you and what are you doing in my daughter's house?"

BRYCE WASN'T SURE what was more nerve-racking, going to the doctor or waiting for Doc Wight to call him with the results. At this particular moment, it was the latter. He decided to call and see if there was an update instead of worrying himself sick.

Mrs. Wight answered the phone and let Bryce know that Doc had not received anything from the lab yet, but planned to follow up with them before the end of the day. She assured Bryce he would hear from him later.

By four o'clock, there was still no news.

Bryce headed out to patrol around town. Goodwell Park, where Camden had T-ball, seemed as good a place as any to do his community policing.

The large park was on the north side of town. Besides the open green space, there was a baseball field, a soccer/football field, a playground and a small duck pond. Growing up, Bryce and his sister had spent many days here playing baseball, softball, football or soccer.

Bryce had had his first kiss over by the monkey bars when he was eleven. Kelly Jo Hansen had recruited all her friends to tell him she liked him and pester him to ask her out. Finally, they had broken him down and he'd kissed her at the park. Had that made her day? Nope. She'd promptly stopped liking him after that. Maybe he had been a bad kisser, or maybe Kelly Jo had been all about the chase. He'd never know. The only girl Bryce had ever understood was April.

Thinking about April made his chest tighten. He hated that feeling and did everything he could to rid himself of it. As he made his way to the baseball field, he spotted Willow sitting on a blanket almost right away.

For some reason the sight of her made him feel lighter. Only she wasn't alone. Delia sat on the blanket next to her.

Bryce's head fell forward and his shoulders slumped. This was not what he needed today. He was surprised Willow hadn't texted him that Delia had shown up. He wondered how long Willow had been entertaining her.

Pasting on a partial smile because that was what was expected of him, he approached them. "I see Camden has quite the cheering section," he said, getting their attention.

Delia was relaxed, her legs stretched out in front of her as she propped herself up on her elbows. "Well, look who made it to see his boy play some ball."

"Good to see you, too, Delia. Where's Lee tonight?"

"Oh, you know him. He was busy working, so I told him I was spending the day with Cam. April and I packed a picnic dinner for all of us after the game."

Bryce's gaze flew to Willow the second Delia called her April. She shook her head ever so slightly as if to warn him not to correct her.

"Delia has been a big help all day," Willow said. "She is very crafty and creative."

Delia's smile lit up her entire face. "Aw, that's so sweet of you to say."

"Willow is very sweet. That's why I hired her as Camden's nanny," Bryce said, hoping to remind her that Willow was not April.

"You're smarter than I thought you were, Sheriff," she replied with a laugh, unfazed by his correction.

Willow got to her feet and smoothed out the skirt of her dress. "Why don't I walk you over to the dugout so you can wish Camden good luck," she said to Bryce.

He was happy to get a moment alone with her to find out what was going on. "Has she been with you all day?'

"Pretty much. She showed up when June was there, thank goodness. She knew who she was. She forgot she'd met me the other day."

Bryce needed to have a serious talk with Lee about giving him a heads-up when Delia decided to pop over. "I hope she wasn't too aggressive. She gets that way sometimes."

"She did not like me at first, but I think I won her over." Willow glanced over her shoulder at Delia. "She seems to love compliments. Eats them up. As long as I point out all the things that make her amazing, she tolerates me."

Impressed, Bryce smiled. "You figured out Delia in one day? I've known the woman most of my life and I still don't know how to relate to her."

"She reminds me a lot of my—" She stopped herself and winced. "My ex-boyfriend's mother."

Bryce nodded. Of course she'd had ex-boy-friends. The background check he'd run on her hadn't listed any other names she would have gone by, which had led him to believe she hadn't ever been married. How was some-one like her still single?

"Dad!" Camden ran out of the dugout and straight for his dad. Bryce often wondered how he could possibly love this kid more than he already did, but somehow Camden stole another piece of his heart daily. Cam slammed into Bryce's legs and gave him a big hug. "You made it."

"I wouldn't miss your first game. Have fun out there."

Camden let go and smiled up at Bryce. "I will, Dad. I'm gonna get a home run."

Bryce tapped the bill of Camden's baseball hat. "We'll be cheering you on."

Willow gave him a high five and he ran off to be with his friends. In their navy blue T-shirts and white baseball pants, they all looked so official. How could his boy be old enough to play ball already? It felt like yesterday that he was a baby, coming home from the hospital.

"I got a couple pictures of him and some of his teammates when we first got here," Willow said. "I'll send them to you." She got on her phone and, in a matter of seconds, his was chiming.

She knew exactly what he needed. He was terrible at remembering to document these milestones. Again, that had been April's department.

"Sheriff!" Kara Sinclair was one of the doers in Bryce's life. She usually reached out to him once a week to see what she could do for him and Camden. She was the one who had suggested that he sign Camden up for T-ball because her son was going to be on the team. "Glad you could make it. I was so surprised when you said Camden didn't need a ride. I didn't realize you hired a nanny. This must be her, huh?"

"Kara, this is Willow. Willow, this is my neighbor Kara. She's the one who helped me get Camden on the team."

"Nice to meet you, Kara."

Kara looked Willow up and down. "Well, aren't you a doll face. Where did you come from exactly? Do they have mail-order nannies?" she asked, cackling at her own joke.

"I'm originally from Dallas. Lucky for me, I was looking for a job here and Camden needed a nanny."

Kara cocked her head to the side and raised an eyebrow. "Now, what would make a big-city girl like you want to settle in our little ol' town?"

Willow didn't flinch at her obvious prying. "My grandmother grew up in Maple Grove and made it sound like a magical place. I was making a change and figured why not here."

"Who is your grandmother?"

"Her maiden name was Rose Everly. I've heard there are Everlys still in the area. I hope to find out if we're related."

Finally satisfied, Kara nodded. "Well, welcome to Maple Grove. If you need anything, don't hesitate to reach out. Alex and Camden get along really well. We could set up some playdates. Bryce has my number."

"I already put your number on the list of emergency contacts," Bryce said to Kara.

"Good. While I have you here, did you get the email from the school about kindergarten registration? You know you have to get all the documents in order and get Camden registered before summer. I know it seems early, but they have strict deadlines."

Bryce faintly recalled seeing something from the school about that. "I think so. I'll have to go back and check."

"I'd be happy to help you. You're going to have to make sure he gets his physical. If you want I can make a copy of my to-do list and send it to you so you don't miss a thing."

"I appreciate that, Kara. Let me look at the email again and if I think I need the list, I'll text you."

"I'll just send it and if you don't need it, you can ignore it." Of course she would. She was a doer. She had to do things for him even if he didn't want them done.

Bryce gave her a thumbs-up. "Great. Enjoy

the game." He headed back to the blanket with Willow.

"She seems nice," Willow said.

"She loves to remind me that I am doing a terrible job of being a single parent."

Willow touched his arm, causing him to look at her. "You are not doing a terrible job at anything. People understand how over-whelming it can be. It's nice that you have the support of people who want to share their experience and tricks of the trade."

He blew a breath out his nose. "Is that what that was? She was sharing the tricks of the trade?"

"I think she was."

Bryce took off his hat and scratched the back of his head. "I guess that's a better way of looking at it," he said, putting his hat back on. "Somedays I wonder if I'll ever manage all this stuff."

Willow smiled. "You'll do the best you can, and Camden will love you for it."

Bryce could only hope that was true. They rejoined Delia and cheered on Camden and his teammates as they took the field. T-ball was a hoot. No one really struck out. No one hit it into the outfield, which was a good thing because the boys and girls out there were more interested in catching butterflies than baseballs. Kids at this age struggled to hit their targets when throwing the ball, leading to lots of singles turning into doubles. Innings were capped at seven runs.

Camden didn't hit a homer, but he got to second base on his first turn at bat and ran all the way home when the girl after him hit it through the shortstop's legs. Between the look of determination as he rounded third and the smile on his face as he crossed home plate, Camden was clearly having the time of his life.

At the start of the third inning, Bryce's phone rang. Doc Wight's number popped up and Bryce's heart sank. Willow caught his eye just as he pressed the button to answer.

"Hey, Doc." Bryce's voice sounded funny even to himself.

"Hey there, Sheriff. I called the lab to check on Camden's blood test. Unfortunately, I think your nanny was right. His glucose levels were extremely high. He should come in for a fasting blood draw, but given all the other symptoms, I think we're looking at type 1 diabetes."

It was a crushing blow. The tightness in his chest made it hard to breathe. How was he going to do this? Doc was still talking, but Bryce couldn't even hold his phone to his ear.

Willow was at his side in an instant. "Breathe in through your nose and out through your mouth. You're okay. Copy me," she said, taking deep breaths. Bryce did as she did.

She took the phone out of his hand. "Hi, Dr. Wight. This is Willow… I think the sheriff needs a minute… Got it. Thanks, Doctor."

She hung up and went back to taking deep breaths with him.

"We got this," she said. In that moment, hiring Willow became the best decision he had ever made.

CHAPTER TEN

It was one week since Camden had been diagnosed with type 1 diabetes. One week of helping Bryce navigate his care. One week of trying to calm the fears that the diagnosis had caused to flare up inside the single dad.

"I organized the pantry," Willow said, showing Bryce how she had spent the morning while June had been over to entertain Camden. "Everything in here is grouped by amount of carbohydrates. This bin is fast sugar—glucose gel packs, some candy and a can of frosting."

"Frosting?"

"I wanted you to have options," she answered with a shrug. Theo had given her a list and she'd gotten everything he suggested. "We only use these things if he has an insulin reaction or his blood sugar drops too low. It's up high because we do not want him to help himself to anything in there."

Bryce scanned the pantry, taking it all in. "This is really impressive."

"Next, we have the refrigerator. Our extra insulin is in here. The bottle we're using, however, is in the cabinet. Here." She opened the cabinet on the end that they had decided would be the new medical cabinet.

"Room temperature makes it less painful for Camden, right?"

"Right." She smiled. He was doing much better at remembering what they needed to do and why they were doing it. "Syringes and everything we need to check his blood sugar are also in here. Just like in the pantry, everything is labeled, thanks to Kara and her amazing label maker."

"Kara's label maker is very impressive."

"I should probably inform you that you have agreed to help her husband trim some branches on a tree in their backyard this weekend to return the favor."

"Happy to do it," he replied genuinely. Willow knew that he felt guilty about accepting so much support from others. Giving him a way to pay back their kindness was exactly what he needed to counteract that feeling.

"I also emailed everything to Dr. Nandi. He

should let us know pretty quickly if Camden
is a good candidate for the continuous glucose monitor."

"I would love to not have to poke him so
many times a day."

Willow couldn't disagree. Between the finger pokes to check his blood sugar and the
insulin shots to keep it in line, Camden got
poked a lot. He was a real trooper, but she
knew he'd also appreciate not having to do
so much.

"According to Theo, the feedback he gets
from parents is much more positive than neg-
ative. He said they report feeling much less
anxious after their child gets one."

Bryce had been nothing but anxious since
Willow had first told him her concern. She
wanted to do whatever she could to alleviate
some of that worry.

"I feel like the person I need to pay back
the most for everything they're doing for me
is you. How am I supposed to do that?" he
asked, taking a seat at the island.

"This is kind of what you hired me for,
isn't it?"

"I hired you to be a nanny, not a private

duty nurse. I'd offer you a raise if I had the money to do it."

She shook her head. "I don't need a raise. I do need a night off, though."

Bryce's brow furrowed. "A night off? For what?"

"Kara invited me to go line dancing with her and some of her friends tomorrow. I thought it might be fun, but she wants to leave right after dinner." She hated to ask. Bryce had not been alone with Camden this whole week. He had relied on Willow to be the one to test his blood and administer the insulin shots. If she went out, he was the one who would have to do it.

"Oh," he said as that realization hit him.

"If you don't want me to go, I totally understand. I can tell her maybe next time would be better."

"No, I don't want you to do that. I mean, technically, you're off duty as soon as I walk in the door. You don't have to ask for the evening off."

"Maybe we could have you do the after-dinner shot and the bedtime check tonight, so if there are any issues, I'm here to talk you through it. That way, you'll be more confident doing it on your own tomorrow."

Bryce looked a little pale and his chest rose and fell faster than it had been a minute ago. She didn't want to send him into a panic. He was quiet and it fed her own anxiety.

"I'm going to tell her that I'll come with her next time. Don't worry about it." There would be plenty of time to go line dancing in the future. Right now, Bryce needed her help. She couldn't let him down.

Bryce shook his head. "Kara will never forgive me if you don't go. There's just one thing." He paused like he needed to consider his words carefully. "You can*not* go line dancing in any of the outfits I have seen you wearing around the house."

That was not what she'd expected him to say. "What's wrong with my clothes?"

Before he could answer, she looked down at her current outfit. Today, she had worn a white maxi dress. There were peanut butter smudges on it from where Camden had decided to hug her after lunch. This fabric also seemed to attract all the dog hair in a five-mile radius. Pink, blue and yellow chalk dusted the skirt from where she had kneeled in the sidewalk chalk they had played with today. Perhaps not the best choice for hanging out with an active four-year-old boy and a constantly shedding golden retriever.

"There's nothing *wrong* with your clothes. They're just too fancy for the dive bar in town that has line dancing. Do you own a T-shirt and jeans or do they not wear those in Dallas anymore?"

Willow was well aware that her vacation wardrobe wasn't very casual. She had been prepared to walk the streets of Greece, not Maple Grove. It was embarrassing that he had noticed.

"I need to go shopping. I planned to do that after I got paid. I sort of used all my cash when I bought my phone."

"You have no money? What about credit cards?"

She had money in a bank and credit cards in her wallet that would alert Hudson to exactly where she was if she used them. She needed at least a couple months for things to blow over and to figure out what she wanted to do with her life. If she could establish herself in Maple Grove, it would make it that much harder for Hudson or her parents to convince her to go back to Dallas.

She shook her head. "I have to wait for my paycheck."

Bryce reached in his back pocket and pulled out his wallet. He opened it and slid out one of his credit cards, placing it on the island in between them. "Use this. Whatever you spend, we'll call a bonus for the nursing skills you bring to the job."

Willow pushed it away. He was already housing and feeding her. She couldn't let him clothe her as well. "I can't do that."

He pushed it back. "Yes, you can. I'm going to come home for lunch tomorrow so you can do some dive-bar clothes shopping."

Bryce was hard to argue with. There was an assertiveness to his tone that made her want to do what he said. A voice like his probably came in handy in his profession.

Willow took the card. "Thank you. I promise not to exceed your credit limit, which is…?"

He cracked a smile.

"I'm kidding," she said. "As much as my current wardrobe does not reflect it, I have a casual style that shouldn't cost very much."

"I trust you," he said, and her heart leaped a little. She knew she hadn't given him much reason to, since she hadn't been totally honest with him and continued to keep secrets, but it meant a lot that he could tell she was trustworthy. She wanted to be trustworthy.

Someday she would come clean about everything. She would be able to speak openly about running away from a marriage she didn't want. She'd be able to thank him for giving her the opportunity to figure out what she did want—once she figured out what that was. If it wasn't for Bryce and this job, she might have been forced to go back to Dallas before she was ready to stand up for herself.

"Do you know how to line dance?" His question pulled her out of her thoughts.

"I do. My friends and I used to go all the time when I was in college." When Kara had mentioned it this morning, so many memories had come rushing back. Before Hudson was in the picture. Back when it had been acceptable to cut loose and occasionally have some fun.

"Where did you go to school?"

"My parents wanted me to stay close to

home, so I went to TCU." She held up two fingers and curled them. "Go, Frogs."

"Where did you want to go?"

Willow was thrown for a second. No one had ever asked her that before. Her parents certainly hadn't. It had been expected that she would go to TCU, so that was where she went.

"I would have loved to have gone to UT Austin. They have the best nursing program in the state, but I didn't even apply."

Bryce seemed surprised by her answer. "That would have been a very different experience. Austin and Fort Worth are nothing alike."

This was so true. What would her life have been like if she had done what she wanted instead of what her parents wanted? Would she have gone back to Dallas to work or would she have stayed in Austin? She would never have met Hudson.

"I guess it's better you didn't go to UT," Bryce said. His blue eyes locked her in place and made her heart thump a little bit harder. "You ended up in Dallas, and whatever was wrong in Dallas is what made you come to Maple Grove. I'm glad you're here."

Her heart was thumping harder now. He

was magnetic. She could feel herself being pulled in his direction. It was wrong for her to give in to that feeling. Thankfully, the island was in between them and she was not going to make a fool of herself and climb over it. She did put her elbows on the counter and lean in.

"I'm glad I'm here, too."

They stayed there, eyes fixed on one another. The feeling rushing through her veins was completely new and made Willow wonder how she could have ever thought being with Hudson would have made her happy. Bryce was setting a whole new standard when it came to men. She wanted someone who asked her about her day, someone who cared about what she wanted out of life and didn't simply tell her what she should want, someone who looked at her like Bryce was looking at her right now.

Camden came running into the kitchen, breaking the spell she was under. "When's dinner? I'm starving. Can I have some juice?"

"You can have some water. Dinner will be ready in…" Willow spun around to check the oven timer. "Ten minutes."

Theo had assured her that the best thing for

Camden was balanced meals served around the same time every day. As if being in charge of the meals hadn't been hard enough, now she had to think about how much protein, carbs and healthy fats were in everything. Yet, she found that if she thought about it through a lens of medicine, it was actually easier. Cooking was like chemistry and she had been a star student in all her chemistry classes.

"Come on, let's go wash up while Willow finishes things up in here," Bryce said, ushering Camden out. He glanced back at her and gave her a small smile as he went.

Willow realized that she didn't want some mystery someone to make her feel special, she liked that Bryce made her feel that way. That was going to get her in trouble.

WILLOW SANDERSON WAS like no one Bryce had ever known. She was smart, but she didn't act like she knew it all. In fact, when she didn't know something, she did some research or she found someone who did know. She was resourceful, compassionate, funny, empathetic, engaging and beautiful.

The last part made Bryce feel guilty. He

shouldn't think about things like that. How beautiful she was shouldn't have been something he ever noticed about her, but it was impossible to deny. As she slung her purse over her shoulder, she ran over the last couple of details he needed to remember.

"Set a timer for thirty minutes after he starts lunch. That's all he gets even if he's not finished. If he finishes before the timer goes off and he's still hungry, he can have the string cheese in the fridge. Reset the timer for thirty minutes and, if for some reason I'm not back, he gets his shot."

"I've got it," he assured her. "Go shopping for your line dancing outfit."

The blue-and-white wrap dress she had on was belted at the waist and hit the floor. When she walked, her tanned legs slashed through the slit in the front. *Beautiful.* Bryce averted his eyes. He shouldn't be looking at her legs or thinking about how gorgeous she was.

"Kara told me where to go so I can be in and out. I'll be back in less than an hour." She was so frazzled, even though there was no need for it. He had been the one who suggested she go on his lunch break. "I know you have to get back to work."

"Go before you waste my entire lunch hour telling me how you'll be back on time."

She laughed at herself and headed for the door. "Bye, Cam."

"Bye, Willow!" Camden shouted without even looking up at her. He was too invested in his current art project.

Bryce loved that she never forgot about him. Camden was always considered. That was what she was hired for, he told himself, but something also told him that she didn't think of him as just a job. She truly cared about Camden.

There was a knock on the door a couple minutes later. Banjo barked and Bryce shook his head. "Would you just go," he said as he yanked open the door, thinking it was Willow coming back for one more thing.

"Wow, Sheriff. Nice manners." Daisy stood on his front porch with her usual scowl. Banjo recognized his walker immediately and welcomed her with open paws. He jumped up on her and she patted him on the head.

"Sorry, I thought you were someone else."

He had forgotten that it was Friday. "Why aren't you at school?"

"No school today," Daisy said with a shrug. Her hair was up in a messy ponytail and her clothes were wrinkled as though she'd slept in them all night. "I thought I'd get Banjo's walk done early so I can have the rest of the day to myself."

"You just woke up, didn't you?"

"I'm a teenager who had no school today. Of course I just woke up."

Bryce blew out a laugh and opened the door wider. "Come on in. I'll get his leash."

"Where's your babysitter? Do you need a new one? Because I could be convinced to be paid to hang out with a kid all day instead of going to school."

Handing her Banjo's leash, Bryce smiled. "Thanks for that very tempting offer, but Willow is just on a lunch break."

"Your loss." She attached the leash to Banjo's collar. "We'll be back."

"I want to go on a walk with Banjo and Daisy," Camden said, racing to the door.

Bryce grabbed him and picked him up. "Maybe next time, bud. You have to eat lunch."

"He can come with if he wants. I don't

mind. I'll have to charge you double, but it's no trouble."

"Double," Bryce murmured with a shake of his head. "He needs to eat lunch. We can take Banjo for another walk after dinner tonight."

"But I want to go with Daisy," Camden said, kicking his legs and squirming in his arms.

"Okay, how about we just add on a five-dollar surcharge for the kid and he can come with me?"

"He can't, Daisy. He has to stick to a really specific schedule because of a medical issue. Take Banjo. We'll see you in a little bit."

Camden decided now was the perfect time to have a meltdown. Bryce shut the door and carried his flailing son to the kitchen. "Buddy, this isn't the way to get what you want. You know that."

His current mood was not going to be conducive to having his blood sugar checked. What if they just skipped that part? Bryce had to dose him according to what he ate, not what his before-lunch blood sugar was.

Willow had a chart that she filled out with all his readings. If he didn't have numbers to put on there, she'd notice.

"Come on, Cam. I need you to settle down. We need to do your poke and eat lunch. Can you calm down?"

Camden was having none of it. He wanted to walk Banjo. He didn't want to be poked. He didn't want to eat lunch. He wanted Willow.

Bryce wanted Willow right now, too. "How about you and Willow take Banjo for a walk when she gets back? Would that be cool? You don't have to wait for me to get home tonight, okay?"

Camden stopped wiggling and nodded. Tears streaked his cheeks. "I don't want to do any more pokes, Dad."

His words squeezed Bryce's heart like a vise. "I know, buddy. I wish you didn't have to get any more. Willow has a friend who is going to give you a cool thing on your arm that tells us your numbers without having to poke as much. That's going to be so much better."

"I want that now."

"I do, too. But can you try to be brave a little bit longer until we can get that for you?"

His sweet little boy nodded before wrapping his arms around Bryce's neck and hugging him. This was a million times harder than Bryce imagined. He knew it would be tough. He knew it was going to break his heart to see Camden struggle, but actually being the one who had to inflict the pain was excruciating.

He kissed the side of Camden's head. Bryce wished Willow was there. She was better at calming Camden down. She knew how to ease his fears and how to say all the right things so both Camden and Bryce were more relaxed. Suddenly, guilt washed over him. That was the first time he had thought that way about Willow instead of April. In moments like this, he always thought about April.

Setting Camden on one of the island stools, Bryce opened the medical cabinet to get the supplies. He only thought about Willow because she was a nurse. She was the one who had been in charge of all this medical stuff. That was why his mind had gone to her absence instead of April's.

After lunch, Bryce reset the timer for thirty minutes. Camden went to play with his zoo animals. A knock on the door stole his attention away from cleaning up.

Daisy and an overheated Banjo walked in.

She unleashed him and the panting dog ran for his water bowl.

"That dog spends more time peeing on every tree than he does walking. Can I get some water while you get my money?" Daisy asked, cutting to the chase.

"Follow me," Bryce said. He pulled a cup from the cabinet and filled it up from the dispenser on the refrigerator.

"Can I get some ice?" she asked as he held the cup out.

Bryce bit back the retort he wanted to give and pivoted back to the fridge, pulling open the freezer door to grab the ice instead of letting it drop into the full cup and making a mess.

"So, what medical condition does Camden have exactly that makes him have to eat on a schedule?"

Bryce bristled at her intrusive question. "That's really not your business, Daisy," he said, handing her the ice water she requested.

She took a sip of the water and glanced around the kitchen, her eyes landing on the container that Willow had on the counter for the discarded syringe needles.

"It's diabetes, isn't it?"

"When someone tells you something isn't your business, it means that you should drop it."

"My mom has diabetes. How long has he had it?" she asked, completely ignoring his requests for privacy.

"He was just diagnosed," Bryce replied, sensing she wasn't going to stop talking about it.

"Oh, wow. My mom's had it since she was a kid, too. You'd think that would mean she'd be better about managing it, but she's terrible. She's so bad at staying on a schedule and even worse at staying away from the sweet stuff. Nothing funner than trying to get your mom to swallow a spoonful of sugar in the middle of the night when her blood sugar crashes because she skipped dinner but then takes her normal dose of insulin. You ever try to get someone who's almost unconscious to swallow granulated sugar? It's like trying to get them to swallow sand."

Bryce didn't know Daisy's mom had diabetes. Why would he? He could see the impact this disease had on Daisy. It had been hard for him to help Camden. What would it be like to be a teenager trying to help someone manage all this?

He went to the pantry and snagged a couple of pouches of the glucose gel and tossed them on the counter. "Willow says these are good if Camden crashes. I think they'd go down easier."

Daisy's eyebrows lifted. "Oh, this is the fancy stuff. We can't afford the fancy stuff, but I'll take these if you're offering."

"They're yours." He had a million questions for her all of a sudden. "Does your mom have any other issues because of the diabetes?"

This was one of his biggest fears. What kinds of problems was Camden going to have as he grew up? Would there be a ton of complications?

"She's got neuropathy in her feet and hands. The doctor says her kidneys aren't the best. I keep telling her she needs to take better care of herself, but she just laughs and tells me not to worry about her." She bit down on her lip as her leg bounced. "Someone's got to worry about her, right?"

"You're a good kid, Daisy."

"Can you remember that the next time you try to arrest me for something?"

They both laughed and Bryce shook his head. He pulled out his wallet and handed her twenty dollars. "Thanks for walking Banjo."

"Thanks for hiring me," she said with absolute sincerity.

Willow came racing into the house. "I'm back. You can go to work. Sorry it took so long."

Bryce glanced at the clock on the oven. She'd been gone forty minutes. "You're fine. Did you get everything you needed?"

"I am going to pay you back for all this. I couldn't resist these boots. Oh!" She had rushed into the kitchen and was startled when she noticed Daisy sitting at the island. "Hi, Daisy. I didn't expect you until this afternoon."

"No school today," Daisy replied. "Let's see your boots."

She sure had a way of making herself at home.

"They're really cute. I'm going line dancing tonight and I couldn't resist." Willow set her shopping bags on the island and pulled out the large box that housed her new cowboy boots. She opened it and Daisy oohed and aahed.

Bryce threw a thumb over his shoulder. "Okay, well, I guess that's my cue to head back to work."

"What else did you buy?" Daisy asked, sneaking a peek into one of the other bags.

Willow's eyes latched on to his. "Did everything go okay?"

"All good. The timer is set. I wrote everything on your chart."

"Good." She smiled and he felt it in the center of his chest. "I'll see you later."

Why was he looking so forward to that?

CHAPTER ELEVEN

IT HAD BEEN quite some time since Willow had gotten herself ready for a girls' night out. She actually couldn't remember the last time. She hoped Bryce wouldn't be disappointed in her for putting a movie on for Camden so she could be all ready when Bryce got home. Kara had said she was picking her up at five forty-five, which didn't leave her much time if Bryce got home from work at his usual time.

She finished applying her makeup and ran the straightener through her hair. Why did she have so much hair? Satisfied, she stepped back and did an outfit check. The new jeans she bought were tight and dark. She loved them. She tied the front of the new blue plaid shirt in a knot over the white cami she already had in her possession. The new cowboy boots were the icing on the cake. Willow was ready to cut loose and have some fun.

Bryce walked in the house at the same time

she stepped out of her room. He froze the moment he saw her.

"What?" She went from feeling good about herself to insecure.

Bryce removed his hat and shook his head. "Nothing. You look ready to line dance."

"This is what people wear to line-dancing dive bars, right?"

Bryce continued into the living room. "Yeah, that's exactly what people wear to line-dancing dive bars. You'll fit right in." He greeted Camden and went into the kitchen.

Willow wasn't sure what had just happened, but she wasn't going to put too much thought into it. She followed him into the other room. The kitchen table was set. Willow had everything prepared so she could eat and run. "I made a Mediterranean salad with chicken for dinner. We can eat whenever you're ready."

"Someone is excited about going out tonight." A sly smirk stretched across Bryce's face.

Was she that obvious? She did like the idea of meeting some new people, seeing another side of Maple Grove, doing something she thought was fun instead of spending a Friday night doing what Hudson wanted to do.

"Let me get out of my uniform and we can eat," Bryce said, taking a swig of his after-work soda.

"Cam, let's do your poke real quick," she said. Her phone rang as she pulled out the blood monitor. It was Kara. Willow answered it. "Wait till you see the boots I got for dancing tonight."

"Oh, Willow, I'm so sorry. Mary Beth's daughter isn't feeling well and Michelle said she hurt her back at CrossFit this morning and that there's no way she can dance tonight. We were thinking maybe we should reschedule for next week."

Disappointment swept over her. "Of course. I totally understand. I am so sorry to hear about Michelle's back and Mary Beth's daughter. I hope everyone feels better soon. Let me know if y'all reschedule."

"For sure. Have a good night."

Willow ended the call just as Camden climbed up on the stool. "Can I have chocolate milk with dinner tonight?" he asked.

She pasted on a smile. "I bought some

sugar-free chocolate sauce, so I would say yes to one glass with dinner."

"Yay!"

"What are we cheering about down here?" Bryce asked, joining them at the island. He had changed into his blue jeans and a fitted black T-shirt, going from a handsome lawman to a casual and cool cutie in a matter of minutes.

"Willow said I can have chocolate milk."

"Well, if Willow says you can, I guess you have a reason to celebrate." He glanced from a beaming Camden to Willow. "What's wrong?"

She hadn't realized she had stopped fake-smiling. "Nothing."

"I can do his poke if you want to get dinner on the table so you can get out of here sooner," he offered.

Willow turned her face to hide the emotion that was bubbling to the surface. How silly to want to cry over a stupid night out. "No rush. Kara called. The other ladies backed out. We're going to reschedule girls' night to next week."

"Oh, Willow, I'm sorry. I know you were looking forward to going out."

She waved a dismissive hand. "No biggie. I've been feeling bad about leaving you alone tonight anyway. Plus, Kara said we could reschedule. I haven't been dancing in years—what's another week or so?"

She ripped open an alcohol pad to run over Camden's finger, trying to focus on the task at hand instead of the giant letdown Kara had handed her. Canceled plans happened. It wasn't the end of the world. This little boy in front of her had much bigger problems than she did. Perspective was good.

They ate dinner and Bryce took Camden out back to play on the swing set while Willow cleaned up. She needed to get out of this outfit and into the new pajamas she'd bought—the ones that weren't silky or sheer and wouldn't embarrass her if Bryce saw. She was about to retreat to her room when Bryce came back in the house.

"Whatcha doing?" he asked, shoving his hands in his pockets.

"I'm going to take these boots off and change out of my dive-bar outfit since that is not where I am headed."

"What if it *was* where you were headed?" he asked with a slight tip of his head.

She scrunched up her face. "What do you want me to do? Go by myself? No thanks."

"Not by yourself. With me."

"With you? Who's going to stay with Camden? We'd spend half the night making sure they knew all the signs of low and high blood sugar and would probably still be too worried to really enjoy ourselves."

Unfazed by her concerns, he grinned at her as he grabbed his keys. "I have a qualified babysitter who can do it all. I just need to go pick her up. I'll be back in fifteen minutes. Don't take those dancin' boots off yet."

As promised, he was back in fifteen minutes. He walked in with none other than Daisy the dog walker. Willow wondered if he had lost his mind.

He must have noticed the look of pure disbelief on Willow's face. "Daisy's mom is diabetic. She probably understands this stuff better than we do."

"Is the dog staying?" Daisy asked, taking a look around.

"Yes, the dog is staying," Bryce replied like that question made no sense.

"If I have to watch the dog, too, that's going to be extra."

Bryce closed his eyes, dropped his head and shook it slightly. The girl never settled for less than she believed she deserved. "Of course it is."

"Are you sure about this?" Willow asked as they walked to the truck.

Bryce stopped and turned to face her at the bottom of the porch steps. He was so handsome it made her weak in the knees. He smiled up at her. "You deserve to go out tonight. Camden will be fine." He held his hand out. "Let's go see how they taught you to line dance in Fort Worth."

She swallowed hard and stared down at his hand. She was going out dancing with her ridiculously attractive boss who let her live in his house. What could go wrong?

BRYCE WASN'T SURE she was going to get off that porch. She stared at his outreached hand with nothing but uncertainty in her eyes. After a few more seconds ticked away, she stepped down and put her hand in his. It felt nice and his heart might have skipped a beat.

She had nearly taken his breath away when he came home tonight. Willow was beautiful when she was dressed in her designer clothes, but she was next level in jeans and flannel. She was a poor country boy's dream.

It was the look on her face when she told him that Kara had canceled that had made him call Daisy, though. He had to find a way to get her out on that dance floor, even if that meant he would take her himself.

The music made Willow sway when they walked into the Whiskey Rose. Wyatt loved country music. It had a way of making it seem like small-town country life was the only kind of life worth having. Bryce couldn't help but tap his foot to the beat as he waited for Hank, the bartender, to pay him some attention. The counter was sticky and when Hank finally came over, he was good about wiping it down before taking Bryce and Willow's order.

"Well, if it isn't Sheriff Koller. What can I get ya?" Hank and Bryce had grown up together in Maple Grove. They were a couple of years apart in age, but both had played baseball in high school. While Bryce had chosen to settle down, get married and start a family, Hank stayed a bachelor and ran the Whiskey Rose with his older brother, Cody.

"Hi, Hank. I'll take a glass of the IPA you

have on draft." He looked over his shoulder at Willow.

"Same," she said, a genuine smile now plastered on her face.

"Make that two."

Hank slid two cardboard coasters in front of him and went to pour the drinks. Some old-timers sipped their beer from pint glasses, sitting at the bar on wooden stools. The younger crowd was on the dance floor and that was where Willow's gaze was fixed. She stood in one spot but her feet were mimicking what was going on out there.

He leaned closer. "If you want to get out there, go ahead."

She shook her head and bumped against him, sending a jolt of electricity through his arm and into his chest. "No, let's have a drink and then we can go out there together. I want to see the Sheriff Shuffle."

Bryce chuckled. How did he get here? More importantly, how did he get here with her? If he was being honest, he'd have to admit he was happy that he was.

Hank came back with the drinks. "Who's your friend?" he asked, nodding in Willow's direction.

Bryce tugged on Willow's sleeve. "This is Camden's nanny, Willow. Willow, this is Hank."

Gracious as ever, Willow offered him one of her gorgeous smiles. "Hi, Hank. Nice to meet you."

Hank leaned forward and his smile was a bit too sly for Bryce's liking. "Well, hello there, Miss Willow. You must be the new woman in town that everyone's been talking about."

Willow's eyes went wide. "Everyone's been talking about me?" She pressed a hand to her chest.

"Someone as pretty as you? Absolutely, everyone's talkin'," Hank replied.

Bryce felt his hackles rise. That sounded a whole lot like flirting. "Small towns, you know. Can you start me a tab?" he asked. "We're going to grab a table."

"You got it, Sheriff. It was nice meeting you, Willow. I hope to see you around. I'd love to find out what brought you to Maple Grove and how I can help convince you to stay."

Bryce had to fight an eye roll. He forced a smile and placed his hand on Willow's lower back to guide her away from the bar and the flirtatious bartender.

"He seems nice. Everyone in this town is *so* nice," Willow said, taking a seat at one of the open tables.

"Yeah, Hank's a nice guy. Although I wish he hadn't made it sound like you were being gossiped about all over town."

She pulled a pretzel from the bowl on the table. "Yeah, that part wasn't my favorite, either." She popped the salty snack in her mouth. Her lips were painted pink. He had a hard time looking away.

"Well, everyone in this town is nice, so even if they are talking about you, it's probably just to say they can't wait to get to know you better."

"Okay, you are being *too* nice."

Bryce shrugged his shoulders and smirked. "I am probably the nicest one here. Don't forget that."

Willow took a sip of her drink. "I won't forget. I knew that about you the minute I met you."

A warmth flowed through him. He liked that she liked him. "Let's finish these drinks and get you on the dance floor and see what those new boots can do."

They did just that. When a Thomas Rhett song came on, Willow couldn't stay seated any longer. She set her beer down and slid off her chair. She pulled on Bryce's arm. "Come on, Sheriff, let's dance."

They found a space on the dance floor and joined in on the dance. It had been a while since he'd been line dancing, but it was like riding a bike. His body remembered what to do even if his head wasn't so sure. Willow didn't seem to have any trouble following along. She laughed when he spun the wrong direction and bumped into her.

"It's right heel, left heel, spin to the *right*," she said with a giggle.

He teasingly scowled at her. "I know, I know."

They laughed and they danced. Willow seemed so carefree, and it encouraged him to let himself set some of his worries aside, at least for a few hours. She was such a light. His world had been so dark since April got sick. Willow made him believe that there was a chance he could find his way out of this grief.

After over an hour on the dance floor, they were both sweaty and parched. Bryce led Willow back to the table before going to the bar to get them another round of drinks.

"It's nice to see you out, enjoying yourself, Sheriff," Hank said, sliding two new glasses in front of him. "It's been a long time."

Bryce tugged on the collar of his shirt. "It has."

It had been almost a year and a half since Bryce could remember letting loose. April had been diagnosed in October and was gone by the first week of April. He wasn't sure if it was the six months before her death or the six months after that had been the worst. All he knew was that the last eighteen months hadn't brought him much happiness. Until tonight.

He went back to the table where Willow was waiting for him. She was dancing in her seat as she watched the dance floor. Bringing her tonight had been so worth it. It was the joy on her face that was making him feel happy.

He set the drink in front of her and she drank it down like she had been denied fluids for days. She set the half-empty glass down and wiped her mouth with the back of her hand.

Willow was glowing. "This is so fun."

It was making his day to make hers. "I'm glad you're having a good time."

She reached across the table and put her hand over his. The physical effect her touch had on him was startling every time. It was scary and thrilling at once.

"Thank you for coming with me. I like spending time with you."

He put his other hand over hers. "I like spending time with you, too."

Her smile was so big that her eyes crinkled at the edges. He wanted to lean over this table and plant a kiss on those lips. That thought alarmed him. He swallowed and pulled his hands away. Touching her made him lose his mind.

Willow's attention went back to the dance floor.

"You should go back out there," he suggested.

"Only if you come with me," she said.

Bryce shook his head. "I'm an old man. I need longer to recover. Go."

Willow stood up and dropped her chin, giving him that look. "You are not an old man."

"It's fine. Go."

She didn't need to be told again. She hustled out there just as a new song came on and a new dance started. She joined some ladies in the line and the one next to her helped coach her through the dance. Bryce watched as she followed along with that big grin on her face.

"Sheriff." Gretchen came up from behind him. "What are you doing here? I mean, obviously you're here to have a drink and do some dancing. That was a dumb question."

"There are no dumb questions. Isn't that what our teachers used to tell us?"

"Oh, they may have said that, but you know they were in that teachers' lounge talking about all the kids who asked dumb questions."

Bryce laughed and nodded. "That is probably true. To answer your not-that-dumb a question, I am here because my nanny got stood up by some ladies who promised to take her line dancing. She seemed so bummed I figured I'd bring her over here and let her have some fun."

"Your nanny is here? Which one is she?" Gretchen scanned the crowd, surely capable of picking out the woman who wasn't familiar. "Is that her, dancing next to Myra Finnley?"

"That's her," he replied. Gretchen pressed her lips together. "What?" he said.

She tipped her head to the side. "Seriously, Sheriff? Sam would absolutely find that woman *cute*. I knew you didn't answer because she was either homely or because she was a knockout. Of course she's a knockout."

"I don't judge people for how they look, Sergeant."

"Wait until Sam lays eyes on her. I'll have to listen to him pine away for the next month." Gretchen seemed a tad bit jealous and Sam hadn't even met Willow yet.

Bryce was surprised that Sam and Gretchen had never dated. There were times they seemed like they would make a perfect couple. Other times, they sounded like they wanted to run as fast as they could in the opposite direction of each other. It was a love-hate relationship, for sure.

"Willow's too nice for Sam. He likes a woman with a little more bite."

"Oh, trust me, she's out of his league. That doesn't mean he won't torture me with his wild fantasies about having someone like that fall for him."

"Why don't you just ask him out?" Bryce accidentally wondered out loud.

"What? Me? Ask Sam out?" Gretchen snorted. "Not in a million years." She took a long pull from her bottle of beer. "He wouldn't say yes anyway." Another pull. "Right?"

Bryce wasn't much for giving relationship advice, especially to his desk sergeant regarding his deputy. An office romance could cause drama he had no time for. Instead, he answered honestly. "I don't think he could ever say no to you, Gretchen."

He didn't miss the way a certain hopefulness flashed in her eyes. Then she turned her head and focused on the dancers. "I don't know about that, Sheriff. Of course, if someone had told me I'd find you here tonight out on a date with your nanny, I would have told them they were losing their minds."

Bryce nearly choked on the sip he had taken from his glass. "I'm not on a date. I told you, she was supposed to come here with friends who had to cancel. I'm just tagging along so she didn't have to come alone or not at all."

Gretchen's eyes turned back on him. "That was actually really sweet of you."

"What can I say? I am a sweet guy."

They both laughed. No one at the station would ever dare call the sheriff sweet when he was on the job.

"Who's home with Camden if you two are here at the Whiskey Rose?" she asked.

He cringed. "Don't judge me when I tell you," he said, knowing she'd promise not to but would absolutely do so when she heard who was babysitting.

"Why would I judge you?"

"Because Daisy Sikes is babysitting Camden tonight."

Gretchen's eyes nearly bulged out of her head. "Daisy Sikes? *The* Daisy Sikes? Sheriff, I'm not judging you, I'm thinking I might need to arrest you for child endangerment."

Bryce confined his laugh to a snort. "I don't blame you. I might arrest myself when I get home and find out what went on while I was gone."

"Why in the world would you hire Daisy to babysit?"

He didn't want to share Daisy's personal business with Gretchen. He wouldn't want people telling the world his son had diabetes. It wasn't his place to share her mother's condition. "You'd be surprised, but I do think that she will do a good job in the end. That's why I did it. *And* I didn't have a lot of time to find someone, honestly."

Gretchen shook her head. "You are a brave man, Sheriff. Brave or stupid. We're going to call it brave for now."

He accepted her teasing because she wasn't wrong. "Who are you here with?"

Gretchen pointed toward the bar and the woman clearly flirting with Hank. "My neighbor, Miranda. We're out celebrating her divorce. She's always had a secret crush on Hank, so here we are. I'm supposed to be her wingwoman, but she seems to be doing fine on her own."

Bryce wasn't going to complain that someone else was there to distract Hank from whatever it was that he thought was going to happen between him and Willow.

"I heard she and Harrison called it quits," he said. "She used to complain to April all the time about his constant traveling."

"Yeah, it's better this way. He moved back to Dallas. Maple Grove wasn't the place for him."

Most of the residents of Maple Grove had

lived here their whole lives. It was rare that people from the big cities could make it in their sleepy small town. That thought caused Bryce to glance over at Willow, dancing her heart out. Would she really be able to make Maple Grove her home? She was enamored by it now, but would it lose its novelty after a few months? Years, maybe? How dangerous was it to get attached?

"You gonna introduce me to your way-too-cute nanny?" Gretchen asked.

"You want to go out there or wait until she takes a break?" he asked, nodding toward the floor.

Gretchen's smile revealed her amusement. "Are you going to come out there with me?"

He rolled his eyes and set his glass down. "Come on, Sergeant. Let me show you how it's done."

"Well, I think I like this nanny before I've even met her. I've been missing this side of you."

Her words sent an avalanche of feelings to drop inside of him. Willow was to blame for his smiles tonight. He hadn't been one for smiling much over the last year and a half. He knew that had made him someone people didn't want to be around. Yet, his improved mood also made him feel guilty. Wasn't he supposed to mourn April forever?

CHAPTER TWELVE

NEW BOOTS AND line dancing for hours had proven to be a terrible combination. Willow nursed some pretty bad blisters for the next week. She was the one who had to back out the following Friday when Kara tried to reschedule their girls' night out.

She didn't feel like she was missing out, though. This Friday, she was having a girls' night in. Well, girls plus Camden.

"When can I make the ones with strings?" Camden asked as he slid a bead on his piece of yarn.

"These ones are kind of hard, bud," Daisy said as she braided the threads of her friendship bracelet.

"Well, the kind you're making is hard, but maybe he could do a simple braid with yarn," Delia said as she worked on an even more complicated bracelet.

"I could help him try," June offered.

"He probably can do a better job than I

am," Willow said with a laugh. "I don't think I'm doing this right."

Daisy stopped what she was doing and leaned over to look at the mess that was Willow's bracelet. "Yeah, you messed it up. Let me fix it."

Willow moved over so Daisy could do her magic. She heard the front door open at the same time Banjo did. He barked and ran to greet his master.

Bryce came around the corner and stopped when he saw there were a few extra people in his house. "Are y'all having a party without me?"

"Dad! Look at the friendship bracelet I made." Camden held up his string of yarn. "I'm going to give it to Kenzie on my T-ball team."

"Kenzie? I thought you were making it for me," Daisy said, looking hurt.

"I'll make you a different one. This one has a lot of green and that's Kenzie's favorite color."

All four women said, "Awww!" at the same time.

"You are the sweetest, Cam," Delia said.

"I'm literally jealous of a four-year-old.

There are no boys at Maple Grove High School who can tell you what my favorite color is," Daisy said.

Willow put her hand on the rueful teenager's shoulder. "I bet that there are boys who wish they knew what your favorite color is."

"Ha."

"You are adorable. Trust me." Willow winked.

"I'm going to change out of my uniform," Bryce said, throwing a thumb over his shoulder.

Willow moved toward him. "We ordered pizza. I hope that's okay. It should be here in a half hour."

He motioned for her to follow him to the stairs. "Do you need me to send everyone home? I know Kara and her friends are heading to the Whiskey Rose later."

"Oh, no. I'm not going line dancing tonight. I'm enjoying having them here." Her face fell. "Unless you want them to go. I didn't mean to assume that you would be okay with people in your house after a long day at work. I can tell them they have to go after dinner."

Bryce held a hand up. "No, no. It's fine. Camden seems to be having fun."

"I think he loves all the attention. Your kid has four different generations of women wrapped around his finger. It's pretty impressive." Impressive but not surprising. Camden was a chip off the old block. She couldn't say that, though. He might notice that she was fighting feelings that she knew she shouldn't be having for him.

"A four-year-old Casanova. I'm in trouble," he said with raised eyebrows.

She nodded and laughed. "You are."

He set his hat on the hook by the door and took the stairs two at a time. Willow caught herself staring at his retreating figure longer than she should. She hustled back to the kitchen.

"Fixed it for you," Daisy said. "Just make sure you don't wrap threads the same color around each other."

"Thank you. Cam, let's do your poke before the pizza gets here."

"I want Daisy to do it."

Willow glanced at Daisy, trying to relay that it was okay for her to say no.

"No problem, little man. Let's do it." The teenager took his hand and walked over to the island with him. Willow grabbed the supplies they needed to check his blood sugar.

"What are you doing?" Delia asked, looking up from her bracelet.

"We have to check Camden's blood sugar before we eat." Willow realized that no matter how many times Delia was around when they had to manage his diabetes, she didn't remember that he had it.

"Why would you need to do that?" She got up from the table and joined them at the island.

"Camden has diabetes," Willow said. "We have to monitor his blood sugar throughout the day."

Delia's confusion made her anxious. The anxiety led to her being more confused. It was a vicious cycle. "Does April know about this? I don't know if you should be poking him without his parents in the room."

Daisy visibly flinched when Delia mentioned April. Willow tried to silently communicate to Daisy not to say anything. She tried her best to keep Delia calm. "We can wait for Bryce to come down. Would that make you feel better if Bryce was here?"

"What is all this stuff?" Delia opened the

cabinet with all the medical supplies. "This is where my daughter keeps her coffee mugs. Where are April's coffee mugs?"

"The mugs were moved right here," Willow said, opening the cabinet that now housed those mugs.

"April! Why are you letting people move things around in your kitchen?" Delia walked out of the kitchen. June and Daisy's eyes were wide and fixed on Willow.

"Check his blood sugar," she said to Daisy before following Delia out. Delia went back to Willow's room and reached for the doorknob. "Let's go back in the kitchen and wait for Bryce," Willow suggested.

"He's probably in here, too." She pushed the door open and stood in the doorway with more confusion furrowing her brow. "What is going on?"

"Delia," Bryce said from behind them. Willow stepped out of the way and let him take over.

"Whose stuff is this?" she asked, her eyes roaming over Willow's things scattered on top of the dresser. "Where's April?"

"We ordered pizza. Why don't you come help me set the table? Did you call Lee and tell him you were having dinner here?" Bryce asked, changing the subject while trying to guide her back out into the living room.

"Where is Lee?" Delia asked, complying and following Bryce out of the bedroom.

"He's at home. We called him earlier to say you were staying for pizza, so he's going to pick you up at seven. Do you still want to stay for pizza?" Willow asked.

"Is Bryce paying?"

Bryce chuckled. "I'm paying."

"Then I'm staying."

Bryce and Willow made eye contact. Crisis averted. Daisy and Camden were back at the table, working on their bracelets.

"Did you make this?" Bryce asked, checking out the one Delia was almost finished with.

"She did. You are so talented, Delia," June said.

She beamed and took her seat. "I used to make these all the time years ago. It's fun. Anyone with patience can do it."

Willow walked over to Camden's blood sugar chart and saw that Daisy had written down his current number. She caught Daisy's eye and gave her a thumbs-up and mouthed, "Thank you."

Daisy gave her a lopsided smile. She would have to explain to her later about Delia's condition. Willow was sure it had been a little scary to hear Delia asking about April.

Bryce walked over to the refrigerator and pulled out his after-work Coke. "What set all that off?" he whispered.

"Testing Cam's blood sugar."

He nodded knowingly.

"Sorry," she whispered.

He shook his head. "You're doing great. Don't apologize." He glanced over her shoulder at the four people sitting at his kitchen table. June and Delia were helping Camden braid some yarn. "You are the reason that my son is surrounded with all that love right now."

It warmed Willow's heart as much as it did his. She was happy to give all these people a place to come together. They were all lost souls in their own way. June lived alone without any family nearby. Delia only had Lee. Daisy was a wayward teenager, struggling to find her place. Willow felt like she fit right in. She was the runaway from Dallas, hiding from everyone who knew her. She loved that none of these people told her what to do or had expectations of her. They just liked her for her.

"I can't believe I almost fired you," Bryce said quietly. "We all would have been worse for it."

She felt those words leave his mouth and enter her chest. He had this way of making her feel important. She hadn't felt important in a very long time. This moment solidified that the best decision she ever made was not getting married to Hudson, who'd made her feel like an accessory. A pretty thing that he wore on his arm at cocktail parties. Someone to be seen and not heard.

"What are you thinking?" Bryce asked, the space between his eyes creased with concern.

"I was thinking about how different things were in Dallas."

He nodded. "I'm sure you miss it."

"Actually, I wish I'd left a lot sooner."

BRYCE WASN'T SURE if he should believe her. Hearing Willow say that she thought her life in Maple Grove was better than her life in Dallas was music to his ears. It seemed hard to believe given all the drama that surrounded them. Between Camden's illness, Delia's condition, and the ghost of his wife still lingering in this house, it was a wonder she wanted to be here at all.

The ladies cleaned up their craft project and everyone helped set the table. The pizzas came and Bryce sat back and enjoyed the conversation and laughter happening around his kitchen table. It had been too long since this much joy lived between these walls.

"I heard the bluebonnets are in bloom in the fields along the Wildflower Trail," June said.

Delia sighed. "I haven't been to see the bluebonnet fields in forever. So beautiful."

"What's the Wildflower Trail?" Willow asked.

June set her slice of pizza down and wiped her hands on her napkin. "Oh, there's this lovely walking trail on the west side of town where, in the spring, the bluebonnets fill the fields on either side of it. It's absolutely one of the prettiest things to see in Maple Grove. Did your grandmother not tell you about the bluebonnets?"

Willow shook her head. "She did not. Maybe she'd never been."

"Well, then you need to go! Both you *and*

your grandmother can't miss out," June said. "Bryce, you should take her this weekend to go see."

His gaze flicked from June to Willow. "We could go over there if you want to."

"You don't have to entertain me on your day off. If you tell me where it is, I can go by myself," she replied.

"You don't want to go by yourself," June admonished her.

"I'll go with you," Daisy said, followed by a loud "Ow!" She reached down and touched her leg, glaring at June, who sat next to her.

"I'm sure you have better things to do. Bryce and Camden can take her," June said firmly.

Bryce was being set up by his eighty-year-old matchmaking neighbor. They were going to talk about that later.

Understanding registered on Daisy's face. "Riiight. Yeah, I totally forgot. I do have lots to do. Sorry, Willow. You're gonna have to go with the sheriff."

"You want to see the bluebonnets, Cam?" Bryce asked. "There's a pond at the end of Wildflower Trail. We could do some fishing. That would be fun."

Camden nodded.

"Sounds perfect. Y'all should have a wonderful time," June said, picking her pizza back up and smiling smugly, as if she'd just gotten away with something. He was on to her, though.

They finished dinner and Lee came to pick up Delia. Bryce offered Daisy a ride home. He watched as Camden threw his arms around the teenager, completely unaware of the fact that she was the town troublemaker. Not that it would matter. In his eyes, Daisy was the coolest babysitter he'd ever had.

Daisy hugged Willow next. As long as he'd known her, he'd never seen Daisy do anything but rebel against adults. Somehow, Willow had come to town and tamed the beast. It was the wildest thing he'd ever seen.

"You've got an awesome family, Sheriff," the teenager said when they got in his truck.

The lump in his throat was unexpected and made it impossible to say anything in return. *Family.* That was such a loaded word for him. He had felt like his family had been irreparably broken the day April died.

He nodded and she continued. "Camden is super lucky he's got Willow for a nanny.

She's so organized when it comes to all that blood sugar stuff."

Bryce cleared his throat. "She was a nurse before, back in Dallas. We're really lucky that she took the job with us. I don't think I would be that organized," he admitted.

"She's also really good with Delia. I was freaking out a little bit when she started talking about April. I didn't realize she has trouble remembering."

"Yeah, if you ever babysit again, remember that you can't leave her alone with Camden, okay? It's important that someone always be there because she has those episodes sometimes. Camden would be really scared."

Daisy nodded. "Thanks for trusting me. With your dog and with your kid. It means a lot to me, even though I might not always act like it."

Bryce could only imagine how hard it was for her to admit that out loud. He gave her a sideways glance and smiled. "As long as you don't give me a reason to not trust you with them, we're good."

He turned on to her street and her leg began to bounce as she stared out the window. She chewed on her fingernail. Going home didn't bring her the same comfort that it did him.

"Have a good weekend. Stay out of trouble."

"I hope *you* have a good weekend. Miss June sure didn't want me to go see the bluebonnets with Willow. Don't disappoint her."

"Yeah, well, June is forgetting that Willow and I are employee and employer." That would be what he would remind her of when they had their heart-to-heart.

"Oh, Sheriff." Daisy laughed. "You are funny."

"I'm not being funny. I'm being real. Y'all can keep your opinions about my relationship status to yourselves." He pulled into her driveway and put his car in Park.

Daisy turned her body to face him. "When you're lucky enough to find someone amazing, you don't worry about things like employee-employer baloney. You hang on with both hands and be grateful."

He wasn't about to take relationship advice from a fifteen-year-old. "Good night, Daisy."

"Goodnight, Sheriff," she said, pushing the door open. "Thanks for the pizza."

Bryce feigned shock, holding his hand over

his heart and letting his mouth drop open. "Did you just use your manners? *You* have manners?"

She shook her head and rolled her eyes as she jogged up to her house. Who was this kid and what did she do with the Daisy he knew?

Willow and Camden were snuggling on the couch reading when he got home. Banjo sat at Willow's feet with his head resting on top of his paws. The dog didn't even bother to get up when he heard the door open.

Family. The word echoed in his head. Only Willow wasn't theirs to keep. She could choose to leave at any time. Unless he gave her a reason to stay. Bryce felt that twist of conflicting feelings again. This was April's family. Was he ready for that to change?

"I think it's getting close to bedtime, Camster."

Camden yawned as he protested, "I'm not tired."

Willow and Bryce both laughed. "Nice try, mister. Come on, let's get ready and I'll read you one more story in bed," Bryce offered.

Willow encouraged him to get up and follow Bryce. Camden shuffled his feet like he was walking through wet cement. Once he was ready, they climbed onto his twin-size bed. Bryce tucked Camden in under the sheets with the colorful dinosaur footprints on them while he lay on top of the dino comforter. The ceiling fan over their heads rattled as it spun. Bryce would try to fix that this weekend.

"Why does Grandma talk about Mom like she's not in heaven?" Camden asked. "Willow said I had to ask you."

Bryce appreciated that Willow hadn't tried to tackle that one on her own. "Sometimes Grandma gets confused. Was that scary for you?"

Camden shook his head. "How come no one told her Mommy was in heaven? You didn't want to make her sad?"

"Kind of. You should let me and Willow handle it if Grandma does it again, okay?"

He nodded. "Do you think Mommy can see us and she knows Grandma sometimes thinks she's still here?"

Camden rarely asked questions about April. Delia's outburst must have really bothered him. "I think Mommy watches over all of us."

"Yeah." He snuggled closer. "I think she still likes us."

"She still *loves* us, bud. She'll always love us and we'll always love her." If there was one thing he never wanted Camden to doubt, it was that his mother loved him and would have given anything to still be here with him.

"Yeah. And it's okay if we love Willow, too. Mommy won't be mad."

Bryce stiffened. "Did someone say that to you?"

"No, I just love Willow and that's okay, right?" He was looking for reassurance that his feelings were not bad. Bryce was having the grown-up version of that same internal conflict.

"Mommy would be happy that you have someone like Willow helping me take care of you."

But would April be happy that Bryce had someone like Willow to make him feel butterflies again? Someone like Willow to put a smile on his face without trying? Someone like Willow to make him forget that he was supposed to be missing April?

CHAPTER THIRTEEN

WILLOW WAS WELL aware that the state flower in Texas was the bluebonnet. However, she had never in all her years seen a field full of bluebonnets before today.

Acres of vibrant blue-violet bluebonnets swayed gently in the spring breeze. As far as her eyes could see, there were flowers on top of flowers. A sea of blue and green.

"This is absolutely breathtaking. Camden, come here and take a selfie with me." She crouched down and put an arm around him, angling her phone to get the best shot of the flower field behind them. "Say bluebonnets!"

"Bluebonnets!" he repeated.

"Do you want me to take a picture of you in the field?" Bryce offered, setting all his fishing gear down. That was the longest sentence he had said to her today. In fact, that was the most he'd said since dinner last night. After he put Camden to bed, he'd informed her he was going up.

"Sure, thanks." She handed him her phone and carefully stepped off the trail and into the sea of bluebonnets. Trying not to step on any of them, she only went a few feet in. Crouching back down, she threw her hands over her head. "Try to get the flowers to fill the whole screen around me," she directed.

He took a couple shots and held her phone out for her as she returned to the gravel trail. "Let me know if those were okay."

Willow scanned through the shots and was pleased with them. "These are perfect. Thank you. Do you want to take a picture with Camden so you have it to look back at?"

"That would be nice," he said. He lifted Camden up, not trusting the little guy to maneuver as carefully through the flowers.

"Can I pick some to bring home?" Camden asked innocently.

"Nope, we leave the bluebonnets where they are so other people who walk the trail can see them. We also leave them so they can grow back next year," Bryce explained. His gaze landed solidly on Willow. "Just because we think something is pretty doesn't mean we should take it and keep it for ourselves."

His words were messing with her head again. Why did it feel like he wasn't talking about the flowers? She had wanted to talk to him about what happened yesterday. Between Delia looking for April and June basically forcing him to bring her here, she felt like they needed to debrief. His avoidance of her made it impossible to know what was going on inside that handsome head of his.

Was he trying to set boundaries for her, or for himself? If it was the latter, she wanted to tell him she was ready for some boundaries to be crossed. Being with Bryce and Camden was exactly where she wanted to be. If she could be with them and get to do things like kiss Bryce, she was 100 percent in. Of course, if he was trying to tell her to back off, she needed to pull it together and respect that.

Willow took a few pictures of father and son before they resumed their hike to the fishing pond. Camden skipped to the water's edge while Willow put down a blanket. The small pond sat in a clearing at the end of Wildflower Trail. In contrast to the blue-bonnet fields leading there, the pond was surrounded by nothing but shades of green. A breeze from the west caused little ripples to form on the water's surface that caught the light and created sparkles.

"Cam, you should have a snack," she said, opening the cooler she had packed. "That was a long hike and you probably need a little fuel."

He had a light sheen of sweat on his face and arms. It was warm outside, so it was very possible it was simply from the heat, but she needed to get a little bit of sugar in him to keep his blood sugar from getting too low.

Bryce came over and grabbed his water bottle. His blue eyes reminded her of the bluebonnets they had just walked through. When he looked at her, she became intensely aware of her heartbeat and the way it raced.

"Have you ever fished before?" he asked her before taking a swig of his water.

"I once went to a lake house with my friend and her family for a weekend. I watched her older brother fish. Does that count?"

Bryce cocked one eyebrow and smirked. "No, that does not count."

"Then I guess today has another first in store for me."

"I'll teach you," Camden said. His little cherub face was already smudged with dirt. "It's *so* easy."

"So easy, huh? What happens if she doesn't catch anything and you told her it was *so* easy?"

Willow's jaw dropped. "Are you implying I won't be able to catch a fish?"

Bryce chuckled. His smirk was back. "I'm teasing. I think you'll catch a fish or two. It's *so* easy."

"Great!" Willow threw her hands up. "Now I'm for sure not going to catch one because you're putting too much pressure on me."

"We'll help you," Bryce said, putting his hand on Camden's shoulder. "We won't leave until you catch one."

Willow wagged a finger in his direction. "I'm holding you to that."

Two fruitless hours later, she was eating those words. None of them had caught a single fish. Not even close.

"Are you sure this pond has fish?" Willow asked.

Bryce shrugged. "I'm beginning to wonder."

"I think we need better bait," Camden suggested.

"Oh, yeah? What do you think we should use as bait?" Bryce asked with a tilt of his head.

As if it was completely obvious, Camden looked at them both and replied, "Cheeseburgers."

Willow and Bryce got lost in their laughter. Willow might have been confused about her feelings for Bryce, but she was undoubtedly in love with Camden Koller.

Bryce reeled in his line and picked Camden up. "Oh, yeah? Well, I think we should go eat some cheeseburgers. How does that sound?"

"Yay!" Camden cheered. Willow wanted to cheer, too. Fishing without fish was only tolerable because of the company she kept.

When they got back to town, Bryce took them to the Hideaway, claiming they had the best burgers in Maple Grove. He wasn't wrong. Willow took one bite of that juicy, cheesy burger and she was in heaven. She couldn't get enough of the soft, buttery, slightly toasted brioche bun. It even came with some yummy dill pickle chips. A blob of ketchup fell on her plate.

"I told you so," Bryce said as she practically moaned.

"How's everything over here?" the waitress asked, coming back to check on them.

"It's delicious," Willow said wholeheartedly.

The waitress quickly shifted her attention back to Bryce. She swept her blond hair over her shoulder. "How about you, Sheriff? All good?"

"It's great, Nadine."

"Let me know if I can get you anything else. It's good to see you. We've missed having you and Camden come in."

Willow wondered how long it had been since he'd eaten at the Hideaway and why he hadn't been there in a while. Nadine clearly missed him.

Bryce smiled. "I won't make the mistake of staying away again."

That seemed to make Nadine's day. She went to check on another table with a little extra bounce in her step.

"How long has it been since you had cheeseburgers here?" Willow asked, unable to ignore her curiosity. "It seems like Nadine *really* missed you."

His jaw tightened for a second. "It's been a little over a year." He scratched the back of his neck. "Nadine and I dated in high school for maybe a millisecond sophomore year. Sometimes she's extra friendly. It used to make April jealous."

That added something to the story. "Oh, former girlfriend. Makes sense. She was very much invested in your happiness in a way I did not think was related to how you were going to tip her at the end of this meal."

Bryce's shoulders seemed to relax and a smile played on his lips. "You think that's real funny, don't you?"

"Come on, Sheriff. You have to have half this town waiting to see when you're going to put yourself back on the market."

"What if I don't want to put myself on the market?"

Willow could see him sinking back into that sad place he liked to go inside his head. "Then there will be lots of broken hearts in Maple Grove, Texas."

He blew a dismissive laugh through his nose and shook his head. Willow knew there'd for sure be one broken heart if Bryce wanted to stay happily unattached—hers.

"Oh my gosh." Bryce sat up a little straighter.

His whole expression softened. "I'll be right back." He got up from the table.

Willow swung her head around, looking over her shoulder to see where he was going. From her spot in the booth, it was hard for her to see who he was talking to. When he came back, he wasn't alone. An older gentleman with silver hair was with him.

"Willow, I'd like you to meet Charlie Everly. Charlie, this is Willow. Her grandmother was Rose Everly. Ring any bells?"

"You're related to Rose?" the man asked.

Willow's heart was fluttering as fast as a hummingbird's wings. She was quite possibly sitting in front of one of her long-lost relatives. "Are *you* related to Rose?"

A smile spread across his face. "I am."

As soon as Willow and Charlie started talking, Bryce regretted not reaching out to him sooner. As it turned out, he was Willow's grandmother's cousin, who had lost touch with Rose decades ago.

"She talked about Maple Grove with so much love. She's the reason I came here, actually."

Charlie and his wife had joined them in

their booth. "I can't believe Rosie ever gave this old town a second thought. After her parents sent her off to marry that guy in Dallas, she never came back. Not even for the holidays. I was only eight when she left, but I figured she couldn't wait to get out of here and was glad to go somewhere bigger and better."

"My grandfather's side of the family used to monopolize all the holidays. They still do," Willow explained. "I think Grandma Rose missed coming home so very much. She used to tell me about all her family traditions. She was especially fond of the Spring Festival."

Charlie's expression turned wistful. "I was so much younger than my cousins, but I used to follow Rose and her sisters around like I was a lost puppy. I remember them having so much fun at the festival. They'd buy me fresh-squeezed lemonade and cotton candy and take me on the carousel."

"Did you go on the Ferris wheel? Willow is taking me on the Ferris wheel when we go to the festival," Camden said.

Charlie smiled at Camden. "I was too afraid to go on the Ferris wheel when I was your age. I really missed out. You're going to love it." He turned to Willow. "I hope we'll see you there next weekend. My whole family will be there and I would love for you to meet them. Some of your other relatives will be there, too. Rosie's sister Greta had two boys who stayed in town. Their families will want to meet you, for sure."

Willow was practically bouncing in her seat. "That would be so wonderful. I would love to meet everyone."

She was still on cloud nine when they got home later that afternoon. Bryce should have thought of this sooner. Connecting her with family was a good way to help her want to plant roots here. If she stayed for them, he wouldn't have to feel guilty about wanting her to be part of his and Camden's life for the long haul.

"I can't believe all these people existed and I didn't know about it. Part of me wants to call my dad and tell him all about the family he has here."

"Why don't you?" She never talked much about her parents. From the little she did say, he could tell that they had been very involved in her life. Perhaps more than she had wanted.

She shook her head. "I can't. Not right now, but someday. Someday, I'll be able to introduce them all to each other." Her voice cracked and her eyes became teary. "Can you excuse me for a second?" She ran back to her room.

Bryce was left confused and concerned. She had been so happy, and now she was crying. He knew she wanted some privacy, but that didn't stop the tug she had on his heart. He needed to know she was okay, but Camden needed his insulin.

Camden was becoming quite the pro at letting Bryce and Willow check his blood sugar and give him his insulin shot. Bryce knew he had Willow to thank for that. Her calming presence and the consistent routine she had put into place were the reason this was going so well.

"High five, bud. You are awesome." Bryce held up a hand so Camden had to jump to hit it.

"Can I read books in my room?" Camden was exhausted. Their busy morning was catching up to him. He didn't want to admit that he wanted to take a nap but reading in his room was code for just that.

"Go for it."

With Camden tuckered out and Willow

taking some time for herself, Bryce used his alone time to clean up. He gathered up the toys that were strewn around the living room and folded the blanket that Camden had been snuggling under when he first woke up this morning. Banjo wanted some attention, so he got down on the floor and rubbed his belly.

Bryce's thoughts kept drifting back to the woman on the other side of the wall. Maybe meeting family had made her emotional. Maybe she'd had a falling out with her dad. Maybe it was something totally unrelated.

The sound of her door opening caused his heart to stutter-step and then break into a run when she came around the corner. She smiled when she saw him on the floor with the dog.

"Where's Cam?"

"Reading in his bed." Bryce made air quotes with his fingers.

She nodded knowingly. "You gave him his shot?"

"I did." He loved that Camden's health was always her priority. "Are you okay?"

She joined him on the floor, gracefully folding her legs under her. Her bubblegum-pink shorts and gray T-shirt made him smile this morning when she had come out of her room. It was such a departure from the wardrobe she'd brought to Maple Grove. Willow always looked lovely, but in something as simple as shorts and a T-shirt she looked at home versus on vacation. That was what he liked the most.

"Thank you for taking me out today and showing me those gorgeous fields and trying to teach me how to fish."

"It would have helped if there had been some fish," he said with a laugh.

Willow smiled as she petted Banjo. "That would have been nice, but it was fun just being together experiencing nature."

"I'm glad. Make sure you tell June how much fun you had."

"Right. She seemed very invested."

Bryce nodded. "She did."

Willow got quiet. "Most of all, thank you for introducing me to Charlie. I lived in the Dallas/Fort Worth area my entire life, but I never felt as at home as I do here in Maple Grove. Most of that has had to do with you and Camden, but meeting the family I have here makes it feel *real*."

Bryce pinched his eyebrows together. "It didn't feel real before?"

Willow pressed a palm to her cheek. "I don't know. I mean, you did almost fire me once. All of this could be gone in an instant if you wanted it to be, but Charlie will always be my cousin."

He knew he had teased her before about the firing, but he needed to clear things up now. The thought of her not being in this house, helping him raise Camden, made his stomach hurt. "I don't ever want to fire you."

"You say that today..."

He reached over and touched her face. "I mean it, Willow. I couldn't do all this without you."

"You could do it all on your own if you had to, but you could easily do it with a nanny. Any nanny."

Bryce shook his head. "I don't want *any* nanny."

Willow's breathing hitched. There was something pulling him to her. An invisible string tugged at him right in the center of his chest. She looked deep in his eyes. It was as if she was trying to get inside his head, make sure he meant what he said.

He leaned in closer and tipped his head ever so slightly. Their lips were almost touching. He closed his eyes, giving in to feelings he wasn't sure he should be having.

"Dad!" Camden screamed from his room, jolting Bryce out of the bubble he and Willow had found themselves in.

Both of them ran into his room. Bryce could tell right away what the problem was. Camden had drunk a ton of water during their hike and then even more during lunch. He should have had him go to the bathroom before he let him fall asleep.

"I'm so sorry, buddy. That was my fault. It's not a big deal. Let's get you cleaned up," Bryce said.

"I'll take care of the bedding," Willow offered.

Bryce lifted Camden up and carried him into the bathroom. He started the bath and got Camden undressed.

"I'm sorry, Daddy."

"It's okay, Cam." All Bryce wanted to do was reassure him. The only one who should be sorry was Bryce. "Daddy totally forgot to remind you to go to the bathroom before you went to your room to read books. It was my fault."

Camden pressed both his hands against Bryce's cheeks. "Next time, don't forget."

Guilt seeped into every pore. He had been thinking about Willow instead of thinking about Camden. He'd almost kissed Willow. What if Camden had woken up before his accident and come into the living room? How confusing would that have been for him? Bryce needed to make sure that moving forward, he considered Camden first.

CHAPTER FOURTEEN

WILLOW FOUND HERSELF touching her lips a million times over the next couple of days. Bryce had almost kissed her on Saturday, she was sure of it. Had Camden not needed them, they would have absolutely kissed. Her lips had never wanted something to happen as badly as they wanted to be kissed by Bryce Koller. They still tingled from the anticipation.

"Hello, hello!" June called as she came through the back door. "I made some low-carb cookies for Camden. Peanut butter. I think he's going to love them."

Camden came running into the kitchen. "Cookies!"

"I think *I'm* going to love them," Willow said, taking them from her before Camden could. "They were made by you, which guarantees they're delicious."

"Can I have one?" Camden jumped up and down on his socked feet.

"After lunch."

He stopped hopping and jutted his bottom lip out in a pout. "Fine." He returned to the living room where he had been playing with his animal figurines.

"How was the Wildflower Trail? Were the bluebonnets beautiful?" June asked as she took a seat at the kitchen table.

"You were right, it was worth seeing. We took some pictures. Want to see?" Willow unlocked her phone and opened her photo app. She handed it to June. "Just swipe with your finger across the screen to see all of them."

June smiled as she went through the photos. "Did you catch any fish?"

"No luck," Willow said with a laugh. "I don't think there were any fish in that pond. Bryce was getting flustered. It was kind of cute."

June glanced at Willow over the phone. "Cute? You think Bryce is cute?"

Willow shook her head and started to make a cup of coffee for her nosy neighbor. "Don't start with me."

"What? Am I wrong in thinking that it wouldn't be the worst thing in the world if you and Bryce explored being more than Camden's dad and nanny?"

Willow warred with herself over whether to tell June what happened on Saturday. In the end, she decided not to. Bryce had gone back to having very firm boundaries. "What if we tried being more and it didn't work out? I would lose this job, this roof over my head, Camden. That would be a disaster."

June stood up and moved closer. "And what if it did work out and you got to have this roof over your head, Camden and Bryce forever?"

That would be a dream come true, but it was only that—a dream. "I am not sure things would work out the way you imagine. Let's not forget that I have only been working for him for a few weeks. I don't think we should get ahead of ourselves."

"I fell in love with my husband after knowing him for one week and we didn't spend nearly as much time as you and Bryce spend together. Not to mention that you two have navigated something as huge as Camden's diabetes together. The two of you are far from strangers."

It was sweet of her to try to make her case. Willow knew it was all coming from a place of love. There was no doubt that June wanted nothing but good things for them. What she didn't know was that there was a huge secret that Willow was keeping from Bryce, from everyone in Maple Grove.

Meeting Charlie Everly this weekend reminded her that there were people back in Dallas who had no idea where she was, were angry with her for leaving like a coward, were going to do everything to get her back in line when she finally reached out.

There was also something Bryce was keeping from her. She felt it. She could see it in his eyes sometimes. It caused him to retreat inside himself, closing him off from her. Until he could let her in, she was not confident that they could be more than what they were.

"I like being here. I'm not ready to put what I have at risk just yet." Bryce was worth keeping in her life even if it meant that their relationship would never be anything other than what it was today.

"I guess I'll just have to keep working on him until you see there's no way you can lose. You won't be able to resist if he truly turns on the charm," June said with a wink.

Willow couldn't imagine him being more charming. Resistance would be fruitless, for sure. She smiled at June and wagged a finger at her. "You are nothing but trouble."

"When you get to be my age, causing trouble is one of the few things worth sticking around for."

Willow had such feelings of adoration for June. She reminded her so much of Grandma Rose. Spending time with June always felt familiar. This was exactly how Willow imagined it would be if her grandmother were still alive. The two of them would sip coffee and chat about the weekend. Grandma Rose would have loved Bryce. There was no doubt she would have played matchmaker just like June.

When Willow could be completely honest with Bryce and he with her, she could think about taking that leap. For now, both of her feet were going to stay on the ground.

June went home and Willow finished some chores. After lunch, Willow let Camden indulge in one of June's cookies. They were delicious, just like she knew they would be. A couple of hours later, they went to the park to meet Kara and her son.

The boys ran off to climb the playground structure shaped like a ship. It had a mini climbing wall and three different purple slides. Camden's favorite part was the lily-pad bridge where he had to jump from dangling saucer to dangling saucer.

"I'm sorry you couldn't come out with us last Friday. How are your blisters?" Kara asked.

"Much better. I think next time I go line dancing, I'm going to choose comfort over fashion and wear my running shoes."

Kara's nose wrinkled. "I cannot be seen with you if you wear tennis shoes to the Whiskey Rose."

Willow bumped her shoulder against Kara's with a smile. "Be nice to me and my feet." Kara raised her eyebrows. "Okay, maybe I should walk around in socks and my boots for a few days and break them in."

"Better plan," Kara said with a laugh. "You have some time to break them in unless you plan to wear them this weekend. Y'all are going to be at the festival, right?"

"I can't wait. I finally met Charlie Everly, and it turns out we are related. He was my grandmother's cousin. I'm going to meet his family and some of my other relatives there."

Kara smiled wide. "I'm so happy for you!

That's so exciting. Now you have no reason not to stay in Maple Grove forever."

"Why are you worried about me leaving Maple Grove?" Willow pulled back.

"It's not unusual for people to come here from Dallas or Austin and not last very long. Our way of life doesn't always compete with the fast pace of the big city."

"Maybe I like the pace of things here. Maybe I like the people, even the ones not related to me."

Kara smirked. "Well, you live with Sheriff Koller, so I can believe that."

"What's that supposed to mean?"

Kara tipped her chin down. "If I wasn't married to my husband, who I love very much by the way, I wouldn't mind it if the sheriff looked at me the way he looks at you."

Oh, goodness. Kara was in cahoots with June, for sure. How many times was she going to have to have this conversation today? "I am very happy being Camden's nanny. It's a good job that I wouldn't want to lose because of something silly like getting caught up in how someone looks at me."

The boys were chasing each other around a little too close to the bigger kids who were on the swings. "Alex! Camden! Get away from the swings, please!" Kara's voice carried across the park. Alex tackled Camden to the ground. Both boys giggled as they rolled around. "Boys," she said with a shake of her head.

It was so funny to Willow that people thought that she would choose Dallas over this town. She loved everything about Maple Grove. She loved the people, the places, the simplicity of things. She loved Camden's giggles. She loved friends who teased her and wanted her to be happy. She loved that she had family here. She loved the way that Bryce looked at her, even though she shouldn't think about that.

When Willow and Camden returned to the house, it was almost time for Bryce to get home. Thanks to June, Willow was trying her first Crock-Pot meal. June swore that all she had to do was stick in all the ingredients, set the cook time and walk away. She went for something easy—salsa chicken. It smelled fantastic, like tomatoes and cilantro.

"Can we play hide and seek?" Camden asked.

"Sure," she said. "Who's hiding first?"

"Me!" Camden ran out of the room before she could even cover her eyes and start counting.

Willow sat down on the couch and, loud enough so he could hear her, slowly counted to ten. "Ready or not, here I come!"

He had clearly decided to stay on the first level. She checked his bedroom first, opening the closet and checking under his bed. When she didn't find him there, she creeped into the bathroom and pulled back the shower curtain.

"Got you!" she shouted to an empty room. He wasn't there, either. Returning to the hall, she realized her door was not closed all the way. Of course, the little stinker had gone into her room to hide.

She checked under the bed and in the bathroom. The only thing left was the closet. She opened the door to the closet that held her clothes, but Camden wasn't there. The sound of a very satisfied four-year-old giggling came from the other closet. The forbidden closet. She knew Bryce didn't want her to go in there, but she had to find Camden. He would understand that she hadn't been snooping.

Willow yanked the door open and flipped on the light. She hadn't thought about what could be in there since being told to stay out. What she saw caused her heart to break a little for Camden and Bryce. All of April's clothes hung on the rod or lay carefully folded on shelves. Her shoe collection was lined up in rows on shelves to the right. There was a counter against the far wall where her jewelry was kept and displayed. A couple of purses sat on the shelf above that. It smelled like perfume. Willow imagined it was the scent April used to wear.

Camden jumped out of the hanging clothes. "You found me!"

Everything must have been exactly as she had left it before she died. Anyone who opened this door would assume she was still very much alive. Bryce had left her things in here because perhaps it was too difficult to give them all away.

"What are you doing in there?" his voice came from behind. It was a mixture of pain and confusion. Instantly, Willow wished she was anywhere but standing in this closet.

WILLOW SPUN AROUND with wide eyes and a closed mouth. Bryce had to take a couple of deep breaths before attempting to ask again.

"Daddy's home!" Camden ran out of April's closet and grabbed on to Bryce's leg. "We were playing hide-and-seek. Willow couldn't find me. I'm a really good hider."

Hide-and-seek? He scrubbed his face with both hands. His heart pounded in his chest as the scent of April's perfume hit him.

"I am so sorry," Willow said, finally finding her voice. She stepped out of the closet, shut off the light and pulled the door closed behind her. "I swear that is the first time I have ever opened that door."

He picked up Camden and carried him out of the room. He didn't like being in there, and seeing April's things made it a million times worse.

"It's Willow's turn to hide!" Camden said as Bryce set him down on the couch.

"No more hide-and-seek. I'm going to get changed out of my uniform and we can go out back and throw a ball for Banjo."

Bryce walked past Willow, who stood in the doorway to the hall that led to the bedrooms.

"Bryce, I'm sorry."

He shook his head and kept walking. He

could hear her feet lightly padding up the stairs behind him.

"Bryce," she said in what sounded like a plea.

He didn't turn around. "It's fine, Willow. I get it. You guys were playing a game. He doesn't understand what that room is. It's fine."

Her hand was on his shoulder and it sent tingles down his spine. His eyes closed as he tried to control his breathing. As soon as he faced her, she wrapped her arms around him and gave him a hug.

"You're hurting and I'm sorry," she said against his chest.

Without overthinking it, he accepted her comfort and put his arms around her as well. He rested his cheek against the top of her head. The giant lump in his throat made it hard to reply, but he tried. "We started remodeling the master bedroom and bathroom right before she found out she was sick. I wanted to stop working on it, but she was determined to see the project finished. She and I had to relocate up here during that time. Chemo wiped her out. I literally had to carry her up and down these stairs so many times. The day they finished, she got to take a look at everything before she collapsed. She died in the hospital a week later."

Willow squeezed him tighter. "Oh, Bryce."

He didn't want her pity. He simply needed her to know why he reacted the way he did. "Delia had put everything in the closet for April. I haven't mustered up the strength to take it all out yet."

Willow pulled back just enough to look up at him. "That's why you stay up here."

"It didn't feel right to sleep in there when she didn't get the chance." It was like that part of the house belonged to someone else. He had no memories of her in that remodeled space. Her clothes had spent more time in there than she did. He chose to stay in the place they'd shared together.

"It is a beautiful space and I am so glad to hear that she got to see it before she died. Besides being the kind of person who was loved by you and so many people in town, she had incredible taste and style. I appreciate getting to know her better through the people and things that meant something to her."

Bryce reached up and cupped Willow's cheek. She reminded him of April in so many ways and, in others, they were complete opposites. It was a big reason for these twisted emotions he felt for her. Was he attracted to her because she reminded him of April or was it because she was different? He feared that if he acted on these feelings without being sure, he'd lose Willow, and Camden would be the one who would lose the most.

He rested his forehead against hers. "I like you so much. I'm a mess right now, though. You should know that my hesitation isn't because of you. It's because of me. I don't ever want to hurt you."

"Thank you for letting me know what's going on inside your head. I want you to know that I'm okay with giving you time to work things out."

This was what made her different from April. April would have thrown a fit if he had told her he couldn't be with her because he was dealing with his feelings about someone who wasn't here anymore. She was a firecracker who always knew what she wanted and wasn't afraid to demand that she get it. Sometimes it hadn't mattered what Bryce wanted or felt.

Willow seemed to spend a lot more time

worrying about what others thought and felt. She adjusted to everyone else's demands instead of making demands of her own. Right now, he appreciated that about her because he didn't want to be rushed, not when Camden was involved.

"I'm going to get things ready for dinner," Willow said, breaking their physical connection.

"Tell Cam that I'll be down in a minute."

Willow nodded and headed down the stairs. Bryce unbuttoned his shirt and tossed it on his bed. He felt lighter. Opening up to Willow had taken some of the weight off his shoulders. His phone rang as he took off his belt. The number on his screen was unfamiliar. He almost didn't answer it, but then figured that if it was some telemarketer, he'd tell them to remove his number from their call list.

"This is Sheriff Koller," he said, imagining the potential scammer's face when he heard that.

"Bryce, this is Andy Boswell. It's been a long time, man."

Andy Boswell was someone Bryce met at the Law Enforcement Leadership Conference he'd gone to a few years back. Andy did some consulting with smaller counties, like the one Maple Grove was in, that didn't have the budgets or the manpower to handle more complex cases.

"Andy, how's it going? It has been a long time. How are you?"

"I've been good. I was hoping you could help me out. I'm doing a little private investigating. I've got a high-profile client who is trying to find someone who took something valuable."

Bryce sat down on his bed. "You're calling me to consult on a theft?"

"The guy is hoping he doesn't have to turn this over to the police. He's willing to pay me a lot of money to find this woman and to keep it quiet."

Bryce's interest was piqued. "Okay, how can I help you?"

"This might be a long shot, but I had a friend in the state police look her up and it turns out her license was run by someone out of your office recently. I thought maybe, just maybe, you could guide me in the right direction."

Suddenly every one of his senses was on high alert. He didn't want to believe it, but feared he knew the answer to the question before he asked it. "Who are you looking for, Andy?"

"Her name is Willow Sanderson. She's been on the run for about three weeks. It looks like she must have been in Maple Grove soon after she disappeared. I'm just wondering if you could find out who pulled her over, what they pulled her over for, if she said where she was headed. Anything would help at this point."

Bryce's blood ran cold. "You said you're trying to find her because she has something valuable that belongs to your client. I mean, what are we talking about here? Is this a diamond thief or some kind of dangerous criminal that I should know about?"

Andy's laughter on the other end of the line told him it wasn't that serious. "Funny you should mention diamonds. That's exactly what I'm looking for. She does have a diamond on her that's worth close to five hundred grand. But she's no mastermind criminal. Runaway bride is more like it."

Runaway bride? Bryce couldn't wrap his head around it. Willow had been living in his house for three weeks and never once mentioned almost being married.

"This woman fled the church right before the ceremony was set to start. Has been off the grid since then. Must have shut off her phone. Isn't using any of her credit cards. Hasn't accessed any money from her bank account. Her parents heard from someone she used to work with that she's alive but didn't want to be found. My client thinks she's probably sold the engagement ring and is living off that for now."

If he only knew. So many things began to make sense. The little things she said and did. The things she didn't do. He knew there had been something else going on that had brought her to Maple Grove.

"This client of yours, is he a good guy?" Bryce asked, curious about the man whom Willow had agreed to marry but ultimately left at the altar.

"His family is part of the Dallas elite. I don't know much about him. He's very demanding. Something tells me this woman ditching him was quite a blow to his ego. He seems very determined to find that ring."

Did this guy care more about the ring than knowing that Willow was safe?

"I'll look into it. Let me get back to you,"

Bryce said, trying to keep his voice even. He needed to talk to Willow before he told Andy he knew exactly where she was. She was going to get one chance to explain herself.

CHAPTER FIFTEEN

BRYCE CAME DOWNSTAIRS in his undershirt and uniform pants. He picked up Camden and went out back, disappearing out of sight without a word. A few minutes later, he stalked back inside without Camden and disappeared into the back hall.

Willow wasn't sure what was happening. They had shared such a real moment upstairs… Maybe that had triggered something. When he reappeared, it was clear he didn't go back there to deal with April's things. He tossed the garbage bag that held her wedding dress and very not lost phone on the living room floor.

"What's in there?" he asked with his hands on his hips.

This didn't make sense. Why would he suddenly be wondering about her wedding dress? It was obvious that he knew something he didn't know moments before.

"What is going on?" she asked instead of answering.

"Why did you really come to Maple Grove? And don't tell me it was because your grandmother grew up here. We both know that's not why."

Willow's whole body felt warm. Surely her face had turned bright red? "I did come here because my grandmother grew up here. I chose Maple Grove for that reason." It wasn't a lie. Had it not been for Grandma Rose, she would not have come.

Bryce's face crumpled. "Why won't you tell me why you left Dallas? Why won't you admit what's in this bag? I think it should be clear by now that I know what's in there, Willow. I just want to hear you say it."

She swallowed hard and decided to put it all out there. If it meant he was going to fire her for not being completely up-front, so be it. Her past had caught up to her and she couldn't run anymore. "It's my wedding dress and my old phone. I left Dallas because I didn't want to get married."

Throwing his hands up in the air, Bryce sounded relieved. "Finally! Why was that so hard? What aren't you telling me? Are you in danger? How can I truly help you if I don't know what's going on?"

Willow felt like she was going to cry. She'd been so afraid of how he was going to react and his first instinct was to wonder how he could help. "I wanted to tell you, but I was afraid you wouldn't give me the job if you knew I was a runaway and hiding from people back in Dallas."

"Why are you in hiding?" Bryce stepped closer and gently gripped her arms. "Are you afraid of this guy? Are we in danger?"

"No!" She hated that he would for a second think that she would be there if someone could hurt them. "I would never put Camden in danger. I'm not afraid of Hudson. He is probably looking for me, though. I'm hiding because I know that if he or my parents find me, they're going to do everything they can to get me to go back with them."

Bryce pulled her against him as if he needed to hold on to her so they couldn't take her away. "No one can make you do anything you don't want to do, Willow. I'll see to that."

She let herself melt against him. It felt nice to have someone care for her this way. To want to fight for what she wanted instead of telling her what to do. Bryce had always made her feel like she had a voice. He appreciated her opinion.

She needed to reassure him that he would not need to go to war with anyone. "It's not like they would use physical force. My parents' weapon of choice has always been good old guilt. I hate to disappoint people, them especially. It makes me unhappy when the people I care about are angry or upset with me. That's why I've been avoiding them—I can't bear their disappointment right now."

"Hudson is your fiancé?" Bryce asked, still holding her.

"Yes, Hudson Carpenter. I feel so bad for running out on him. I can only imagine the mess I left for him to clean up when I ran off, but I couldn't do it. I couldn't live the life he wanted me to live. I would have been unhappy. I deserve to be happy, right?"

Bryce cleared his throat and he let her go. "Of course you deserve to be happy, Willow. You also deserve to decide what it is that makes you happy. I get the sense that's not how things have been in the past."

Willow shook her head. "It hasn't."

"Well, Hudson is looking for you. I got a

call tonight from a friend of mine who's doing some private investigating. He was hired to find you and he tracked you here because of the background check I did on you."

Willow sat down on the couch and let her face fall into her hands. "Oh no."

"They don't know that you're *here* here. They know that you were in Maple Grove three weeks ago. That's it. It sounds like Hudson wants the engagement ring back. Do you still have the ring?"

Willow's head snapped up. The stupid ring! She should have left it behind at the church, but she'd been in such a hurry to get out of there that she'd taken off with it still on her finger. "Yes. I have it. I planned to give it back to him when I finally mustered up the courage to tell everyone where I was."

Bryce sat down next to her and placed a hand on her knee. "Well, what if I make arrangements to get the ring back to Hudson without him knowing you were here? I think I could talk my buddy into taking the ring without disclosing how he got his hands on it."

"I think that would be amazing. Do you really believe he wouldn't tell the man paying him where I am?"

"It sounded like he was looking for the ring. If that's all he wants, let's give it to him and see if that's the end of it. Your family would know you're safe, but they would still have to wait for you to be ready to face them."

Willow threw her arms around Bryce. She felt so ridiculous for not trusting him with what was going on sooner. "Thank you for helping me. I'm sorry I wasn't honest with you right from the start."

"Is there anything else I need to know?" Bryce asked, pulling back to look her in the eye. "Let's get everything out in the open."

She shook her head. "Nothing. I have nothing else to hide."

Bryce's exhale sounded relieved.

"I'm sorry I hid my drama from you. I'm sorry you have to fix my mess," she said, truly remorseful.

Bryce gently brushed away the tear on her cheek with his thumb. "Don't be sorry. I want to be the person you come to with your drama. I want to be the one who helps you fix your messes."

Emotion nearly choked her. Hearing him say that meant everything in the world to her. She had never felt like she could ever burden anyone with her troubles. It had been ingrained in her that she was to appear undaunted at all times.

"Thank you," she pushed out.

Bryce gave her a small smile. "I'm going to go get Camden over at June's. You, get me that ring and I'll take care of it."

Willow had to fight the urge to kiss him. She knew that he was not ready for that, but it was difficult to resist. She appreciated that he wanted to help her keep living the way she wanted to live. It had been forever since someone cared about what she wanted when it came to her own life.

When he left, she went to the bedroom and straight to the bathroom where she kept her makeup bag. She dug through the bag and pulled out the diamond ring that had always felt too heavy on her finger. Hudson had chosen it simply because it was bigger and more expensive than the ones his friends had bought their fiancées. It never mattered what Willow wanted or liked. It was all about status. She couldn't wait to give it back.

The next time she accepted a ring from someone, she was going to make sure that she was saying yes because she was in love with the man giving it to her. Willow had a better idea of what it meant to be loved now. Someone who really loved her wouldn't have to ask her what kind of ring she'd like; he would know because he'd care enough to know her. She also knew that when she was in love, she wouldn't be afraid to tell the man how she felt. There would be compromises and understanding. She would feel like a partner, an equal.

The way Bryce made her feel.

Bryce and Camden came back just as she was putting dinner on the table. She handed Hudson's ring to Bryce and hoped that was the end of one life and the beginning of another.

"I'll take care of this tomorrow," he said, putting the ring in his pocket. "Let's just have a normal night."

"Normal sounds really good."

He reached for her hand and gave it a squeeze. What the three of them had was exactly the kind of normal she had been searching for her whole life. Grandma Rose would have approved.

BRYCE PROCRASTINATED CALLING ANDY. He felt better calling him from work than from home, not that Andy couldn't find out where he lived if he tried. Protecting Willow was his number one objective, though. He wanted to keep her safe. All night, he'd contemplated what to say to Andy so he'd take the ring without question. He wasn't sure he had come up with the right words, but it was time to get this over with.

Andy picked up on the second ring. "Bryce Koller. I knew you were the right one to call. What did you find out?"

"You said that all this guy wants is the ring, right?"

"That's what he hired me for, yes."

Bryce paced around his office, unable to sit still. "So, if I was able to get you the ring, that could be the end of it? Could you keep the details of how you got the ring to yourself?"

"Do you have the ring? What kind of magical police work are you capable of down there in Maple Grove?"

"I need to know that you will leave me and Maple Grove out of it. Can you do that?"

"I could, but why? This guy is loaded—I could probably convince him to donate a ton of money to your station. Get you some equipment I know you have to be hurting for in a small town like yours."

"We don't need anything." That was a lie. They could use a lot of new equipment, but he wasn't trading Willow for new radios. "All I want is to stay out of the narrative. Completely."

"She's there, huh?" Andy wasn't clueless. He could put two and two together. "You know her?"

"You called me for a favor and all I'm asking for is a favor in return. Can you do that?" Bryce pleaded.

"Yeah, sure. If I retrieve the ring, that could probably be the end of it," Andy said, not sounding too sure.

"And if he asks you to find Willow after you give him the ring, you'll call me and give me a heads-up?"

"What's going on, man? Is there something I should know about this guy? You asked me yesterday if he was a good guy. Do you know something that I don't that would tell you he's not?"

Willow had assured Bryce that Hudson wasn't dangerous, but Bryce got the strong sense that he was controlling. There was a very selfish part of Bryce that didn't want Hudson Carpenter to come to Maple Grove to convince Willow she had made a mistake leaving Dallas. She didn't seem very certain she could resist whatever influence he had over her.

"What I do know is that the woman who left him is a good person and she does not want to be found. Not yet. Her intention was never to take the ring for her own benefit. She's happy to return it and cut all ties. I sure hope I can trust you with all this."

"I'm coming to get the ring, Bryce. I'll do everything I can to keep her whereabouts under wraps. I'm not sure how you got yourself mixed up in this, but it sounds like it's pretty personal to you. You could have told me you had nothing, but you're trying to help me out, so I want to do the same."

"Thanks, Andy. You can come by the station whenever. I've got the ring here."

"Great. I can be there in a couple hours." He paused and then added, "I hope you know what you're doing, buddy."

So did Bryce.

A couple of hours later, Bryce handed over the ring to Andy and then texted Willow that it was done. She replied with a thank-you and a bunch of exclamation points. He wanted her to feel safe. He wanted her to feel like this place could be her home. Hopefully, he had made those two things possible today.

He had told her that he needed time to get his emotions in order, but the thought of her going back to Hudson put things into perspective. Bryce had feelings for Willow. Real feelings that weren't as mixed up as he thought they were.

When he got home later that evening, there was no one in the family room, no one in the kitchen. He checked the bedrooms without finding Camden or Willow. In fact, even the dog was missing.

"Banjo, come here!" someone who sounded a lot like Daisy screamed from outside.

Bryce cringed. *What was that dog up to now?*

Out back, Willow, Camden and Daisy were spread out in a triangle formation with Banjo in the middle. The dog was filthy like he had rolled in the mud.

Willow crouched down and held out a hand. "Come on, Banjo. Come here, boy. Want some cheese?"

The dog did not care about cheese. He was having too much fun running wild. He ran at each of them but not close enough for them to grab him.

Bryce whistled. "Banjo, come!"

Without hesitation, the dog ran right to him and sat down at his feet. His dirty tail swished back and forth as he stared up at Bryce. Not only did Banjo look like he'd been in a mud pit, he smelled like a sewer.

"What happened?" Bryce asked, plugging his nose so he didn't pass out from the odor.

"Your dog is a maniac," Daisy said without explanation.

Willow's hair was falling out of her ponytail and she had mud on her face and paw prints on her shirt where Banjo had clearly jumped up on her. "We had a tiny problem getting Banjo to cooperate with letting us bathe him after he got loose during his walk with Daisy."

Bryce grimaced. "Why does he smell like that?"

"Banjo rolled in poop!" Camden came running over with the biggest smile on his face. "It's so gross!"

Bryce looked to Willow. "That's not what's all over him, is it?"

"No, no. He rolled in some…poop, and then we tried to bathe him out here using the hose. When we got him wet, he took off and got muddy. It's been a fun couple of hours." She sounded exhausted, but he couldn't help but be amused by her adorableness.

"Okay, well, does anyone have his leash?" he asked.

Daisy ran over to one of the chairs on the back deck and grabbed the leash. "Here."

Bryce leashed Banjo and handed it back to Daisy. "Do you think you can hold on to him for five minutes while I get the right supplies for a dog wash?"

Daisy rolled her eyes. "Yeah, I think I can handle that, Sheriff."

Bryce ran around the house and grabbed the old plastic baby pool they used to put Camden in when he was a toddler. He also found Banjo's dog shampoo and some rubber dishwashing gloves.

Willow came over to help him when she spotted him coming around the side of the house. "Let me take something for you."

Camden helped fill the pool up with water

and Banjo was more than excited to get in and splash around. "He loves water when it's not spraying out of the hose at him, so this is my trick to giving him a bath. It's like his personal outdoor bathtub," Bryce explained.

"So much easier," Daisy said. "By the way, I charge extra for bath time."

Bryce glanced at Willow, who couldn't hide her smile before turning toward Daisy. "Of course you do."

The four of them worked together to give Banjo a very much needed bath. Willow suggested they do a rinse and repeat to make sure they got all the stink off him. No one disagreed.

Camden's giggles were a healing balm on Bryce's heart. His resilience was such a blessing. He couldn't help but notice that Daisy was laughing right along with Cam. She was such a tough talker and had walls higher than Bryce's to keep people out, but today she was lighter. She told Banjo he was a good boy even though he had been a bad boy earlier. Her smile made her look like the kid she was. It was nice to see her without that scowl that always aged her.

When Bryce's eyes landed on Willow, his

heart seriously fluttered. She was joy personified. Positivity flowed from her and touched everyone around her. Bryce felt it. He could tell Camden and Daisy did, too. She was happy here, and he wanted her to stay.

Andy had to be back in Dallas by now. He probably had gone straight to Hudson Carpenter and returned the ring. Willow's ties to him had been cut for good. He could see that she felt it—the feeling of being untethered from something she hadn't been able to free herself from until today.

Banjo shook the water from his fur and everyone threw their arms up to cover their faces before falling into a fit of laughter.

"I'm gonna have to charge you a little extra for the cost of my laundry bill after this bath, Sheriff," Daisy said.

Bryce shook his head. If she needed to get her clothes washed, he could help her with that. "Why pay for laundry when I can wash everything here?" Bryce picked up the hose nozzle and pressed down on the handle, shooting her and Camden with the spray.

"What the heck?" Daisy screamed and jumped up.

Camden held his hands out. "Dad! Stop!" he shouted through his laughter.

Bryce looked at Willow, who was already on her feet. "Don't you dare," she warned.

"You're the dirtiest of them all," he said as he showered her with water.

"Camden, we have to stop him," Daisy said, and before Bryce knew what hit him, he was tackled and Willow came over to wrestle away the hose.

"Get him, Willow!" Camden encouraged.

Bryce raised his hands up like she was the sheriff pointing her weapon at him. She twisted the nozzle to change the setting from shower to something he could only assume was going to be more painful. "Think about this, Willow. I'm your boss. You should give that ba—"

Before he could finish his sentence, she shot him right in the chest with the high-pressure jet stream. He fell back, and Camden and Daisy cheered.

Camden hopped up and down. "Get him again, Willow!"

"I think he's had enough." Willow set the hose down and offered him a hand up.

He reached up and took her hand. As she

tried to help him up, her feet slipped on the wet grass and she fell on top of him instead. Bryce felt the wind knock out of him. She looked down on him with her hair a mess and those pretty brown eyes of hers. They were both out of breath and frozen in this moment. He had never wanted to kiss someone as much as he wanted to kiss Willow. He reached up and brushed some hair from her face. His hand lingered longer than it should on her cheek.

"Sorry," she said, her face warming under his touch. He wished she would lean down and put her lips on his. Instead, she placed her hands on the ground on either side of his head and lifted herself off him.

"She is way too nice to you, Sheriff. I would have soaked you to the bone," Daisy said, ending the moment he was having with Willow. "Come on, Cam. Let's get some towels to dry everyone off."

The kids went inside and Bryce sat up. Willow was beside him, soaking wet.

"The plan was to have him cleaned up before you got home, but Banjo always finds a way to make things interesting."

"I'm glad it worked out this way. I had fun

giving him a bath with y'all. Seeing Camden laugh like that made my whole day."

Willow smiled. "*You* made my whole day. Thanks again for taking care of the ring. I finally feel like I can relax. It's a nice feeling."

He placed his hand on top of hers. "I'm glad."

"Now I just have to work up the courage to call my parents."

"Cam and I will be here for you when you do."

"Careful, Sheriff," she warned. "Keep talking like that and I won't be able to stop myself from kissing you next time."

Bryce felt the heat travel up his neck. Did he want that to be a warning or was he hoping that was a promise?

CHAPTER SIXTEEN

"Daisy, do you have any threes?" Delia asked.

Delia, Daisy and June had decided it was time to teach Camden how to play Go Fish. He sat on Willow's lap so she could be his partner and help him out.

"Nope," Daisy replied, popping her *p*. "Go fish. Cam, my man, do you have any twos?"

Willow pointed out the two he had in his hand.

"I think I want to keep that one," he said.

"You can't keep it, bud," Willow explained. "If you have it and she asks for it, you have to give it to her. Those are the rules."

He let out a heavy sigh. "Fine."

The game continued until Daisy won. June gathered up the cards and began to shuffle. Willow turned her head to check the clock on the microwave. Bryce would be home soon.

"Are you excited to go to your first Spring Festival?" June asked.

Willow might have been more excited to go to the Spring Festival than every other person in Maple Grove. She had been waiting for this day ever since her grandmother had told her about the festival.

"I can't wait. I hope I haven't built it up in my mind so much that it struggles to live up to my expectations."

"Spring Fest is the best," Daisy reassured her. "It's always fun. They have this ride called the Gravitron where you spin around superfast and they drop the floor and you stick to the wall. It's so awesome."

"I want to stick to the wall," Camden said, his eyes alight with the possibility of a thrill.

"You're going to have to talk to your dad about that one. That sounds like a ride that would make me lose my lunch." Willow stuck out her tongue, pretending to retch.

Camden's nose scrunched up. "Why would you lose it? You already ate it."

"It means she would barf. I'll take you on it, Cam," Daisy offered.

Willow loved how Daisy seemed to enjoy taking Camden under her wing. "That's very sweet of you, but I think we still should ask his dad."

As if on cue, the front door opened and Bryce walked in. "Whose idea was it to play cards without me?" he asked as he approached the table.

"You want me to deal you in?" June asked.

"No, that's okay. I need to get out of this uniform and ready for the festival." Bryce put a hand on Willow's shoulder. His thumb gently brushed up and down the back of her neck, sending the most amazing tingle down her spine.

Did it mean something that he was touching her in front of the others? Could this be a sign that he was ready to see if this thing between them was more than a working relationship? June and Daisy's gazes moved from his hand to Willow's face. They then shared a knowing smile with each other. They approved, for sure. Would Delia?

"Maybe we all should start getting ready to go," Willow said.

"What time are you meeting up with your family?" Bryce asked.

He was still touching her and making it hard to think straight. "Um, Charlie said to meet them by the popcorn stand at six."

Bryce gave her shoulder a squeeze before

letting go. "Okay, good. That gives us time to grab something to eat and maybe play a couple games if we get going."

"I want to go on the Gravitron with Daisy. Can I, Dad?" Camden asked, his eyes pleading.

Bryce scrunched up his nose. "I'm not sure I know what the Gravitron is, but sometimes rides have rules like you have to be a certain height to go on them."

Camden stood on the kitchen chair and put his hand on his head. "I'm tall. I can do it, Dad."

He ruffled Camden's hair. "We'll see, buddy. I'm going to go change."

Once they heard Bryce climb the stairs, Daisy slid her chair back with a grin on her face. "Well, well, well. Glad to see the sheriff is finally making his move."

Willow shook her head. "Don't start."

Daisy chuckled as she made her way around the table. "I'll see y'all at the festival."

June put the cards away. "She's not the only one who's happy to see he's coming around."

"Coming around to what?" Delia asked.

"Coming around to letting Camden go on

some rides this year," Willow deflected. "It's going to be a fun night, isn't it?"

Camden threw both hands up. "Yes!'

June gave Willow a pat on the same shoulder Bryce had touched earlier. "I'll see y'all at the festival as well. I better go home and freshen up."

The doorbell rang, sending Banjo into a tizzy. Before Willow could get to the door, Lee opened it and let himself in.

"You don't have to ring the doorbell, Lee. You're family," Bryce said as he jogged down the stairs at the same time. He had changed into jeans and a gray T-shirt that was snug in all the right places.

"Sorry about that. I always forget about the dog." Lee bent down and scratched Banjo behind the ears. His thick salt-and-pepper hair was slicked back and he was dressed like he had come from the golf course. "Was she okay today? She was talking about April this morning and I was a little worried when she asked to come over here that there might be some issues."

"No issues," Willow assured him. "We all took Banjo on a walk with Daisy and then came home and played some games."

"I'm so glad I pay a dog walker to walk the dog with the whole family," Bryce grumbled. She knew he didn't mean it. He liked giving Daisy a job to do.

"She's a good kid."

"I know she is," he said, grinning at her. She loved that, even as sheriff, he saw the good in people and not just the bad.

Lee said hello and goodbye to Camden and took Delia home for dinner, promising to meet up at the festival later that evening. Bryce smiled at Willow with the same sparkle in his eyes that his son had a few minutes ago.

"Who's ready to go to the Spring Festival with me?"

"I am!" Camden jumped up and down with his hand raised above his head.

Bryce feigned surprise. "You are?"

Camden nodded. "Yes!"

Bryce turned that mischievous gaze on Willow. Stepping toward her, he closed the space between them until they were toe to toe. "What about you? Are you ready to go to the festival with me?"

Willow tilted her head up, her smile matching his. "There's no one else I'd rather go with."

He took her hand and interlocked their fingers. His hand was warm, but it was his touch that made her feel on fire. Willow's heart beat double time as he grinned down at her, more relaxed than she had seen him the entire time she'd known him.

"I feel exactly the same way," he said with a sincerity that she felt in her chest.

Willow couldn't remember ever feeling this way. All the times in her life that she had thought she was in love with a man paled in comparison to how she felt in this moment with this man. There was something about Bryce that made her not only feel safe but accepted. He liked her for who she was even though she wasn't a very good cook and once flooded his kitchen with bubbles. She didn't have to pretend to be perfect.

Willow didn't have to wonder how she got here. Grandma Rose had led her to this town and to this man. Her grandmother had always pushed for Willow to trust her heart, and her heart was becoming very attached to Sheriff Bryce Koller.

BRYCE WANTED TO show Willow everything. He wanted her to experience all that Maple

Grove's Spring Festival had to offer. First up, the food.

"Does everything come on a stick?" she asked as she dipped her chicken-on-a-stick into the barbecue sauce.

"Almost everything." Bryce handed Camden a napkin. The four-year-old had a blob of ketchup on the corner of his mouth after taking a bite of his corn dog.

The three of them sat at one of the picnic tables that had been set up close to the food trucks. It seemed that the whole town had turned out for the first night of the festival.

"What do you want to do first?" Willow asked Camden.

"I want to go on the Gravitron with Daisy."

"I think we need to let your dinner settle before you go on something called the Gravitron," Bryce said. "How about we start by playing some games? I saw one where you have to knock down some milk bottles with a softball."

Camden scrunched up his face. "What's a softball?"

"It's like a big baseball," Willow explained. "I bet you would be awesome at that game."

Camden beamed at her encouragement.

"Let's do that. Can I win one of those?" He pointed at a little girl carrying a teddy bear almost as big as she was.

Bryce knew he was going to have to do everything he could to win one of those giant bears. "I bet we can do it if we try our best."

The way Willow smiled at Bryce heated his skin. Her dark hair was pulled over a shoulder exposing one side of her neck. He imagined what it would feel like to press his lips to that curve and how intoxicating her perfume would be if he was that close.

"Sheriff Koller, it sure is nice to see you out having some fun." Doc Wight and his wife held hands. "And check out this big guy," he said, mussing Camden's hair. "Someone is doing an excellent job managing your sugars. You look healthy as a horse."

"A horse? I don't look like a horse!" Camden replied, making everyone laugh.

Doc held up a hand. "Sorry, I meant healthy as a superhero."

Camden seemed pleased with that comparison and went back to his corn dog.

"He's doing really well. He's sleeping better, his energy is up, and you can tell being regulated helps his mood. We've noticed so many positive changes," Willow told Doc Wight.

"That's excellent news. You're a lucky kiddo, Camden. Nanny Willow is an excellent nurse as well as a nanny. When you outgrow her, I hope she remembers we could use a nurse like her at the clinic."

Bryce felt the possessive urge to jump over the table and wrap his arms around Willow to keep anyone from thinking they could take her away. Instead of making a fool of himself, he tried to remind himself she would never leave him and Cam to go work at the clinic. "She's stuck with us for a while, Doc. I don't know if you'll be able to wait that long."

Doc chuckled. "You underestimate me, Sheriff. For someone as sharp as Willow, I might just offer her a deal she can't resist."

Bryce forced a smile, but the thought of Willow taking a different job made him anything but happy.

"That's very sweet of you, Doc," Willow replied. "But I am kind of attached to my current employer. I mean, to the family. To Camden." She glanced at Bryce before her cheeks turned red and she ducked her head. Little did she know she had nothing to be embarrassed about. He was more than attached to her as well.

"We all know you can't compete with Camden, Dale," Mrs. Wight said, giving her husband a pat on the arm. "Y'all have fun tonight. We need to get in line for some food. I'm starving."

"Everything on a stick is delicious!" Willow held up her chicken-on-a-stick.

She made Bryce smile for real. It was her charm that had caught his attention when they first met. It was why he'd helped her get her engagement ring back to the man she'd chosen not to marry. It was the reason he wanted her to stay with him and Camden for as long as possible.

When they finished their dinner, they took Camden over to the game booths. Camden bounced up and down with a huge grin on his face. Bryce paid for all three of them to take a shot at knocking down the milk bottles.

The young man behind the counter skillfully juggled three softballs. "Who wants to go first?"

Camden's hand shot up in the air. "Me!"

"All right, little guy." The guy set the three balls in front of him. "You're up."

Camden picked up the first ball and could barely hold it with one hand. His eyes widened. "This is a *big* baseball."

"You can throw it with two hands if that will make it easier," Willow suggested.

Camden held it over his head with two hands and launched it toward the milk bottles. It hit the one on top of the pyramid and it fell over.

"Yes! Nice one, Cam!" Bryce patted him on the back as Camden reached for the next ball.

"Do it just like you did the last time but aim a little lower," Willow said.

Camden tried again but missed. His little face scrunched up in disappointment.

"Shake that off. You got this," Bryce told him.

Willow nodded. "You can do it."

Camden picked up the third ball and his little pink tongue poked out between his lips as it often did when he was concentrating. He held it above his head and tossed it at the milk bottles. One fell right away and the other wobbled. Willow leaned in closer and took Bryce's hand while she shouted at that one wobbling bottle to fall over.

To their dismay, that bottle settled back into its spot.

Camden groaned, both hands pressed to the top of his head. Willow squeezed Bryce's hand tighter. He gave her a squeeze back. "Don't worry, buddy. Willow and I each get to throw three. We'll win that bear, I promise."

Bryce had rarely felt so determined. He let go of Willow's hand and stepped up to the counter. The young man reset the bottles and placed the three balls in front of him. Bryce picked up the first one and quickly tossed it at the bottles. It missed but hit the back of the booth with a loud thwack.

"Too eager," he whispered with a shake of his head. "Sorry about that, Cam."

Camden embraced his new role of encourager. "You can do it, Dad. Try again."

His second throw knocked down two of the bottles much to Camden's delight. Willow gave him the prettiest smile. He wanted to win a bear for Camden and anything she wanted as well. It had been a long time since he'd felt the urge to impress a lady as much as he wanted to dazzle Willow.

Like he was some kind of major league pitcher, he wound up and threw that last ball like it was the bottom of the ninth and he needed one more strike to win the World Series. The ball whizzed right past that last bottle but didn't make contact.

Camden's shoulders slumped. Bryce felt the weight of his disappointment. Wasn't a kid's dad supposed to be the hero?

"Hey, we still have three more balls to throw. I will admit that I never played softball when I was younger, but I was a baton twirler and I could toss that thing so high and catch it behind my back," Willow said, pulling both Bryce and Camden out of their gloom. "That means I am super accurate when I throw something. You start thinking about which bear you want, Camden, because I've got this."

Once the bottles were reset and the softballs were placed in front of her, Willow picked one up and gave it a kiss. She winked at Camden and threw the ball, knocking all three bottles down at once.

Camden's arms went up as he shouted, "Yes! We won! We won! I want the panda bear!"

The kid behind the counter went to get Camden his prize and Bryce couldn't help himself. He lifted her off her feet and spun her around. She laughed and wrapped her arms around his neck. Their gazes were locked and his skin tingled. Bryce's heart was pounding.

He set her down and gave in to temptation, kissing her cheek. "Thank you for doing what I couldn't."

She appeared a bit dazed. "It was just luck. You would have done it if you had gone again."

"Thanks to you, my ego doesn't have to risk failing twice. I'm not sure how to repay you for that."

Her hand pressed against the spot his lips had touched. "I think you did."

Bryce's whole body felt alive. She had liked that he kissed her, and that made him want to do it again.

"This is awesome!" Camden interrupted Bryce's thoughts of making out with Willow by thrusting a giant panda in between them.

Bryce grabbed the stuffed animal. "This is the biggest stuffie I have ever seen. How is it going to fit in our house?"

"It can fit, Dad."

"I don't know. Willow, what do you think?"

"Oh, come on, Sheriff! I think there's plenty of room for Mr. Panda. We can have him move into your room and you can sleep on the couch."

Bryce feigned shock. "You're going to kick me out of my own room for Mr. Panda?"

"No, Mr. Panda is going to sleep in my room," Camden announced. "He can sleep on the floor."

"That sounds like a much better idea." Bryce playfully narrowed his eyes at Willow. "But if he needs more room, Willow has the biggest bed in the house. He can sleep with her."

Willow giggled and smacked his arm. "I won the bear. I shouldn't have to sleep with him, too."

Bryce chuckled as his phone chimed with a text. He checked it and saw the notification that he had a message from Andy. His heart dropped as he clicked on it to open the message.

This is your heads-up.

CHAPTER SEVENTEEN

WILLOW NOTICED THE black clouds that gathered over Bryce's head as soon as he read his texts. His brow furrowed and his smile was replaced by a frown.

"Is everything okay? Is it police business?"

Bryce shoved his phone back in his pocket. He clearly was forcing a smile. "It's nothing. It's fine. Who wants to go on some rides?"

"Me!" Camden exclaimed. "And Mr. Panda."

"I don't know about bringing Mr. Panda on the rides. We might need to put him in the truck."

Willow glanced at her watch. "I'm supposed to meet up with Charlie and the rest of the family in a few minutes. Do you guys want me to hold on to Mr. Panda while you hit the rides?"

Both father and son's faces fell. "But I want to go on the wheel thing with you," Camden whined.

"I forgot about the Everlys. We don't have to go on rides right now. Do you want us to come with you?" Bryce asked.

"You don't have to do that. Go, have fun. Cam, you and I will go on the Ferris wheel before we leave. I promise."

"What about me?" Bryce asked. "Do I get a ride on the Ferris wheel, too?"

The flutters in Willow's stomach were extreme. First, he'd kissed on the cheek, and now he wanted to take a ride on the Ferris wheel with her? That was the perfect setting for a first kiss if she'd ever heard of one. His feelings for her had gone from confusing to not so subtle really quick.

"We've got all night, Sheriff. I bet I can squeeze in a ride with you, too. Let's do a quick blood sugar check and give Camden his insulin before I take off."

Bryce nodded. "Always on top of things. What would we do without you?"

"Let's hope you never have to find out," she replied jokingly.

"You have no idea how much I hope that."

His response was delivered so seriously it gave her pause. Why in the world would he ever have to worry about her leaving? Had she not made her feelings clear? Not only did she love Camden, but she was head over heels for the boy's father as well. Bryce was everything Hudson had not been. He offered her a level of support that she hadn't known was possible in a partner. Willow knew the smart thing was to hold on with both hands and never let go. If he felt the same way, this was the beginning of something amazing.

"I'm not going anywhere, Bryce. I've got nowhere to go, and even if I did, I don't want anything but what's right in front of me."

He touched her hand and the sparks were all too real. *This* was real. His smile and that realization melted her insides. "Go meet your family. I can take care of Camden."

Willow handed him the bag full of Camden's medical supplies. She was proud of him for showing confidence in being able to handle his son's needs. He had come so far from the scared dad in the clinic's waiting room.

"Remember to take into account all the excitement ahead of him this evening when you give him his dose," she said. Bryce nodded. "And make sure he drinks water."

"I remember."

"And text me if you need me."

He shot her a crooked smile. "I've got it. Go see your family."

Willow trusted him to handle this and she didn't want him to think any different. She stepped away and gave them a wave as she spun around and headed for the popcorn booth. Excitement twirled through her body as she made her way to meet Charlie and her other relatives.

Her grandmother's cousin stood by the booth along with his wife, Rhonda. Charlie had a little girl in his arms, who was probably just a year or two younger than Camden. A younger man and woman chatted with Rhonda and another couple. First impressions were Willow's specialty, but her nerves were still getting the best of her.

"There she is," Charlie said as soon as he set eyes on her. "Willow! You made it."

Willow took a deep breath and moved swiftly in his direction. "I have been thinking about this since we met at the restaurant. I am so excited to meet everyone."

Charlie handed off the little girl to the man next to him and opened his arms for a welcoming hug. "Well, the feeling is mutual. Convincing everyone to wait until six and not hunt you down as soon as they got here has been a challenge."

It meant so much that they were as eager as she was to finally meet. Charlie got right to introductions. Grandma Rose had a big, beautiful family. Charlie and Rhonda had two children, Christina and Damon. Since Charlie was ten years younger than Rose, his children were at least a decade younger than Willow's mother. Both of them were married and had two or three kids each, most of whom were in high school or college.

Grandma Rose's sister, Greta, had two sons who lived in or near Maple Grove. Aaron and Cody were Willow's mother's first cousins. Both were married, but only Aaron and his wife had kids. Brandy, their eldest daughter was there with her little girl, Hannah. She was the little girl Charlie had been holding when Willow first saw him this evening.

Everyone was so sweet and treated Willow like close family instead of some long-long relative. They all wanted to know about Grandma Rose and Willow's mother. They asked Willow questions about growing up in Dallas. Brandy was also in healthcare and wanted to know about Willow's nursing background.

Willow lost all sense of time as she got to know her extended family better. The sky began to darken, and the carnival lights took over for the setting sun. Cody and his wife, Holly, convinced Willow to come dance with them over by the beer garden. They had a band playing on a raised stage and the line dancing was in full swing.

Her phone buzzed in her pocket. Willow got off the dance floor and fished her phone out. There was a picture of Bryce, Camden, June, Delia, Lee and Daisy with the texted message WE MISS YOU in all caps underneath it on her screen. As much as Willow was enjoying meeting the Everly family, her heart belonged to that messy patchwork of a family in the photo.

"Are you having a good time?" Charlie asked, sneaking up beside her.

"I've been dreaming about the Maple Grove Spring Festival for as long as I can remember, and it is definitely living up to expectations."

"I'm happy to hear that, sweetheart. I think Rosie would be over the moon knowing you were here delighted by something that brought her so much joy as a young girl."

Willow agreed that her grandmother was smiling down on her from heaven right now. "I'm having the best time, but I've got a little boy, a sheriff, and some sweet friends waiting for me to join them on some rides. I think I need to head over to the Ferris wheel."

Charlie grinned. "Sheriff Koller is a good man. One of the best. It makes me happy to know that you have someone like that in your life."

Willow was happy to have him as well. "Thank you for connecting me with everyone tonight. I hope we all can get together again soon."

"Absolutely! You're one of us now, Willow. Get ready to be invited to all the family gatherings from now on."

His kindness swelled her heart. "I cannot wait to get my dad down here to meet y'all. I know he's going to love you as much as I already do."

"Please tell him he always has a place to stay when he comes to town. We'd love to have him and your mom."

This time his sweet words made her heart

clench. These last few weeks were the longest she had ever gone without talking to her parents. It pained her to think about what her disappearance had done to them and how much her decision to run might have damaged their relationship permanently.

"I hope they'll come visit soon," she said, trying to hide her hurt.

Willow quickly said goodbye to everyone and promised to not be a stranger any longer. She needed Bryce to tell her that everything was going to be all right. That together they would handle whatever the fallout was with her parents. Now that the ring had been successfully returned to Hudson, perhaps it was time to come clean about where she'd been hiding.

The Spring Festival was a celebration of new beginnings, of a renewal of life. Willow was in the midst of her own revival, and it was thanks to the sheriff and his son, who'd let her be part of their lives, that she was thriving. She sent Bryce a text that she was on her way to the Ferris wheel and she wanted her first ride to be with him.

BRYCE'S WHOLE BODY was thrumming with anticipation of Willow's return. He had this terrible fear that her ex-fiancé was going to show up at the festival and whisk her back to Dallas. It was ridiculous. She wasn't going to disappear. Still, he knew he'd feel better when he could see her.

He'd fought the urge to text her earlier, telling himself not to interrupt her time with her family. Daisy had joined him and Camden, and she was the one who said exactly what he was thinking out loud—everything was better when Willow was around. It had been her idea to take the group selfie when everyone was together and send it to Willow so she would come find them. He had to admit, the teenager's plan worked perfectly.

"Where have you been? Camden and I have been on the Dancin' Daisy like five times," Daisy said when Willow arrived in front of the Ferris wheel.

Willow's smile lit up her whole face. She put her arm around Daisy and squeezed. "I love that you missed me and that you went on a ride that has your name in it."

Bryce could tell that Willow's affection and attention meant the world to Daisy. "Of course we missed you. You're a million times more fun than this guy," she said, throwing her thumb over her shoulder in Bryce's direction. "He won't even let me take Cam on the Spinner 5000."

"The Spinner 5000?" Willow glanced between Daisy and Bryce.

"The Spinner 5000 is that," Bryce replied, pointing at the death trap that Daisy thought was a good idea to take a four-year-old on. "I like my child with his dinner inside his stomach, not all over his shoes."

"Lame," Daisy said.

"Yeah, lame," Camden repeated with the same disillusioned tone.

"Where's Mr. Panda?" Willow asked.

"He needed to go take a 'nap' in the truck," Bryce said, making air quotes.

Willow nodded, then glanced around. "Where's June, Delia and Lee?"

"Grandma and Lee are on the Ferris wheel already," Camden replied.

"And Miss June is on there with her *friend*— Mr. Douglas Whipple," Daisy said with waggling brows.

"Mr. Douglas Whipple?" Willow looked to Bryce. "Who is that?"

"He used to be the only accountant in town," he explained. "He lives one block over from us. You've probably seen him walking a little dog down our street in the evenings."

Willow's eyes went wide when her memory made the connection. "Yes! I have seen him." She nudged Daisy. "I bet he walks down our street, hoping to bump into June. I'm going to have to grill her when I get her alone."

Daisy jumped right into the gossip. "He asked her to go on the Ferris wheel with him and she made Delia and Lee get in line with them. You should have seen how she blushed when he complimented her hair and her outfit. It was kind of adorable."

Willow's hand covered her heart. "Awww."

Bryce chuckled. He loved that she was so invested. That had to mean she cared about more than just him and Camden. If her ex came to find her, maybe all the connections she had here would be enough for her to refuse him.

"All of you old people are falling in love, and I can't even get a dumb boy to talk to me," Daisy complained.

Willow quirked a brow. "All of us *old* people?"

"You, specifically, are not that old, but you know what I mean."

Bryce wasn't stuck on the fact that Daisy called them old, he was fixated on the comment about them falling in love. Was that what she saw going on? Love was a big word. Besides his family, he had never used that word with anyone other than April. He still loved April. He would always love her. Could he even fall in love with Willow if he was still in love with his wife?

Camden tugged on Bryce's arm. "I want to go on a ride."

"What if I let you and Daisy ride the Ferris wheel?" Bryce suggested. "That wouldn't be lame, would it?"

He looked up at Daisy to check for her reaction before answering.

"That could be pretty cool, Cam-da-lam. If you go with me, Willow can go with the sheriff. Otherwise, I would have to go with him and that would definitely be lame."

Bryce knew what she was doing, but he still had to act offended. "For your information, I don't go on rides with juvenile delinquents. It's a bad look for a man of the law like myself."

"What she sees in you, I'll never understand," Daisy said, giving it as good as she got it.

"Hey, now. I don't want you to ever settle for anything less than a man like Sheriff Koller when you grow up," Willow said. "You could do a lot worse than a guy who always has your back, forgives you when you mess up, makes you laugh, and isn't just sweet to you but everyone in his life. Those are qualities you should not only be looking for but should demand in a guy."

Daisy turned and smiled up at Bryce. "Well, now we know." She reached for Camden's hand. "Come on, Cam. Let's get in line."

How in the world did Bryce let Daisy Sikes get comfortable enough to think it was okay to comment on his life…his *love* life? Of course, it was kind of nice to hear what Willow thought of him. His mom used to call those sorts of compliments "warm fuzzies" because that was how they made the person feel, and that was how Bryce felt right now— warm and fuzzy.

"I make you laugh?" he asked when they were alone.

Willow's cheeks blushed. "Do you want to

go on the Ferris wheel with me or am I going to have to go by myself?"

"I'm coming because I've always got your back," he teased. "I'm sweet like that. But you're not the only one I'm sweet to."

She narrowed her eyes. "*So* funny."

It was too late, she had already admitted she enjoyed his sense of humor. Bryce placed his hand on the small of her back and guided her toward the Ferris wheel line. There were a few people in line separating them from Camden and Daisy. He watched as Daisy gave her full attention to his little boy. She was a good kid; giving her a chance to feel included was the best thing he could have done for her.

"Did you have fun meeting all of your relatives?" he asked, turning his attention back to Willow.

She clasped her hands to her chest. "I did. They are all so nice. They're so different from my dad's other side of the family. More down-to-earth, I guess. The family I grew up with tends to care more about status and how much money someone makes than the actual person. The Everlys wanted to learn things about me and where I came from. They wanted to know what kind of music I like and if I'd seen some show on Netflix. It was refreshing."

Everything about Willow's life before coming to Maple Grove made Bryce nervous, maybe because she shared so little about it. He wanted to believe that his little hometown had made an impression that couldn't be easily erased. Still, this doubt niggled at the back of his mind as it had ever since Andy sent that text. What if the people from her old life came here and tried to take her back? Would she leave?

"I'm glad they made you feel welcome here. You somehow fit right in with everyone in Maple Grove from the start," he said, hoping that she would affirm that she felt that way, too.

Willow gave him a wry smile. "I don't know if that's true," she said.

How could she say that? The way he saw it, she blended in so seamlessly. If she didn't feel like she fit in, would it be easy for someone to lure her back to Dallas? Too easily his fear shouted inside his mind.

Willow reached for his hand. "You keep going to some sad place inside your head. What's going on in there?"

"I hope I've never made you feel like you don't belong here. I know I've had my moments where I was defensive and gruff. I'm sorry if I ever gave you the impression that you didn't belong."

She placed her other hand on their joined hands, squeezing his between hers. "Bryce, you have been the best. What I meant was that I don't think that the person I was when I arrived is the same person I am now. Maple Grove and everyone in it brought out a different side to me. I feel like I was this puzzle piece that never really fit in, no matter how much I tried back in Dallas. When I came here, I didn't know where I belonged, but I knew I wanted to be part of this picture."

"We want you in this picture, too," Bryce admitted. The knot in his stomach tightened even as her smile widened.

"I feel that. I've realized my puzzle piece was flipped upside down. You and Cam helped me get it right side up and I'm finally clicking into place."

Bryce wanted to kiss her so she knew how much he wanted her to click into the empty space next to him. He didn't kiss her, though, because the thought of opening up like that completely terrified him. Things were moving too fast, and as quickly as these feelings had developed, they could just as easily evaporate.

"Next," the ride operator called out, snapping them out of their bubble.

Willow let go of him so they could take their seat on the Ferris wheel. June and Douglas happened to exit as they got on.

"How was the ride?" Willow asked June.

"We'll compare notes when you get done," she replied with a wink.

Bryce and Willow took their seats and the operator lowered the bar that was supposed to keep them from falling out. The seat rocked back and forth as they started their ride.

"What a view," Willow said as they lifted up in the air.

It wasn't the world below them that had Bryce's attention, it was the woman sitting next to him. Should he tell her that her ex-fiancé was still looking for her? Should he tell her how scared he was? His heart beat fast. The mixture of fear and attraction had him in this constant state of fight or flight. Should he fight for her or run away to save himself from getting hurt?

She turned her head and gripped his knee. "I feel like things are shifting between us. Am I misreading things? I work for you. I'm living in your home. I don't want to mess any of that up, but I can't deny that I got on this ride hoping you were going to kiss me."

No words could get past the ball of emotion caught in Bryce's throat. It wasn't like him to do anything without considering all the possible consequences. In his line of work, the repercussion of a bad decision could get him or someone else hurt. This wasn't life or death, but his heart was already battered and he was afraid to put it back in harm's way.

Of course, if he risked nothing, he could lose everything. He should tell her about her ex. He should trust that she wanted to make a new life here and leave her old one behind. Words continued to fail him, so he acted instead.

He gently cupped her cheek and closed his eyes the moment their lips touched. It had been a long time since Bryce had kissed someone and even longer since he had shared a first kiss with someone. Those butterflies in his stomach were shaking off the dust and fluttering up a storm.

Willow let him control the pace but she did have a tight grip on his arm. Her kisses were as sweet as she was. He selfishly hoped that this would convince her not to go anywhere, to stay in Maple Grove no matter what the people from her old life did or said.

Fear crept back into his consciousness. What were the chances that this kiss could make all the difference? How could Bryce compete with someone that she had cared about enough to almost marry?

He pulled back and her eyes stayed shut for a few extra seconds. Her lips curled into a smile. His chest warmed. When she opened her eyes, she sighed.

"That didn't feel messy at all," she said with a hum. "It was even better than I imagined it would be."

Her satisfied grin made him temporarily forget that he should be worried. She leaned over and kissed him one more time. It was almost comical that he had wondered if he could be falling in love with her, because, in this moment, he knew he was.

The ride attendant unlocked the bar on the seat. Bryce had been so absorbed in Willow that he hadn't noticed they made it all the way around. He stepped out of the Ferris wheel cart and offered his hand to Willow so she got off the ride safely.

"We need to talk when we get home," he said before they rejoined the rest of the group waiting for them on the other side of the gate.

Camden waved them over. "Did you like it, Dad? We were so high in the sky!"

Bryce picked him up. "I thought it was pretty awesome, bud."

"I bet you did," Daisy said with a snicker.

"Looks like Willow thought it was awesome, too," June teased.

"Where's April? Why isn't she with you?" It was late, and when Delia got tired, her memory suffered.

"She's not here, sweetheart," Lee answered. He put an arm around her. "Maybe we should head home. It's getting late."

"I think we should head home, too. This little guy is up way past his bedtime."

"Why wouldn't April come to the festival?" Delia asked, undeterred. "She loves the Spring Festival."

Lee tried again to convince her to head home. She thankfully relented and Lee wished everyone a good night. Everyone else exchanged nervous glances. All the reasons it had been a bad idea to kiss Willow came rushing back.

Bryce hiked Camden higher up on his hip. "Do you need a ride home, Daisy?"

"I'm good, Sheriff."

"June?"

"I'll make sure she gets home safely," Douglas offered.

Bryce nodded and motioned for Willow to follow him. They walked to the truck in uneasy silence. Bryce buckled Camden into his car seat next to Mr. Panda. The little boy's eyelids had grown heavy.

"Are you okay?" Willow asked when he started the truck.

He wanted to say yes, but something stopped him. He wasn't okay. He had crossed a line, kissed Willow even though there was so much in their way.

"We can talk about everything when we get home."

Willow didn't argue. The drive home was short. As soon as he pulled onto their street, he noticed the car in front of his house. He pulled into the driveway and his headlights illuminated the figure standing on his front porch.

Bryce didn't recognize the car or the man. He feared this visitor had something to do with the text he had received earlier in the evening. Willow gasped and his stomach dropped.

"What's wrong?" He knew as soon as he asked. This wasn't some investigator looking deeper into the situation.

"It's Hudson," Willow said in a breath.

CHAPTER EIGHTEEN

WHAT WAS HUDSON CARPENTER doing on Bryce's front porch? How did he know where to find her?

"Stay in the truck," Bryce said, his voice not as calm as Willow would have liked.

"No." She touched his leg. "He's here to talk to me, and it's time I faced him."

"You don't need to do this tonight. I can go out there and tell him to come back tomorrow."

Willow glanced over her shoulder at Camden, who was fast asleep in the back seat. "I ran away on the day of our wedding. I owe him a conversation. I'm the bad guy here, not him."

"You are not a bad guy for not committing to someone you didn't want to commit to. You did him a favor by calling it off," Bryce tried to reason.

It was kind of him to make her behavior

seem less selfish. "I should have been honest with him. I ran off like a coward with no explanation. He deserved better than that. Take Camden inside and put him to bed. I'll be okay."

By the look on his face, Bryce wasn't convinced, but he shut off the truck and opened his door. "I'm going to put him to bed and then I am going to stand by the front door, listening for trouble. I will send him away if I hear him be anything less than respectful."

Willow smiled at his protectiveness. "Got it."

He got out of the truck and opened the back door to retrieve Camden. The inside of the cab was now lit up by the interior light and there was no way Hudson didn't see her. She took a deep breath and tried to muster up the courage to face the man she had been hiding from for weeks.

With her heart pounding in her chest, Willow stepped out of the truck and her eyes met the stare of the man she had agreed to marry all those months ago. Her whole body trembled as she made her way to the front porch.

"Look who's alive and well." Hudson's voice was wrapped in suppressed anger.

Bryce came up beside her and up the steps. "I'm Sheriff Bryce Koller. This is my house. You are?"

"Hudson Carpenter. I was actually here to talk to you to see what you could tell me about the ring you helped return, but apparently you know much more than my investigator let on."

"I work for Bryce. I'm—"

"She's my son's private nurse," Bryce interrupted. It wasn't exactly a lie, but it was interesting that he used that title instead of nanny. He turned to Willow. "I'm going to put him to bed. Let me know if you need anything."

She pressed her lips together and nodded. Bryce unlocked the door and pushed it open, disappearing inside with a still sleeping Camden.

As soon as the door closed, Hudson let out a sharp laugh. "Wow, you took off and started a new life, huh? What are you wearing? Where are your clothes?"

Willow had on jeans and a T-shirt, something Hudson had never seen her in. Casual was not in the Carpenter fashion vocabulary. She had forgotten how blunt he could be. "We just got back from the fair. This is what people wear to the fair," she said, embarrassed that she had to explain herself.

"The fair." He rubbed his chin. "Wow, how small town of you. So you ran away to this place to become a private nurse. Do you live here?"

"I do."

Hudson paced back and forth on the porch. His hands were clasped behind his back. He glanced her way, his head cocked to the side. "Are you and the sheriff…together?" he asked as if he just thought of it. "How long have you known this man? Was this going on before you left?"

The first question was harder to answer than it should have been. Given that Bryce had wanted to talk about things after they kissed on the Ferris wheel, she wasn't sure what to call them.

"I did not know Bryce until I got to town. I was looking for a job and he was looking for someone to help him with his son. I did not leave because of anyone but myself."

"Where's the boy's mother?"

"That's not really your business, Hudson. Listen, I'm sorry. I'm sorry I was too chicken to face you and tell you to your face that I couldn't go through with the wedding. I was scared and afraid of what everyone would say, so I ran."

Hudson stopped moving and raised his hands to his sides. "Well, I can tell you what everyone said because I was there. I had to face all of the wedding guests. Your family, my family. Business associates. Friends— ours and our parents'. I had to answer all the questions even though I had no idea what was happening."

Guilt hit her like a wave. "I know I put you in a terrible position. It was wrong. I should have acted like an adult and faced up to what I was doing. I know saying I'm sorry isn't nearly enough to make up for what I did to you."

"You're right, your apology means nothing. I want to know what happened. I want to know why you would do that to me, Willow. I have never done anything but treat you like a princess, but you ran away and hid like I was some kind of monster."

Willow rubbed her forehead, knowing she deserved all of his ire. "I didn't mean to make you feel that way. I was sitting in that bridal suite and started thinking about what our life was going to be like, and I realized that it wasn't the life I wanted." He started to speak, but she talked over him because she knew what he was going to say. "I know that you were offering me a wonderful life. I am not saying the life we would have had would have been terrible, but I realized it just wasn't what I wanted."

"What do you want, Willow?" His hands smacked down against his sides. "Maybe if you had talked to me, I could have given you exactly what you wanted. You didn't even give me the chance."

Willow took a deep breath. Tension tightened her shoulders. As much as he wanted to believe he would have listened and done whatever she asked, she knew better. He would have dismissed her fears as nonsense. He would have told her that what she wanted wasn't really what she wanted. He would have insisted that his way was the best and her parents would have agreed. She would have been bullied into going along with the plan.

"I'm aware that I'm not very good at asserting myself. I was raised to be a people pleaser. It's something I'm working on, but I knew that I wasn't prepared to stand up for myself, so I left."

"There's nothing wrong with being a people pleaser. Until this little runaway bride stunt, I was nothing but proud to have you on my arm. Your parents were so happy for us, so proud of you and the life you were living. Your mother has been completely devastated by this whole fiasco. Do you even care about the fact that you tarnished their reputation in the entire Dallas/Fort Worth area?"

She could feel the new Willow slipping away as he shook that part of her that hated disappointing the people in her life. She had thought about her mother often since she left. She knew she had left both of her parents in a bad position. It was one of the reasons she had stayed hidden. The thought of facing her mother had been the scariest.

Hudson stepped closer and clasped her hands in his. "I know getting married is a big step. Everyone gets cold feet. Even I was feeling nervous that day. But what we had was good, Willow. I know that if you come home, we can work things out. I know we can find our way back to each other."

Willow's chest rose and fell with heavy

breaths. She could handle his anger better than she could his request to give him another chance. Everyone in Dallas expected her to do as she was told, as if she didn't have an opinion. Not only did she not have one, she didn't need one because it didn't matter. The only thing that mattered was what everyone else wanted.

She had spent enough of her life trying to live up to all those expectations. It was exhausting. Going back to that would be her undoing.

"I never meant to hurt anyone. Especially you. I also know I have a lot of work ahead of me to repair the damage I've done to my relationship with my parents, but I'm not ready to go back to Dallas. I have a job and friends here. I have been learning so much about myself, and I don't want to give up on who I'm becoming."

Hudson let go of her and jammed his hands into his pockets. "Then I'll stay here until you're ready to come home."

Shocked, Willow actually flinched. "You're going to stay in Maple Grove?"

"Why not? You seem to think it's a good place to be. Thanks to technology, I can literally work from anywhere. Once you figure yourself out, we'll work on us."

How could she tell him she never wanted to go back to Dallas? Not only that but she never wanted there to be an *us* with anyone other than the man inside the house.

"Hudson—"

He stopped her. "Don't. I know you weren't expecting me to show up at your doorstep tonight. I wasn't expecting this to be your doorstep. Get some sleep. We can talk tomorrow after we both get some sleep and think about what we really want. I know that the woman I fell in love with and who fell in love with me is still in there somewhere. I'm not giving up on her yet."

He had no idea how much it scared her to think that might be true.

BRYCE DIDN'T WANT to be rude and eavesdrop, but he also needed to make sure Willow was safe. She had promised Hudson Carpenter wasn't dangerous, but desperate people did desperate things.

Hudson was desperate; Bryce could hear it in his voice. He listened to him try to convince Willow that she should go back to

Dallas with him and act like none of this happened. It took everything inside him to stay in the front room and not run out there and demand Hudson get off his property.

When Hudson said he was going to stay in Maple Grove, Bryce's heart sank. This man was going to wear her down until she agreed to go back to Dallas with him. How long would that take? A few days? A few weeks? Why did he have this sinking feeling that it would eventually happen? Willow already felt guilty and maybe there was still a part of her that loved him. She had to have loved him at some point. Love didn't just disappear.

Willow opened the front door and startled when she found Bryce standing in the foyer. Her hand pressed to her chest. "I knew you were going to be close. I didn't realize you were going to be *that* close."

"Sorry. I was worried about you. Are you okay?"

She had asked him the same question on their way home and he hadn't been able to answer. When she didn't answer right away, he feared she was about as okay as he had been.

"I thought your friend wasn't going to tell him where I was."

It wasn't an accusation, but it felt like one. "He promised me that he would do everything he could. I asked him to give me a heads-up if Hudson didn't want to give up finding you after the ring was returned."

"Clearly, that's exactly what happened. Nice of him to warn you."

Bryce kept his gaze on his feet, unable to look at her when he confessed what he knew. "He texted me today."

"What?"

He glanced up at her surprised expression and regretted not telling her sooner. "I never in a million years thought he would show up in Maple Grove tonight. I thought I had some time to figure out what to do."

"What do you mean? All you had to do was tell me. I'm the one who needs to do something. I could have called him or called my mom. You can't solve this problem for me. I need to take care of this myself."

"I know that." He stepped closer to her, but she held a hand up to stop him.

"It's been a wild night. My head is so full it feels like it's going to burst. I think I need to go to bed so I can sort it all out." She stepped around him and down the hall. He wanted to hold her, comfort her in some way, but knew that wasn't what she wanted from him at this moment. She stopped before slipping into the doorway to the bedroom. "Did you kiss me tonight because you knew Hudson was going to come for me?"

Bryce wasn't sure which answer she wanted to hear. She'd probably say the one that was the truth, but he also wasn't certain which one that was. "I don't know," he admitted.

She inhaled through her nose and nodded sadly. Clearly, that wasn't the answer she wanted, but it was the most honest that he could be. There had been some fear mixed in there with all the other reasons for wanting to kiss her.

Sleep evaded him most of the night. He wondered if she was downstairs having the same issue. When he got up in the morning, she was already in the kitchen making some coffee. The dark circles under her eyes answered his question.

"You're up early on a Saturday," she said. "Would you like some coffee?"

"Sure. I didn't get much sleep last night. Figured it might be a more productive use of my time to get up than stare at the ceiling for another hour."

She nodded as she pulled another mug from the cabinet. "Same."

They waited in silence for the coffee to brew. There were so many things he wanted to say, but nothing felt right. Better to be quiet than to ruin everything by saying the wrong thing.

Willow poured them each a cup and slid his across the island. "Cheers," she said, holding hers up.

"Let's hope the caffeine can work its magic before Camden gets up."

She laughed, and even though it was quiet, it made him feel better to hear it.

"I was going to take Camden back downtown to the festival this morning and visit the farmer's market, maybe take him on a few more rides. You're welcome to come with us if you want."

She held on to her mug with both hands and stared down at the coffee inside it. "There are things I need to take care of. I don't know that I'll make it to the festival today."

Bryce nodded. "Weekends are always yours to do as you please. You are off duty."

"I know."

"I heard Hudson say he was staying indefinitely. I know you can handle it, but I am the sheriff. If he starts to harass you, I'm happy to help in whatever way you need me to."

"He's not going to harass me. I don't know what he's thinking, but I'm positive I won't need the police to get involved."

He couldn't tell if she was defending Hudson or simply didn't want Bryce to worry. He was too tired to make an educated guess.

Willow snapped him out of his thoughts. "Can I ask you something?"

"Of course."

"Why did you tell Hudson I was Camden's private nurse instead of his nanny?"

It was a valid question. He had jumped in and called her that on purpose. "Maybe I'm wrong, but he seems like the kind of guy who puts more emphasis on titles than other people. Something made me think he would see a nanny as a glorified babysitter, and you are so much more than that."

"He's not really that impressed with the fact that I have a nursing degree, either, but I appreciate what you were trying to do."

Bryce moved around the island so they

were on the same side, needing to be closer to her. He had also hoped that if Hudson thought her job was important, then he wouldn't ask her to go back to Dallas with him. No wonder that plan hadn't worked, since he didn't respect anything that she did professionally.

"I am very impressed that you have a nursing degree."

The right side of her mouth curved into a lopsided smile. "Thanks."

Bryce's fingers twitched. He wanted to touch her, hold her, tell her that he never wanted her to leave, but he didn't want to mess with her head the way Hudson did. If Willow was going to stay, he wanted it to be her decision, not something she felt she had to do because it would make him or Camden happy.

He set his coffee on the island. "I'm going to jump in the shower before Cam wakes up."

"Good plan," she said as she lifted her mug to her lips. He had kissed those lips last night and it was everything. Now he feared that one kiss was going to be the first and last. He couldn't tell her that, though. He wouldn't pressure her no matter how much it scared him to simply trust her not to leave.

Camden was awake when Bryce got out of the shower. After a quick breakfast, he got Cam ready to go downtown.

"Can you go on the Ferris wheel with me today instead of Dad?" Camden asked Willow, not realizing that she was not going with them.

"Oh, buddy. Willow's going to stay home today. It's Camden and Dad Day. I think we should go on the Ferris wheel together since you went with Daisy last night."

Camden was not on board with this idea.

"Maybe I'll meet you guys up there a little later," Willow offered. "I'll text your dad when I finish talking to my parents, okay?"

"Your parents are coming?" Camden brightened, as if this was good news. Bryce saw little upside to Willow talking to her parents. They were sure to be in full support of her going back to Dallas.

"No, I have to talk to them on the phone. You go enjoy your Daddy time. Maybe you can play another game and win me a prize."

Camden thought that was a great plan. He wanted to win another giant bear so Mr. Panda would have a friend. Bryce opened the front door, only to be greeted by Hudson holding two coffees from the Coffee Depot.

"Oh, hi. I'm here for Willow."

"Who are you?" Camden asked innocently.

"I'm Willow's fiancé," Hudson replied, as if they were somehow still engaged. As if she hadn't returned the ring, officially ending the engagement. "Who are you?"

"I'm Camden. What's a fiancé?"

Bryce picked him up to hasten their exit. "We'll talk about it in the truck, buddy. Willow, you have a guest!" he shouted back into the house. He couldn't bear to witness Hudson trying to win Willow back. He needed to get out of there immediately.

Hudson hadn't been bluffing last night about sticking around. Bryce could only hope that when he went back to Dallas, he went alone.

CHAPTER NINETEEN

WILLOW CAME TO the door, knowing exactly who was going to be waiting for her on the front porch. She watched as Bryce flew out of the driveway like he couldn't leave fast enough.

Things were so messy right now. Her lack of sleep was not helping her process anything that Bryce did or said this morning, either.

"I brought you some coffee. Just the way you like it." Hudson handed her one of the cups.

"You didn't have to do that."

"I know. I wanted to. I was hoping we could talk and it looks like your boss and your patient are gone for a little bit. Perfect timing, I guess."

Willow held the door open wider and welcomed him in. Banjo realized that there was someone new in the house and came to investigate. One sniff of Hudson and the retriever began to bark.

"What in the world?" Hudson almost bolted back outside.

"Banjo, it's okay." Willow grabbed him by the collar and tugged him away from Hudson, who was not a dog person. "Come on, let's get a bone to keep you busy."

"I can't believe you live here with a kid and a dog. This is like some kind of alternative reality."

Maybe it seemed that way to him, but Willow had never felt more at home anywhere than here at Bryce's. This was not just a house filled with things, but a home filled with love.

Willow gave Banjo a bone and he took off to eat it in private, leaving the two of them alone.

Hudson followed her to the living room. "Isn't this place…quaint."

She picked up some toys that Camden had left on the couch. "Sorry, it's a little messy."

He ran his hand over the couch cushion like he needed to sweep away dirt before sitting down. "This reminds me of that apartment you had when we first met. Tiny and in need of a good cleaning lady."

He was judging Bryce's home and she didn't

like it. "This house is much bigger than my first apartment."

"Right, I'm just saying it reminds me of it. Not that they're identical."

Willow took a breath and reminded herself that she at least owed him a conversation after running out on him on their wedding day. "I feel like I didn't answer all of your questions last night. I think that once I do, we will both be more on the same page."

"I want nothing more than to be on the same page with you. I talked to your mother and father this morning. Let them know that I found you and that I will be bringing you home as soon as you come to your senses."

Willow's brain was not functioning at full capacity thanks to her sleepless night, but there was one thing she knew for certain— she was never getting back together with Hudson. How to convince him was the part she hadn't figured out yet.

"I was planning on calling my mother today and explaining things to her. I know I need to do that. There's no reason to put it off any longer."

"I'm glad you're coming around. You know what would be better than you calling her?

We could surprise her. If we leave within the next hour, we could be back in Dallas by lunch. She would love that."

"I'm not going back to Dallas with you, Hudson. I want to stay in Maple Grove. I came here because this is where my dad's mom was from. Grandma Rose used to talk about it all the time. I have family here. My dad's cousins live here, I have quite a bit of family in the area and they are all very sweet."

Hudson stared at her like she had lost her mind. "Willow, it's wonderful that you found some branches of your family tree, but your actual family is back in Dallas. Your parents have been worried sick about you. They are expecting you to come home and clean up the mess you made."

The shame of disappointing her parents was intense. She could only imagine how furious they were with her. Repairing that relationship was important to her. She wanted her parents to be part of her life, but she also wanted that life to be here, in Maple Grove.

"I plan to make amends with my parents, Hudson. I realize that my disappearing act hurt them, but I'm not going back to Dallas."

"You keep saying that, but I can't figure out why not. What is keeping you here? A job? You don't need to work, Willow. I can take care of you."

"I don't need you to take care of me. And yes, I want a job. I liked having a job. A job gives me a reason to wake up every day with some purpose."

Hudson rested his elbows on his knees and leaned forward. "Then go back to work in Dallas. I'm sure I can make a few phone calls and get you your job back at the hospital. Or if you enjoy doing private nursing work, I'm sure there are plenty of jobs like that in Dallas."

"I don't need you to make phone calls for me. I like *this* job. I like this town. Besides all the relatives I've met, I've made more real friends in the few weeks I've been here than I did in all my years in Dallas. There are so many reasons I want to stay."

Hudson set his coffee down and pulled at his hair. "It's like I don't even know who you are right now."

"Exactly! I'm not the same person I was before I came here. The woman you were in love with isn't me. I was trying to be that person, but I realized I couldn't keep pretending for the rest of my life. You deserve better than that, Hudson. You deserve someone who is able to be herself around you. Someone who wants the same things you want. I'm sure she's out there. What you have to offer someone is amazing. That person is not me. I am so sorry."

The front door opened and shut. Daisy started talking before she even made it into the living room. "Before the sheriff gets back, you have got to tell me right now if he kissed you on the—" As soon as she noticed Willow wasn't alone, Daisy closed her mouth.

"Hey, you're early. I thought teenagers slept 'til noon on Saturdays," Willow joked, forcing a laugh. "Um, Daisy, this is Hudson. Hudson, this is our dog walker, Daisy. Let me get Banjo's leash for you." She did everything in her power to wordlessly communicate with Daisy.

"Cool. Yeah, I'm early. I'm the dog walker. You are?"

"Willow's fiancé," Hudson replied.

"*Ex*-fiancé," Willow clarified when Daisy's eyes almost popped out of her head. "Here's

Banjo's leash. Banjo, come here, boy. Time for your walk."

If there was one thing Banjo loved more than a bone, it was a walk. He did not hesitate to reappear.

Willow followed them to the front door. "I know it's not your day to walk the dog, but please just bear with me."

"What is going on?" Daisy whispered. "Since when do you have an ex-fiancé?"

"Since I ran away from my wedding and hid here in Maple Grove."

Daisy struggled to keep her voice low. "What?"

Willow opened the front door and gave the nosy teenager a push. "I'll tell you all about it later. Like when he's gone later." She shut the door and raced back into the living room. "Sorry, I totally forgot she was coming."

"Who was going to kiss you last night? Don't lie to me, Willow. After everything you did, I deserve the truth."

He did deserve the truth, and maybe the truth was what he needed to hear to accept that they were never getting back together. "Bryce and I have feelings for each other. I didn't plan for that to happen, it just did."

Hudson scrubbed his face with both hands. "Bryce, the sheriff? Your boss?"

"Yes."

"Where is the boy's mother, Willow? What is going on here?"

"She passed away almost a year ago. He's a widower. We seriously haven't even had a chance to talk about what's happening between us because you showed up last night."

Hudson rose to his feet. "Oh, well. I apologize. I didn't realize I was interfering in your new romance with your live-in boss. Excuse me for not assuming that you would catch feelings for the first guy who showed you a little bit of attention after you ran out on me."

"I don't want to hurt you. I am not trying to hurt you. I can't help the way I feel."

"Poor, naive Willow," Hudson said with a shake of his head. "I can't believe you don't even see what's going on. This guy's wife died and he's been taking care of his kid by himself. He's lonely. He hires the first pretty girl he sees and then convinces you that you're falling in love with him so he can have his cake and eat it, too. It's so obvious! Do you know how many guys at my firm start dating the nanny after they get divorced?

Almost all of them! Do you know how many marry their nanny? None!"

His words were like daggers hitting her in the center of her chest. "Bryce is not like the guys at your firm, Hudson. You have no idea what you're talking about."

"I'm not trying to hurt *you*, Willow," he said, throwing her words back at her. "If you think your boss is different from all the rest, good for you. I hope when he comes home today, you ask him if he really thinks you're the woman for him. If he says yes, then I apologize. But if he doesn't say yes, I want you to think about what you're doing and who you're hurting by staying here, pining for a guy who isn't going to be what you want him to be."

Heat flushed through her whole body. With gritted teeth, she said, "You don't know what you're talking about."

"We'll see, won't we."

BRYCE HAD NEVER been so distracted. His body was at the festival, but his mind was solely focused on what was happening back at the house. Camden wasn't a fan of Distracted Dad.

"I want to go home," he said.

Trying to be present, he crouched down to Camden's level. "What do you mean? We haven't won a bear for Willow yet."

"I want Willow to win another bear."

Yeah, well, Bryce wanted Willow to kick her ex-fiancé to the curb, but people didn't always get what they wanted.

"Sheriff!" Daisy called as Banjo ran ahead of her.

"What are you doing here with Banjo? We did not have a dog walking appointment. Do you need extra money for something?"

"Who is this Hudson guy and why is he at your house with Willow right now saying he's her fiancé?"

Bryce raked a hand through his hair. That was a great question and one he did not want to answer in front of Camden.

"What's a fiancé?" Camden asked again.

"It's a special word for a special friend," Bryce replied, begging Daisy with his eyes not to disagree.

"She said he was her ex-friend. Is that true?" Daisy asked.

"Yes." It was a relief to know that was how Willow referred to him. "Why are you walking Banjo? Was everything okay over there?"

"I walked in without knocking and I wanted to know if there had been any K-I-S-S-I-N-G on the Ferris wheel last night and there was this guy acting like he had some claim to our Willow. I didn't like it one bit."

Join the club, kid. "Why are you so interested in two old people, as you so kindly called us last night, and if we're K-I-S-S-I-N-G?"

"Because she's perfect for you! She's like the nicest, coolest person around. You smile when you're together and that's a good thing after the last year, wouldn't you say?"

It was better than good. Willow was exactly what he needed when he had reconciled himself to being miserable for the rest of his life. She had brought joy back into his life.

"I appreciate you looking out for me, Daisy. But this is grown-up stuff, okay? You need to let us figure it out."

She shoved Banjo's leash into his hand. "Fine. Figure it out. Just don't blow this. You aren't the only one who likes her."

Bryce swallowed hard. He understood that losing Willow would hurt more than just him. He looked at Camden, who was petting Banjo. Loss was something his little boy knew all too well.

"Let's take Banjo home."

Hudson's car was gone when they returned. Bryce braced himself, wondering if Willow had gone with him. Banjo and Camden ran ahead of him when he opened the door, and relief flooded his body when he heard her greet them. She was still here.

She was sitting at the kitchen table on her computer. "You guys are back early. I thought you'd spend more time down there."

"Daisy found us and returned the dog. I didn't want to walk around the festival with Banjo," he said instead of admitting that he wanted to be with her.

Camden told Willow the festival wasn't as fun without her and that he wanted to play with Mr. Panda, so off to his room he went. Bryce got a glass of water and joined her at the table.

She closed her laptop. "Can we talk?"

His jaw clenched. That was a loaded question. "Sure."

"You told me that you wanted to talk about what happened at the festival last night, but my surprise guest kind of took things in another direction. Can we talk about what happened?"

There was a war going on inside Bryce. There were so many things he wanted to say about last night, but he was terrified that he was going to ruin everything. He didn't want to pressure her while she was at this crossroads. He wanted to be the opposite of Hudson. She had made it clear that in her old life the people important to her had always asked her to put them and their needs before her. He didn't want to do that to her.

"I'm not sure what happened matters anymore," he said, waiting for her reaction.

She tipped her head and her brows pinched together. "Why not?"

"I know Hudson asked you to come back to Dallas with him. I think you need to make a decision about that first."

"Well, I think knowing how you felt about last night matters."

"I don't see why. I'm not going to say something to make you stay. If you want to go back to Dallas, that's your choice."

She flinched as if he had slapped her. Maybe it was shocking to hear someone tell her that her opinion mattered more than his did.

"If I went back to Dallas, you wouldn't try to stop me?"

Bryce fought the urge to beg her to stay. Every fiber of his being wanted her to choose him and Cam, but he wasn't going to be that guy. He forced himself to shake his head.

She lifted a shaky hand to her lips before she pushed away from the table and got to her feet. She cleared her throat. "Thank you for being honest."

"Always."

Willow moved with a quickness that caught him off guard and disappeared into her bedroom. She probably didn't know what else to say. It had to be a relief to know that he was letting her make her own choices without any guilt trips. She could make her choice without worrying about how he was going to feel about it.

She would choose to stay with Bryce and Camden because he had not pressured her. She had to.

June knocked on the back door and waved at Bryce when she noticed him sitting here.

"Hi, neighbor."

She held up a plate covered in aluminum foil. "I made some sugar-free cookies and thought maybe there was a sugar-free boy who might like to be my taste tester."

"I have a feeling you'll find a very eager taste tester over here." He turned his head and shouted, "Cam, Mrs. Holland is here with a surprise!"

Camden came running and was thrilled that cookies were involved in this surprise. "I can have one?" he said, looking at Bryce.

"They're sugar-free, so yep."

"I used stevia in the batter and sugar-free chocolate chips that Douglas told me were the best-tasting brand."

Bryce smirked. "I didn't know Douglas was so knowledgeable about sugar-free chocolate chips."

"His wife was diabetic, so he knows all kinds of stuff. I told him he should talk to Willow. He has a bunch of recipes he could share with her."

"That's very nice of him."

"Can I give a cookie to Mr. Panda?"

Bryce knew that Mr. Panda's cookie was going to end up being Camden's cookie. Thankfully, two sugar-free cookies couldn't do too much harm.

"Fine, but then that's it for today."

Camden grabbed another cookie and ran back to his room, shouting his thanks as he went.

June glanced around. "Where is Willow?"

"In her room."

"Everything okay after last night? I know it's hard when Delia has an episode."

Bryce had forgotten all about Delia's memory episode. It had rattled him at the time, made him once again question if he was moving too fast. Maybe not enough time had passed. April had only been gone a year. But Hudson's arrival had changed all that. Bryce didn't want to lose Willow. It wasn't the same as losing April, but it was close enough.

"I have bigger issues than Delia's memory loss." He lowered his voice. "Willow's ex showed up last night and asked her to come back to Dallas with him."

June's eyes went wide. "What? Did you tell her not to go? Did you tell her you're in love with her?"

"How do you know I'm in love with her?"

"Bryce Koller, stop it. It's written all over your face. I've known for a long time. I've just been waiting for you to figure it out."

"Well, maybe I have, but I'm not going to

make this decision about me. I want her to choose to stay because it's what *she* wants, not because it's what *I* want."

"Did you tell her that?"

"Pretty much."

"Did you tell her you want her to stay, but you want it to be her choice?"

"How is it supposed to be her choice if I tell her I want her to stay? She left Dallas because no one ever asked her what she wanted, they only told her what they wanted. I don't want to be like that."

June didn't seem totally convinced that was the best plan. The doorbell rang and Willow rushed out of the bedroom. When she came back into the living room, she noticed June at the table.

"Oh, June. Good. I'm glad you're here."

"Who was at the door?" Bryce asked.

"Hudson is here to get me."

Bryce felt like all the air had been sucked out of him. "Get you for what?"

"I'm sorry to do it this way. I'm giving you my notice. I'm going back to Dallas tonight. I hope June can help you with Camden until you can find a permanent replacement."

"What do you mean you're going to Dallas?" June was on her feet. "Willow, sweetheart. Please don't go. I don't want you to go."

Willow wrapped June up in an embrace. "Thank you for saying that. You have no idea how much it means to me that you feel that way."

Bryce was pinned to his seat. It was as if someone had reached in his chest and ripped out his heart, the heart that still had stitches from the loss of April.

Willow was leaving. She had made her choice, and it wasn't him.

CHAPTER TWENTY

LEAVE IT TO June to say exactly what Willow wanted to hear. Only it hadn't been June she needed to hear it from. It was the man sitting at the kitchen table. He didn't even bother to say or do anything when she announced that she was leaving. He just sat there with a blank look on his face. Did he even care that she was going?

"You can't leave without saying goodbye to Daisy. What about Delia? Willow, tonight is too soon," June pleaded.

"It's probably best that no one mentions anything to Delia. I don't think she will remember I was ever here. I'll text Daisy." The lump in her throat grew bigger. She knew Daisy would be sad, but teenagers were resilient, and Willow wasn't vain enough to think that she had made that much of an impression. "I'm going to put my stuff in the car and then say goodbye to Camden."

"He's going to be heartbroken. Are you sure about this?"

The only thing Willow was sure of was that Bryce didn't care. If he didn't care, then there was no point dragging this out. She had feelings that weren't going to go away. It was foolish to try to live together when those feelings were going to remain unrequited. He'd basically told her to go.

"It's going to be okay. When I come back to visit the Everlys, I'll stop by your house to say hello. Maybe Bryce can send over Camden when I'm there."

It wasn't like Bryce would want her to visit. He continued to say nothing from the kitchen.

"Bryce, don't you have something to say to Willow?" June asked.

It took him a minute, but he got to his feet. "Let me help you with your stuff."

His words cut deeper than a knife. She'd spent nearly a month in his home and kissed him less than twenty-four hours ago, and all he had to say about her leaving for good was could he help her carry her luggage out? This was an absolute nightmare. She'd already spent time in her room, crying her eyes out. She needed to hold it together long enough to get in the car. She would not give him the satisfaction of seeing her cry over him.

June threw her hands up and huffed. Bryce ignored her and walked into Willow's bedroom, where her bags were packed. He grabbed the suitcase and headed for the door.

"He doesn't want this," June said. "I know he doesn't want this. Please reconsider."

"It's okay. He's fine with this. He told me to do what I wanted."

"This can't really be what you want. This is your home. It has been since the moment you moved in."

The tears were threatening to fall again. She had to let June believe what she wanted to believe. Willow grabbed her toiletry bag and the garbage bag that still held her wedding dress. Her mother was going to be so angry with her.

Bryce returned, his hollow eyes making Willow feel even more uncomfortable. "Want me to take that stuff out?" he asked in a strangely detached tone.

"I've got it. I'm going to say goodbye to Camden and then I'll be out of your hair."

His Adam's apple bobbed along his throat, and he nodded.

Willow knocked on Camden's door. She pushed it open. "Hey, buddy. I need to talk to you for a second." Tears pricked at the corners of her eyes. This was going to be hard to do without losing it completely. She took a deep breath and sat down on the floor next to him. "I have to go back to Dallas. Miss June is going to watch you until your dad can find a new nanny. But I want you to know that I love you very much, and anytime I come to town, I am going to try to visit you, okay?"

"Why do you have to go to Dallas? I don't want a new nanny."

"I know. I need to go back because I guess that's where I'm supposed to be. I need to go see my parents."

"You said you were going to talk to them on the phone. I don't want you to go," he said, clinging to her.

Tears streamed down her face as she rubbed his back. "I did say that, but things have changed and I need to go to where they are. I will never forget about you, Cam. You are the best."

"Daddy and I can come with you. We'll drive you. You don't have to go alone."

Again, he was saying all the things she

wished his father would have said. Why was it that everyone else wanted her here more than Bryce did?

"She needs to go, buddy. Without us. Her friend is taking her back," Bryce said, pulling him off her lap.

Camden began to cry and reach for her. Bryce held him tighter. "She said she's going to visit you. Don't worry, you'll see her again. She has to go, though."

She didn't have to go. She was going because he didn't care enough to ask her to stay. If only he would say that, she would bring all her things back inside and never leave.

Willow kissed the side of Camden's head. "I promise I will see you again."

About to lose it, she ran from the room. She couldn't say anything to Bryce. He didn't care anyway. She climbed into Hudson's car and covered her face with her hands.

"It's better to leave now," he said, rubbing her back. "Once you're back in Dallas, you'll see. We can figure all this out with your mom and dad's help."

That was the moment she knew she'd never really loved Hudson. When she left him at the altar, she'd felt sad because she knew she was causing problems for the families. She'd never mourned him and what they had together. Not the way her heart was breaking as they pulled out of Bryce's driveway. Knowing she was never going to be part of their family was a pain that might never go away.

"WHAT ARE YOU DOING?" June asked Bryce after Willow left. "How did you two go from kissing on the Ferris wheel yesterday to breaking each other's hearts?"

"I can't talk about this, June." She'd left. She'd gotten into her ex's car and let him take her back to Dallas. He had done everything he thought she wanted him to do. He hadn't pressured her, hadn't tried to make her feel guilty. He'd wanted her to feel safe making the best decision for herself, and she'd chosen to leave. She'd chosen the people who never let her choose. Maybe she wasn't who he thought she was.

"Bryce, you know me. I am not trying to get into your personal business, but I feel like what happened was a big mistake. Something needed to be said that wasn't said."

"She made herself pretty clear. She chose to leave."

"She also made it clear when I told her I didn't want her to go that she wanted to hear that. I think she wanted to hear it from you, not from me."

Camden cried in his arms, and it took everything Bryce had to comfort him instead of cry along with him. June was not making things any easier.

"Bryce Koller, I am an old woman, but I am stubborn as a mule. Give me that boy and go chase them down and stop that woman from leaving. You tell her how you really feel. Don't tell her what you think she wanted you to say. Say what is in here." She tapped on her chest. "Give me Cam." She held out her arms.

"It won't make a difference."

"Prove me wrong, then. If you don't, I'm going to call Daisy and she is going to make your life insufferable. You know she will."

Just what he needed—an eighty-year-old and a fifteen-year-old who thought they knew what was best for him. "I don't need Daisy in the middle of any of this."

"Then I suggest you hand me Camden and you get in your truck and you bring Willow back."

"It's not—"

"Don't tell me what's not going to work. Show me."

When he didn't hand over Camden, June pulled her phone out of the pocket of her cardigan. "I'm calling Daisy."

"Goodness, woman." He set Camden down on the ground. "Camden, you stay with Mrs. Holland. I'll be right back."

June put her arms around the crying little boy. "I've got him. Go get her."

This was pointless, but he knew that if he didn't do as she said, he would never hear the end of it. And he needed there to be an end to this. If stopping Willow and telling her exactly how he felt was going to prove to June that it didn't matter, that was what he would do.

He jumped in his truck and turned on the police siren. He was breaking the rules, but if there was anyone he'd break them for, it was Willow. If they were heading for Dallas, he knew the exact route that any GPS would take them to get to the highway.

Speed limits didn't matter. Thankfully, Maple Grove wasn't full of stop lights. Bryce did his best to make up for their head start. It took ten minutes, but he caught up to Hudson's fancy sports car. Hudson pulled over as soon as Bryce got behind him.

Suddenly, his nerves got the best of him. What was he going to say exactly? How was he going to accept her rejection when whatever he said didn't work?

He slammed the door shut once he climbed out of the truck and made his way to the passenger's side of the vehicle. He could hear the sound of the window going down as he approached.

"I just need a minute," he said, ducking his head to get a look at her, but the passenger's seat was empty. His forehead creased. "Where is she?"

Hudson pinched the bridge of his nose. "Did you seriously chase me down five minutes after she begged me to let her out so she could go back?"

CHAPTER TWENTY-ONE

WILLOW THANKED THE rideshare driver for the lift. If she hadn't had her giant suitcase, she probably would have just walked back, but she had too much stuff to drag along the roadside.

Bryce's truck wasn't in the driveway, making her wonder if she'd made a huge mistake. He'd probably taken Camden back to the festival to cheer him up.

Before she could knock to make sure, sirens blared as Bryce's truck came flying down their quiet residential street. He didn't even pull all the way into the driveway, abandoning his truck halfway in and halfway out. He ran toward her.

"What's wrong? What happened? Is Camden okay?" Stress could trigger an insulin reaction. Panic set in. "Where is he?"

"He's inside with June, I think."

"Why are you driving down the street like a madman?"

"Because I was looking for you."

The adrenaline coursing through her veins must have caused her to misunderstand him. "What do you mean?"

He was slightly out of breath. "I chased down Hudson, thinking you were still in the car, only to find out that you made him drop you off at the gas station. When I got to the gas station, they told me they saw a woman fitting your description with a huge suitcase and a garbage bag get in a car. I came here, hoping this was the place you had that car take you. I was right."

"You chased down Hudson."

"You came back."

"I don't want to live in Dallas."

"I don't want you to live in Dallas. I want you to live here with Camden and me. I want you to choose us and never leave again. I want to fire you as his nanny and ask you to be my person instead, because I've fallen in love with you. I know that might be scary because it happened so fast, but it's how I feel. I still don't want you to choose us because *I* want you to. I want you to choose us because *you* want us—me—as much as we—I—want you."

Willow could feel the tears reemerging. This time she didn't fight them and let them fall freely. "You want me?"

Bryce gripped both of her hands and pulled her closer, leaving little space in between them. "More than I want anything. I love you, Willow."

"Why didn't you say that before? Why did you tell me to go?"

"I didn't tell you to go. I told you to make up your own mind. I thought that's what you wanted from me. I didn't want to treat you like Hudson did, emotionally manipulating you, using Camden's feelings, or mine, as a weapon against your free will."

Willow dropped her head against his chest. "I thought you were saying all that stuff because you didn't feel the same way that I feel."

He tipped her head up so she had to look at him. "And how do you feel?"

"I love you. I love Camden. I love Maple Grove. I love being part of your family. I don't want to be anywhere but here."

"Then, stay," Bryce said without hesitation. It was almost like a dream, but her feet were planted firmly on the ground.

Willow wrapped her arms around his neck

and lifted up on her tiptoes. She brushed her nose against his. "You won't be able to get rid of me."

"Am I not being clear? I love you. Where you go, Cam and I go. You're stuck with us," he said, tipping his head down and capturing her lips with his.

Willow thought the kiss on the Ferris wheel was good, but this one she felt from the top of her head to the tip of her toes. There was no confusion, no doubt. He loved her and she loved him.

"It's about time," June said. They hadn't even heard her open the door. "Daisy is on her way over, so keep kissing. It's the only way she's going to accept everything is fine." She smiled as she shut the door.

Bryce shrugged his shoulders. "You heard the woman. I don't want to be on June or Daisy's bad side. Do you?"

Willow couldn't help but laugh. This was their funny little family, and she wouldn't trade it for the world. "Not for a second."

EPILOGUE

"WHERE ARE YOUR SHOES?" Bryce asked Camden as he got down on his hands and knees to search under his bed.

Camden was too busy playing pirate to help look. He was in a serious sword fight with Mr. Panda.

"You need to wear shoes at school, buddy. They have to be somewhere."

"I think Mr. Panda hid them with the treasure! Where did you put my shoes, you bad pirate?"

"I found the shoes!" June called from the other room.

Bryce hauled himself up off the floor. "Hallelujah. Come on, Cam. You don't want to be late for your first day of kindergarten."

"First day of school! Can I please bring Mr. Panda? He promises to be quiet."

"Sorry, no pandas allowed in school. You will be much too busy with all your new friends to keep an eye on him anyway. Go out there and have Mrs. Holland help you with your shoes."

Camden gave Mr. Panda a hug goodbye and skipped out of his room. Bryce stood up and readjusted his uniform. In the hallway, he almost ran right into Willow.

"Good morning," he said, wrapping his arms around her waist and pulling her in for a kiss.

She was dressed in her new scrubs and in the process of putting in one of her earrings.

"Good morning, Sheriff," she said, letting him have his way with her anyway. She kissed him one more time before wiggling out of his grasp. "If we keep this up Camden will miss school and Doc will fire me for being late on my first day."

There was no way that was going to happen. Doc had been over the moon when Willow reached out to him about working at the clinic part-time. With Camden starting school, she wanted to get back to what she loved, and that was nursing. Doc had hired her on the spot, and June had offered to help with the couple hours after school that Camden needed a sitter.

"You are the most responsible person in this house."

"Someone has to be," she said with a wink. Between monitoring Camden's sugars, planning a wedding and starting a new job, Willow had her hands full.

This summer, she had been the one to set up Camden with her friend Dr. Nandi in Dallas to get an insulin pump inserted into his arm. It was the first time she had been back to the city since she'd run away in the spring. Bryce and Camden had met her parents, and Willow believed that because they wore shirts and ties, they were able to win the Sandersons over. Bryce knew it had more to do with the fact that there was no way for her parents to deny that their daughter was truly happy.

With her parents' blessing they'd gotten engaged on the Fourth of July and planned to get married later that fall. Willow was excited to have her college roommate, her best friend from Dallas, and June and Daisy as her bridesmaids. It was an eclectic group, for sure. Bryce didn't care. He loved seeing her light up every time she talked about something related to the wedding.

"Speaking of being responsible, don't forget that you and Camden need to go to your tux fitting on Thursday instead of Wednesday. Camden's soccer practice is Mondays and Wednesdays, so I had to reschedule."

"Got it. Thursday, tux. Monday and Wednesday, soccer."

Camden was ready to go. June helped him get his backpack on.

"Oh my goodness, you are too cute!" Willow gushed. "Let's go on the front porch and get your first-day pictures. Where's that board I made last night?"

"By the front door where you left it so you wouldn't have to look for it in the morning," Bryce reminded her.

"Right. Come on, Cam. Humor me and smile for a couple of pictures."

"It's your first day, too. I think we need a few pictures of you on the front porch," June said, following them all out.

"I think that's a great idea," Bryce said, pulling out his phone. "I'll take those after you finish with Cam."

She scowled at him. "I am not posing for pictures."

"Yeah, me, either," Camden said.

Bryce smirked at how her refusal to play along backfired on her.

"No, no, no, Camden. If you take a picture, I'll take a picture. Fair?"

"Fine," he said as she handed him the First Day of School sign.

How did his little boy grow up so fast? How could he already be going to kindergarten? It felt like he was a tiny little baby just yesterday. Willow snapped way more than one picture before begrudgingly posing for a couple of her own.

"Perfect." Bryce kissed her on the nose. "You are the cutest nurse ever. I hope you have an amazing first day."

"I'm going to be home late tonight because I am meeting with the wedding planner to go over a few details."

"No problem. Camden and I will take care of dinner. It'll be ready and waiting for you."

Her smile lit up his entire world. "Come here and give me a hug, Mr. Kindergartner." Willow crouched down and opened her arms wide. Camden didn't hesitate to run right into them. "Have an amazing day, buddy. I can't wait to hear all about how it went."

"I hope you have an amazing day, too," he replied.

"I love you, buddy."

"I love you, too." Camden kissed her on the cheek. Nothing warmed Bryce's heart more than to see the two of them together like that. Their bond was so tight, and as much as he missed April, he knew that she had sent Willow to be their person when she couldn't be there herself.

Bryce wrapped Willow up in one more hug. "You got this, Nurse Willow. Love you."

"Love you more."

Willow might have come into his life as a runaway bride, but Bryce had no doubt that when it was time for her to walk down that aisle for him, she'd be there, taking his breath away.

They were already family.

* * * * *

Get 3 FREE REWARDS!

We'll send you 2 FREE Books plus a FREE Mystery Gift.

FREE Value Over **$20**

Both the **Love Inspired**® and **Love Inspired**® **Suspense** series feature compelling novels filled with inspirational romance, faith, forgiveness and hope.

YES! Please send me 2 FREE novels from the Love Inspired or Love Inspired Suspense series and my FREE gift (gift is worth about $10 retail). After receiving them, if I don't wish to receive any more books, I can return the shipping statement marked "cancel." If I don't cancel, I will receive 6 brand-new Love Inspired Larger-Print books or Love Inspired Suspense Larger-Print books every month and be billed just $6.49 each in the U.S. or $6.74 each in Canada. That is a savings of at least 16% off the cover price. It's quite a bargain! Shipping and handling is just 50¢ per book in the U.S. and $1.25 per book in Canada.* I understand that accepting the 2 free books and gift places me under no obligation to buy anything. I can always return a shipment and cancel at any time by calling the number below. The free books and gift are mine to keep no matter what I decide.

Choose one:
☐ **Love Inspired Larger-Print** (122/322 BPA GRPA)
☐ **Love Inspired Suspense Larger-Print** (107/307 BPA GRPA)
☐ **Or Try Both!** (122/322 & 107/307 BPA GRRP)

Name (please print)

Address   Apt. #

City   State/Province   Zip/Postal Code

Email: Please check this box ☐ if you would like to receive newsletters and promotional emails from Harlequin Enterprises ULC and its affiliates. You can unsubscribe anytime.

Mail to the Harlequin Reader Service:
IN U.S.A.: P.O. Box 1341, Buffalo, NY 14240-8531
IN CANADA: P.O. Box 603, Fort Erie, Ontario L2A 5X3

Want to try 2 free books from another series! Call 1-800-873-8635 or visit www.ReaderService.com.

*Terms and prices subject to change without notice. Prices do not include sales taxes, which will be charged (if applicable) based on your state or country of residence. Canadian residents will be charged applicable taxes. Offer not valid in Quebec. This offer is limited to one order per household. Books received may not be as shown. Not valid for current subscribers to the Love Inspired or Love Inspired Suspense series. All orders subject to approval. Credit or debit balances in a customer's account(s) may be offset by any other outstanding balance owed by or to the customer. Please allow 4 to 6 weeks for delivery. Offer available while quantities last.

Your Privacy—Your information is being collected by Harlequin Enterprises ULC, operating as Harlequin Reader Service. For a complete summary of the information we collect, how we use this information and to whom it is disclosed, please visit our privacy notice located at corporate.harlequin.com/privacy-notice. From time to time we may also exchange your personal information with reputable third parties. If you wish to opt out of this sharing of your personal information, please visit readerservice.com/consumerschoice or call 1-800-873-8635. **Notice to California Residents**—Under California law, you have specific rights to control and access your data. For more information on these rights and how to exercise them, visit corporate.harlequin.com/california-privacy.

LIRLIS23

THE NORA ROBERTS COLLECTION

Get to the heart of happily-ever-after in these Nora Roberts classics! Immerse yourself in the beauty of love by picking up this incredible collection written by, legendary author, Nora Roberts!

YES! Please send me the **Nora Roberts Collection**. Each book in this collection is 40% off the retail price! There are a total of 4 shipments in this collection. The shipments are yours for the low, members-only discount price of $23.96 U.S./$31.16 CDN. each, plus $1.99 U.S./$4.99 CDN. for shipping and handling. If I do not cancel, I will continue to receive four books a month for three more months. I'll pay just $23.96 U.S./$31.16 CDN., plus $1.99 U.S./$4.99 CDN. for shipping and handling per shipment.* I can always return a shipment and cancel at any time.

☐ 274 2595   ☐ 474 2595

Name (please print)

Address   Apt. #

City   State/Province   Zip/Postal Code

Mail to the Harlequin Reader Service:
IN U.S.A.: P.O. Box 1341, Buffalo, NY 14240-8531
IN CANADA: P.O. Box 603, Fort Erie, Ontario L2A 5X3

NORA2022

Get 3 FREE REWARDS!

We'll send you 2 FREE Books <u>plus</u> a FREE Mystery Gift.

FREE Value Over **$20**

Both the **Romance** and **Suspense** collections feature compelling novels written by many of today's bestselling authors.

YES! Please send me 2 FREE novels from the Essential Romance or Essential Suspense Collection and my FREE gift (gift is worth about $10 retail). After receiving them, if I don't wish to receive any more books, I can return the shipping statement marked "cancel." If I don't cancel, I will receive 4 brand-new novels every month and be billed just $7.49 each in the U.S. or $7.74 each in Canada. That's a savings of at least 17% off the cover price. It's quite a bargain! Shipping and handling is just 50¢ per book in the U.S. and $1.25 per book in Canada.* I understand that accepting the 2 free books and gift places me under no obligation to buy anything. I can always return a shipment and cancel at any time by calling the number below. The free books and gift are mine to keep no matter what I decide.

Choose one: ☐ **Essential Romance** (194/394 BPA GRNM) ☐ **Essential Suspense** (191/391 BPA GRNM) ☐ **Or Try Both!** (194/394 & 191/391 BPA GRQZ)

Name (please print)

Address _____ Apt. #

City _____ State/Province _____ Zip/Postal Code

Email: Please check this box ☐ if you would like to receive newsletters and promotional emails from Harlequin Enterprises ULC and its affiliates. You can unsubscribe anytime.

Mail to the **Harlequin Reader Service:**
IN U.S.A.: P.O. Box 1341, Buffalo, NY 14240-8531
IN CANADA: P.O. Box 603, Fort Erie, Ontario L2A 5X3

Want to try 2 free books from another series? Call 1-800-873-8635 or visit www.ReaderService.com.

---

*Terms and prices subject to change without notice. Prices do not include sales taxes, which will be charged (if applicable) based on your state or country of residence. Canadian residents will be charged applicable taxes. Offer not valid in Quebec. This offer is limited to one order per household. Books received may not be as shown. Not valid for current subscribers to the Essential Romance or Essential Suspense Collection. All orders subject to approval. Credit or debit balances in a customer's account(s) may be offset by any other outstanding balance owed by or to the customer. Please allow 4 to 6 weeks for delivery. Offer available while quantities last.

Your Privacy—Your information is being collected by Harlequin Enterprises ULC, operating as Harlequin Reader Service. For a complete summary of the information we collect, how we use this information and to whom it is disclosed, please visit our privacy notice located at corporate.harlequin.com/privacy-notice. From time to time we may also exchange your personal information with reputable third parties. If you wish to opt out of this sharing of your personal information, please visit readerservice.com/consumerchoice or call 1-800-873-8635. **Notice to California Residents**—Under California law, you have specific rights to control and access your data. For more information on these rights and how to exercise them, visit corporate.harlequin.com/california-privacy.

STRS23

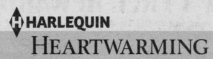
#483 TO TRUST A HERO
Heroes of Dunbar Mountain • by Alexis Morgan

Freelance writer Max Volkov recently helped solve a mystery in Dunbar, Washington, and now he's staying in town to write about it! But B and B owner Rikki Bruce is perplexed by another mystery—why is she so drawn to Max?

#484 WHEN LOVE COMES CALLING
by Syndi Powell

It's love at first sight for Brian Redmond when he meets Vivi Carmack. Vivi feels the same but knows romance is no match for her recent streak of bad luck. Now Brian must prove they can overcome anything—together.

#485 HER HOMETOWN COWBOY
Coronado, Arizona • by LeAnne Bristow

Noah Sterling is determined to save his ranch without anyone's assistance. But then he meets Abbie Houghton, who's in town searching for her sister. Accepting help has never been his strong suit...but this city girl might just be his weakness!

#486 WINNING OVER THE RANCHER
Heroes of the Rockies • by Viv Royce

Big-city marketing specialist Lily Richards comes to Boulder County, Colorado, to help the community after a devastating storm. But convincing grumpy rancher Cade Williams to accept her advice is harder than she expected...